Fritz Leiber, the son of a noted stage and screen performer, was born in the United States in 1910. A former actor, he has written many fantasy and science fiction stories, and contributed to *Weird Tales* before the Second World War. Leiber is well known and held in high regard by readers of both science fiction and fantasy: he has received several Hugo and Nebula awards for the former, and he is seen as the doyen of fantasy writers, as the man who practically invented the sword and sorcery genre as it is known today. Most of the leading writers in the field acknowledge their debt to him, but, as is often pointed out, what makes Leiber's fantasy adventures superior to those of the many writers who have followed in his footsteps is the strong vein of dry wit that permeates his work.

Fritz Leiber

Ship of Shadows

A MAYFLOWER BOOK

GRANADA

London Toronto Sydney New York

Published by Granada Publishing Limited in 1982

ISBN 0 583 13309 6

First published in Great Britain by
Victor Gollancz Ltd 1979
Copyright © Fritz Leiber 1979

Granada Publishing Limited
Frogmore, St Albans, Herts AL2 2NF
and
36 Golden Square, London W1R 4AH
866 United Nations Plaza, New York, NY 10017, USA
117 York Street, Sydney, NSW 2000, Australia
100 Skyway Avenue, Rexdale, Ontario, M9W 3A6, Canada
61 Beach Road, Auckland, New Zealand

Printed and bound in Great Britain
by Cox and Wyman Ltd, Reading
Set in Plantin

Granada ®
Granada Publishing ®

Contents

Ship of Shadows

'Issiot! Fffool! Lushshsh!' hissed the cat and bit Spar somewhere.

The fourfold sting balanced the gut-wretchedness of his looming hangover, so that Spar's mind floated as free as his body in the blackness of Windrush, in which shone only a couple of running lights dim as churning dream-glow and infinitely distant as the Bridge or the Stern.

The vision came of a ship with all sails set creaming through blue, wind-ruffled sea against a blue sky. The last two nouns were not obscene now. He could hear the whistle of the salty wind through shrouds and stays, its drumming against the taut sails, and the creak of the three masts and all the rest of the ship's wood.

What was wood? From somewhere came the answer: plastic alive-o.

And what force flattened the water and kept it from breaking up into great globules and the ship from spinning away, keel over masts, in the wind?

Instead of being blurred and rounded like reality, the vision was sharp-edged and bright – the sort Spar never told, for fear of being accused of second sight and so of witchcraft.

Windrush was a ship too, was often called the Ship. But it was a strange sort of ship, in which the sailors lived forever in the shrouds inside cabins of all shapes made of translucent sails welded together.

The only other things the two ships shared were the wind and the unending creaking. As the vision faded, Spar began to hear the winds of Windrush softly moaning through the long

passageways, while he felt the creaking in the vibrant shroud
to which he was clipped wrist and ankle to keep him from
floating around in the Bat Rack.

Sleepday's dreams had begun good, with Spar having
Crown's three girls at once. But Sleepday night he had been
half-waked by the distant grinding of Hold Three's big
chewer. Then werewolves and vampires had attacked him,
solid shadows diving in from all six corners, while witches and
their familiars tittered in the black shadowy background.
Somehow he had been protected by the cat, familiar of a slim
witch whose bared teeth had been an ivory blur in the larger
silver blur of her wild hair. Spar pressed his rubbery gums
together. The cat had been the last vision of the ship.

His hangover hit him suddenly and mercilessly. Sweat
shook off him until he must be surrounded by a cloud of it.
Without warning his gut reversed. His free hand found a
floating waste tube in time to press its small trumpet to his
face. He could hear his acrid vomit gurgling away, urged by a
light suction.

His gut reversed again, quick as the flap of a safety hatch
when a gale blows up in the corridors. He thrust the waste
tube inside the leg of his short, loose slopsuit and caught the
dark stuff, almost as watery and quite as explosive as his
vomit. Then he had the burning urge to make water.

Afterwards, feeling blessedly weak, Spar curled up in the
equally blessed dark and prepared to snooze until Keeper
woke him

'Sssot!' hissed the cat. 'Sssleep no more? Sssee? Sssee
shshsharply!'

In his left shoulder, through the worn fabric of his slopsuit,
Spar could feel four sets of prickles, like the touch of small
thorn clusters in the Gardens of Apollo or Diana. He froze.

'Sspar,' the cat hissed more softly, quitting to prickle. 'I
wishsh you all besst. Mosst ashshuredly.'

Spar warily reached his right hand across his chest, touched short fur softer than Suzy's, and stroked gingerly.

The cat hissed very softly, almost purring. 'Ssturdy Sspar! Ssee ffar! Ssee fforever! Fforessee! Afftssee!'

Spar felt a surge of irritation at this constant talk of seeing – bad manners in the cat! – followed by an irrational surge of hope about his eyes. He decided that this was no witch cat left over from his dream, but a stray which had wormed its way through a wind tube into the Bat Rack, setting off his dream. There were quite a few animal strays in these days of the witch panic and the depopulation of the Ship, or at least of Hold Three.

Dawn struck the Bow then, for the violet forecorner of the Bat Rack began to flow. The running lights were drowned in a growing white blaze. Within twenty heartbeats Windrush was bright as it ever would be on Workday or any other morning.

Out along Spar's arm moved the cat, a black blur to his squinting eyes. In teeth Spar could not see, it held a smaller grey blur. Spar touched the latter. It was even shorter furred, but cold.

As if irked, the cat took off from his bare forearm with a strong push of hind legs. It landed expertly on the next shroud, a wavery line of grey that vanished in either direction before reaching a wall.

Spar unclipped himself, curled his toes round his own pencil-thin shroud, and squinted at the cat.

The cat stared back with eyes that were green blurs which almost coalesced in the black blur of its outsize head.

Spar asked, 'Your child? Dead?'

The cat loosed its grey burden, which floated beside its head.

'Chchchchild!' All the former scorn and more were back in the sibilant voice. 'It izzzz a rat I ssssslew her, issssiot!'

Spar's lips puckered in a smile. 'I like you, cat. I will call you Kim.'

'Kim-shlim!' the cat spat. 'I'll call you Lushshsh! Or Sssot!'

The creaking increased, as it always did after dayspring and noon. Shrouds twanged. Walls crackled.

Spar swiftly swivelled his head. Though reality was by its nature a blur, he could unerringly spot movement.

Keeper was slowly floating straight at him. On the round of his russet body was mounted the great, pale round of his face, its bright pink target-centre drawing attention from the tiny, wide-set, brown blurs of his eyes. One of his fat arms ended in the bright gleam of pliofilm, the other in the dark gleam of steel. Far beyond him was the dark red aft corner of the Bat Rack, with the great gleaming torus, or doughnut, of the bar midway between.

'Lazy, pampered he-slut,' Keeper greeted. 'All Sleepday you snored while I stood guard, and now I bring your morning pouch of moonmist to your sleeping shroud.

'A bad night, Spar,' he went on, his voice growing sententious. 'Werewolves, vampires, and witches loose in the corridors. But I stood them off, not to mention rats and mice. I heard through the tubes that the vamps got Girlie and Sweetheart, the silly sluts! Vigilance, Spar! Now suck your moonmist and start sweeping. The place stinks.'

He stretched out the pliofilm-gleaming hand.

His mind hissing with Kim's contemptuous words, Spar said, 'I don't think I'll drink this moring, Keeper. Corn gruel and moonbrew only. No, water.'

'What, Spar?' Keeper demanded. 'I don't believe I can allow that. We don't want you having convulsions in front of the customers. Earth strangle me! – what's that?'

Spar instantly launched himself at Keeper's steel-gleaming hand. Behind him his shroud twanged. With one hand he twisted a cold, thick barrel. With the other he pried a plump finger from a trigger.

'He's not a witch cat, only a stray,' he said as they tumbled over and kept slowly rotating.

'Unhand me, underling!' Keeper blustered. 'I'll have you in irons. I'll tell Crown.'

'Shooting weapons are as much against the law as knives or needles,' Spar countered boldly, though he already was feeling dizzy and sick. 'It's you should fear the brig.' He recognized beneath the bullying voice the awe Keeper always had of his ability to move swiftly and surely, though half-blind.

They bounced to rest against a swarm of shrouds. 'Loose me, I say,' Keeper demanded, struggling weakly. 'Crown gave me this pistol. And I have a permit for it from the Bridge.' The last at least, Spar guessed, was a lie. Keeper continued, 'Besides, it's only a line-shooting gun reworked for heavy, elastic ball. Not enough to rupture a wall, yet sufficient to knock out drunks – or knock in the head of a witch cat!'

'Not a witch cat, Keeper,' Spar repeated, although he was having to swallow hard to keep from spewing. 'Only a well-behaved stray, who has already proved his use to us by killing one of the rats that have been stealing our food. His name is Kim. He'll be a good worker.'

The distant blur of Kim lengthened and showed thin blurs of legs and tail, as if he were standing out rampant from his line. 'Assset izz I,' he boasted. 'Ssanitary. Uzze wasste tubes. Sslay ratss, micece! Sspy out witchchess, vampss ffor you!'

'He speaks!' Keeper gasped. 'Witchcraft!'

'Crown has a dog who talks,' Spar answered with finality. 'A talking animal's no proof of anything.'

All this while he had kept firm hold of barrel and finger. Now he felt through their grappled bodies a change in Keeper, as though inside his blubber the master of the Bat Rack were transforming from stocky muscle and bone into a very thick, sweet syrup that could conform to and flow around anything.

'Sorry, Spar,' he whispered unctuously. 'It was a bad night and Kim startled me. He's black like a witch cat. An easy mistake on my part. We'll try him out at catcher. He must earn his keep! Now take your drink.'

The pliant double pouch filling Spar's palm felt like the philosopher's stone. He lifted it towards his lips, but at the same time his toes unwittingly found a shroud, and he dived swiftly towards the shining torus, which had a hole big enough to accommodate four barmen at a pinch.

Spar collapsed against the opposite inside of the hole. With a straining of its shrouds, the torus absorbed his impact. He had the pouch to his lips, its cap unscrewed, but had not squeezed. He shut his eyes and with a tiny sob blindly thrust the pouch back into the moonmist cage.

Working chiefly by touch, he took a pouch of corn gruel from the hot closet, snitching at the same time a pouch of coffee and thrusting it into an inside pocket. Then he took a pouch of water, opened it, shoved in five salt tablets, closed it, and shook and squeezed it vigorously.

Keeper, having drifted behind him, said into his ear, 'So you drink anyhow. Moonmist not good enough, you make yourself a cocktail. I should dock it from your scrip. But all drunks are liars, or become so.'

Unable to ignore the taunt, Spar explained, 'No, only salt water to harden my gums.'

'Poor Spar, what'll you ever need hard gums for? Planning to share rats with your new friend? Don't let me catch you roasting them in my grill! I should dock you for the salt. To sweeping, Spar!' Then turning his head towards the violet forecorner and speaking loudly, 'And you! Catch mice!'

Kim had already found the small chewer tube and thrust the dead rat into it, gripping tube with foreclaws and pushing rat with aft. At the touch of the rat's cadaver against the solid wrist of the tube, a grinding began there which would continue until the rat was macerated and slowly swallowed away towards the great cloaca which fed the Gardens of Diana.

Three times Spar manfully swished salt water against his gums and spat into waste tube, vomiting a little after the first gargle. Then facing away from Keeper as he gently squeezed the pouches, he forced into his throat the coffee – dearer than moonmist, the drink distilled from moonbrew – and some of the corn gruel.

He apologetically offered the rest to Kim, who shook his head. 'Jusst had a mousse.'

Hastily Spar made his way to the green starboard corner. Outside the hatch he heard some drunks calling with weary and mournful anger, 'Unzip!'

Grasping the heads of two long waste tubes, Spar began to sweep the air, working out from the green corner in a spiral, quite like an orb spider building her web.

From the torus, where he was idly polishing its thin titanium, Keeper upped the suction on the two tubes, so that reaction sped Spar in his spiral. He need use his body only to steer course and to avoid shrouds in such a way that his tubes didn't tangle.

Son Keeper glanced at his wrist and called, 'Spar, can't you keep track of the time? Open up!' He threw a ring of keys which Spar caught, though he could see only the last half of their flight. As soon as he was well headed towards the green door, Keeper called again and pointed aft and aloft. Spar obediently unlocked and unzipped the dark and also the blue hatch, though there was no one at either, before opening the green. In each case he avoided the hatch's gummy margin and the sticky emergency hatch hinged close beside.

In tumbled three brewos, old customers, snatching at shrouds and pushing off from each other's bodies in their haste to reach the torus, and meanwhile cursing Spar.

'Sky strangle you!'

'Earth bury you!'

'Seas sear you!'

'Language, boys!' Keeper reproved. 'Though I'll agree my helper's stupidity and sloth tempt a man to talk foul.'

Spar threw the keys back. The brewos lined up elbow to elbow around the torus, three greyish blobs with heads pointing towards the blue corner.

Keeper faced them. 'Below, below!' he ordered indignantly. 'You think you're gents?'

'But you're serving no one aloft yet.'

'There's only us three.'

'No matter,' Keeper replied. 'Propriety, suckers! Unless you mean to buy by the pouch, invert.'

With low grumbles the brewos reversed their bodies so that their heads pointed towards the black corner.

Himself not bothering to invert, Keeper tossed them a slim and twisty faint red blur with three branches. Each grabbed a branch and stuck it in his face.

The pudge of his fat hand on glint of valve, Keeper said, 'Let's see your scrip first.'

With angry mumbles each unwadded something too small for Spar to see clearly, and handed it over. Keeper studied each item before feeding it to the cashbox. Then he decreed, 'Six seconds of moonbrew. Suck fast,' and looked at his wrist and moved the other hand.

One of the brewos seemed to be strangling, but he blew out through his nose and kept sucking bravely.

Keeper closed the valve

Instantly one brewo splutteringly accused, 'You cut us off too soon. That wasn't six.'

The treacle back in his voice, Keeper explained, 'I'm squirting it to you four and two. Don't want you to drown. Ready again?'

The brewos greedily took their second squirt and then, at times wistfully sucking their tubes for remnant drops, began to shoot the breeze. In his distant circling, Spar's keen ears heard most of it.

'A dirty Sleepday, Keeper.'

'No, a good one, brewo – for a drunken sucker to get his blood sucked by a lust-tickling vamp.'

'I was dossed safe at Pete's, you fat ghoul.'

'Pete's safe? That's news!'

'Dirty Atoms to you! But vamps did get Girlie and Sweetheart. Right in the starboard main drag, if you can believe it. By Cobalt Ninety, Windrush is getting lonely! Third Hold, anyhow. You can swim a whole passageway by day without meeting a soul.'

'How do you know that about the girls?' the second brewo demanded. 'Maybe they've gone to another hold to change their luck.'

'Their luck's run out. Suzy saw them snatched.'

'Not Suzy,' Keeper corrected, now playing umpire. 'But Mable did. A proper fate for drunken sluts.'

'You've got no heart, Keeper.'

'True enough That's why the vamps pass me by. But speaking serious, boys, the werethings and witches are running too free in Three. I was awake all Sleepday guarding. I'm sending a complaint to the bridge.'

'You're kidding.'

'You wouldn't.'

Keeper solemnly nodded his head and crossed his left chest. The brewos were impressed.

Spar spiralled back towards the green corner, sweeping farther from the wall. On his was he overtook the black blob of Kim, who was circling the periphery himself, industriously leaping from shroud to shroud and occasionally making dashes along them.

A fair-skinned, plump shape twice circled by blue – bra and culottes – swam in through the green hatch.

'Morning Spar,' a soft voice greeted. 'How's it going?'

'Fair and foul,' Spar replied. The golden cloud of blonde hair floating loose touched his face. 'I'm quitting moonmist, Suzy.'

'Don't be too hard on yourself, Spar. Work a day, loaf a day, play a day, sleep a day – that way it's best.'

'I know. Workday, Loafday, Playday, Sleepday. Ten days make a terranth, twelve terranths make a sunth, twelve sunths make a starth, and so on, to the end of time. With corrections, some tell me. I wish I knew what all those names mean.'

'You're too serious. You should – Oh, a kitten! How darling!'

'Kitten-shmitten!' the big-headed black blur hissed as it leapt past them. 'Izzz cat. IZZZ Kim.'

'Kim's our new catcher,' Spar explained. 'He's serious too.'

'Quit wasting time on old Toothless Eyeless, Suzy,' Keeper called, 'and come all the way in.'

As Suzy complied with a sigh, taking the easy route of the ratlines, her soft taper fingers brushed Spar's crumpled cheek. 'Dear Spar . . .' she murmured. As her feet passed his face, there was jingle of her charm-anklet – all gold-washed hearts, Spar knew.

'Hear about Girlie and Sweetheart?' a brewo greeted ghoulishly. 'How'd you like your carotid or outside iliac sliced, your—?'

'Shut up sucker!' Suzy wearily cut him off. 'Gimme a drink, Keeper.'

'Your tab's long, Suzy. How are you going to pay?'

'Don't play games, Keeper, please. Not in the morning, anyhow. You know all the answers especially to that one. For now, a pouch of moonbrew, dark. And a little quiet.'

'Pouches are for ladies, Suzy. I'll serve you aloft, you got to meet your marks, but—'

There was a shrill snarl which swiftly mounted to a scream of rage. Just inside the aft hatch, a pale figure in vermilion culottes and bra – no, wider than that, jacket or short coat – was struggling madly, somersaulting and kicking.

Entering carelessly, likely too swiftly, the slim girl had got parts of herself and her clothes stuck to the hatch's inside margin and the emergency hatch.

Breaking loose by frantic main force while Spar dived towards her and the brewos shouted advice, she streaked towards the torus, jerking at the ratlines, black hair streaming behind her.

Coming up with a *bong* of hip against titanium, she grabbed together her vermilion – yes, clutch coat with one hand and thrust the other across the rocking bar.

Drifting in close behind, Spar heard her say, 'Double pouch of moonmist, Keeper. Make it fast.'

'The best of mornings to you, Rixende,' Keeper greeted. 'I would gladly serve you goldwater, except, well—' The fat arms spread '—Crown doesn't like his girls coming to the Bat Rack by themselves. Last time he gave me strict orders to—'

'What the smoke! It's on Crown's account I came here, to find something he lost. Meanwhile, moonmist. Double!' She pounded on the bar until reaction started her aloft, and she pulled back into place with Spar's unthanked help.

'Softly, softly, lady,' Keeper gentled, the tiny brown blurs of his eyes vanishing with his grinning. 'What if Crown comes in while you're squeezing?'

'He won't!' Rixende denied vehemently, though glancing past Spar quickly – black blur or pale face, black blur again. 'He's got a new girl. I don't mean Phanette or Doucette, but a girl you've never seen. Name of Almodie. He'll be busy with the skinny bitch all morning. And now uncage that double moonmist, you dirty devil!'

'Softly, Rixie. All in good time. What is it Crown lost?'

'A little black bag. About so big.' She extended her slender hand, fingers merged. 'He lost it here last Playday night, or had it lifted.'

'Hear that, Spar?' Keeper said.

'No little black bags,' Spar said very quickly. 'But you did leave your big orange one here last night, Rixende. I'll get it.' He swung inside the torus.

'Oh, damn both bags. Gimme that double!' the black-haired girl demanded frantically. 'Earth Mother!'

Even the brewos gasped. Touching hands to the sides of his head, Keeper begged. 'No big obscenities, please. They sound worse from a dainty girl, gentle Rixende.'

'Earth Mother, I said! Now cut the fancy, Keeper, and give, before I scratch your face off and rummage your cages!'

'Very well, very well. At once, at once. But how will you pay? Crown told me he'd get my licence revoked if I ever put you on his tab again. Have you scrip? Or . . . coins?'

'Use your eyes!' Or you think this coat's got inside pockets?' She spread it wide, flashing her upper body, then clutched it tight again. 'Earth Mother! Earth Mother! Earth Mother!' The brewos babbled scandalized. Suzy snorted mildly in boredom.

With one fat hand-blob Keeper touched Rixende's wrist where a yellow blur circled it closely. 'You've got gold,' he said in hushed tones, his eyes vanishing again, this time in greed.

'You know damn well they're welded on. My anklets too.'

'But these?' His hand went to a golden blur close beside her head.

'Welded too. Crown had my ears pierced.'

'But . . .'

'Oh, you atom-dirty devil! I get you, all right. Well, then, *all right!*' The last words ended in a scream more of anger than pain as she grabbed a gold blur and jerked. Blood swiftly blobbed out. She thrust forward her fisted hand. 'Now *give!* Gold for a double moonmist.'

Keeper breathed hard but said nothing as he scrabbled in the moonmist cage, as if knowing he had gone too far. The brewos were silent too. Suzy sounded completely unimpressed as she said, '*And* my dark.' Spar found a fresh dry sponge and expertly caught up the floating scarlet blobs with it before pressing it to Rixende's torn ear.

Keeper studied the heavy gold pendant, which he held close to his face. Rixende milked the double pouch pressed to her lips and her eyes vanished as she sucked blissfully. Spar guided Rixende's free hand to the sponge, and she automatially took over the task of holding it to her ear. Suzy gave a hopeless sigh, then reached her whole plump body across the bar, dipped her hand into a cool cage, and helped herself to a double of dark.

A long, wiry, very dark brown figure in skintight dark violet jumpers mottled with silver arrowed in from the dark red hatch at a speed half again as great as Spar ever dared and without brushing a single shroud by accident or intent. Midway the newcomer did a half somersault as he passed Spar, his long, narrow bare feet hit the titanium next to Rixende. He accordioned up so expertly that the torus hardly swayed.

One very dark brown arm snaked around her. The other plucked the pouch from her mouth, and there was a snap as he spun the cap shut.

A lazy musical voice inquired, 'What'd we tell you would happen, baby, if you ever again took a drink on your own?'

The Bat Rack held very still. Keeper was backed against the opposite side of the hole, one hand behind him. Spar had his arm in his lost-and-found nook behind the moonbrew and the moonmist cages and kept it there. He felt fear-sweat beading on him. Suzy kept her dark close to her face.

A brewo burst into violent coughing, choked it to a wheezing end, and gasped subserviently, 'Excuse me, coroner. Salutations.'

Keeper chimed dully, 'Morning . . . Crown.'

Crown gently pulled the clutch coat off Rixende's far shoulder and began to stroke her. 'Why, you're all gooseflesh, honey, and rigid as a corpse. What frightened you? Smooth down, skin. Ease up, muscles. Relax, Rix, and we'll give you a squirt.'

His hand found the sponge, stopped, investigated, found the wet part, then went towards the middle of his face. He sniffed.

'Well, boys, at least we know none of you are vamps,' he observed softly. 'Else we'd found you sucking at her ear.'

Rixende said very rapidly in a monotone, 'I didn't come for a drink, I swear to you. I came to get that little bag you lost. Then I was tempted. I didn't know I would be. I tried to resist, but Keeper led me on. I—'

'Shut up,' Crown said quietly. 'We were just wondering how you paid him. Now we know. How were you planning to buy your third double? Cut off a hand or a foot? Keeper . . . show me your other hand. We said show it. That's right. Now unfist.'

Crown plucked the pendant from Keeper's opened hand-blob. His yellow-brown eye-blurs on Keeper all the while, he wagged the precious bauble back and forth, then tossed it slowly aloft.

As the golden blur moved towards the open blue hatch at unchanging pace, Keeper opened and shut his mouth twice, then babbled, 'I didn't tempt her, Crown, honest I didn't. I didn't know she was going to hurt her ear. I tried to stop her, but—'

'We're not interested,' Crown said. 'Put the double on our

tab.' His face never leaving Keeper's, he extended his arm aloft and pinched the pendant just before it straight-lined out of reach.

'Why's this home of jollity so dead?' Snaking a long leg across the bar as easily as an arm, Crown pinched Spar's ear between his big and smaller toes, pulled him close and turned him round. 'How're you coming along with the saline, baby? Gums hardening? Only one way to test it.' Gripping Spar's jaw and lip with his other toes, he thrust the big one into Spar's mouth. 'Come on, bite me, baby.'

Spar bit. It was the only way not to vomit. Crown chuckled. Spar bit hard. Energy flooded his shaking frame. His face grew hot and his forehead throbbed under its drenching of fear-sweat. He was sure he was hurting Crown, but the Coroner of Hold Three only kept up his low, delighted chuckle and when Spar gasped, withdrew his foot.

'My, my, you're getting strong, baby. We almost felt that. Have a drink on us.'

Spar ducked his stupidly wide-open mouth away from the thin jet of moonmist. The jet struck him in his eye and stung so that he had to knock his fists and clamp his aching gums together to keep from crying out.

'Why's this place so dead, I ask again? No applause for baby and now baby's gone temperance on us. Can't you give us just one tiny laugh?' Crown faced each in turn. 'What's the matter? Cat got your tongues?'

'Cat? We have a cat, a new cat, came just last night, working as catcher,' Keeper suddenly babbled. 'It can talk a little. Not as well as Hellhound, but it talks. It's very funny. It caught a rat.'

'What'd you do with the rat's body, Keeper?'

'Fed it to the chewer. That is Spar did. Or the cat.'

'You mean to tell us that you disposed of a corpse without notifying us? Oh, don't go pale on us, Keeper. That's nothing. Why, we could accuse you of harbouring a witch cat. You say he came last night, and that was a wicked night for witches. Now don't go green on us too. We were only putting you on. We were only looking for a small laugh.'

'Spar! Call your cat! Make him say something funny.'

Before Spar could call, or even decide whether he'd call Kim or not, the black blur appeared on a shroud near Crown, green eye-blurs fixed on the yellow-brown ones.

'So you're the joker, eh? Well . . . joke.'

Kim increased in size. Spar realized it was his fur standing on end.

'Go ahead, joke . . . like they tell us you can. Keeper, you wouldn't be kidding us about this cat being able to talk?'

'Spar! Make your cat joke!'

'Don't bother. We believe he's got his own tongue too. That the matter, Blackie?' He reached out his hand. Kim lashed at it and sprang away. Crown only gave another of his low chuckles.

Rixende began to shake uncontrollably. Crown examined her solicitously yet leisurely, using his outstretched hand to turn her head towards him, so that any blood that might have been coming from it from the cat's slash would have gone into the sponge.

'Spar swore the cat could talk,' Keeper babbled. 'I'll—'

'Quiet,' Crown said. He put the pouch to Rixende's lips, squeezed until her shaking subsided and it was empty, then flicked the crumpled pliofilm towards Spar.

'And now about that little black bag, Keeper,' Crown said flatly.

'Spar!'

That latter dipped into his lost-and-found nook, saying quickly, 'No little black bags, coroner, but we did find this one the lady Rixende forgot last Playday night,' and he turned back holding out something big, round, gleamingly orange, and closed with drawstrings.

Crown took and swung it slowly in a circle. For Spar, who couldn't see the strings, it was like magic. 'Bit too big, and a mite the wrong shade. We're certain we lost the little black bag here, or had it lifted. You making the Bat Rack a tent for dips, Keeper?'

'Spar—?'

'We're asking *you*, Keeper.'

Shoving Spar aside, Keeper groped frantically in the nook, pulling aside the cages of moonmist and moonbrew pouches. He produced many small objects. Spar could distinguish the largest – an electric hand-fan and a bright red footglove. They hung around Keeper in a jumble.

Keeper was panting and had scrabbled his hands for a full minute in the nook without bringing out anything more, when Crown said, his voice lazy again, 'That's enough. The little black bag was of no importance to us in any case.'

Keeper emerged with a face doubly blurred. It must be surrounded by a haze of sweat. He pointed an arm at the orange bag.

'It must be inside that one!'

Crown opened the bag, began to search through it, changed his mind, and gave the whole bag a flick. Its remarkably numerous contents came out and moved slowly aloft at equal speeds, like an army on the march in irregular order. Crown scanned them as they went past.

'No, not there.' He pushed the bag towards Keeper. 'Return Rix's stuff to it and have it ready for us the next time we dive in—'

Putting his arm around Rixende, so that it was his hand that held the sponge to her ear, he turned and kicked off powerfully for the aft hatch. After he had been out of sight for several seconds, there was a general sigh, the three brewos put out new scrip-wads to pay for another squirt. Suzy asked for a second double dark, which Spar handed her quickly, while Keeper shook off his daze and ordered Spar, 'Gather up all the floating trash, especially Rixie's, and get that back in her purse. On the jump, lubber!' Then he used the electric hand-fan to cool and dry himself.

It was a mean task Keeper had set Spar, but Kim came to help, darting after objects too small for Spar to see. Once he had them in his hands, Spar could readily finger or sniff which was which.

When his impotent rage at Crown had faded, Spar's thought went back to Sleepday night. Had his vision of vamps and werewolves been dream only? – now that he knew the werethings had been abroad in force. If only he had better eyes to distinguish illusion from reality! Kim's 'Sssee! Sssee shshsharply!' hissed in his memory. What would it be like to see sharply? Everything brighter? Or closer?

After a weary time the scattered objects were gathered and he went back to sweeping and Kim to his mouse hunt. As Workday morning progressed, the Bat Rack gradually grew less bright, though so gradually, it was hard to tell.

A few more customers came in, but all for quick drinks, which Keeper served them glumly; Suzy judged none of them worth cottoning up to.

As time slowly passed, Keeper grew steadily more fretfully angry, as Spar had known he would after grovelling before Crown. He tried to throw out the three brewos, but they produced more crumpled scrip, which closest scrutiny couldn't prove counterfeit. In revenge he short-squirted them and there were arguments. He called Spar off his sweeping to ask him nervously, 'That cat of yours – he scratched Crown, didn't he? We'll have to get rid of him; Crown said he might be a witch cat, remember?' Spar made no answer. Keeper set him renewing the glue of the emergency hatches, claiming that Rixende's tearing free from the aft one had shown it must be drying out. He gobbled appetizers and drank moonmist with tomato juice. He sprayed the Bat Rack with some abominable synthetic scent. He started counting the boxed scrip and coins but gave up the job with a slam of self-locking drawer almost before he'd begun. His grimace fixed on Suzy.

'Spar!' he called. 'Take over! And over-squirt the brewos on your peril!'

Then he locked the cash box, and giving Suzy a meaningful jerk of his head towards the scarlet starboard hatch, he pulled himself towards it. With an unhappy shrug towards Spar, she wearily followed.

As soon as the pair were gone, Spar gave the brewos an eight-second squirt, waving back their scrip, and placed two small serving cages – of fritos and yeast balls – before them. They grunted their thanks and fell to. The light changed from healthy bright to corpse white. There was a faint, distant roar, followed some seconds later by a brief crescendo of creakings. The new light made Spar uneasy. He served two more suck-and-dives and sold a pouch of moonmist at double purser's price. He started to eat an appetizer, but just then Kim swam in to show him proudly a mouse. He conquered his nausea, but began to dread the onset of real withdrawal symptoms.

A pot-bellied figure clad in sober black dragged itself along the ratlines from the green hatch. On the aloft side of the bar there appeared a visage in which the blur of white hair and beard almost hid leather-brown flesh, though accentuating the blurs of grey eyes.

'Doc!' Spar greeted, his misery and unease gone, and instantly handed out a chill pouch of three-star moonbrew. Yet all he could think to say in his excitement was the banal , 'A bad Sleepday night, eh, Doc? Vamps and—'

'—And other doltish superstitions, which wax every sunth, but never wane,' an amiable, cynical old voice cut in. 'Yet I suppose I shouldn't rob you of your illusions, Spar, even the terrifying ones. You've little enough to live by, as it is. And there *is* viciousness astir in Windrush. Ah, that smacks good against my tonsils.'

The Spar remembered the important thing. Reaching deep inside his slopsuit, he brought out, in such a way as to hide it from the brewos below, a small flat narrow black bag.

'Here Doc,' he whispered, 'you lost it last Playday. I kept it safe for you.'

'Dammit, I'd lose my jumpers, if I ever took them off,' Doc commented, hushing his voice when Spar put finger to lips. 'I suppose I started mixing moonmist with my moonbrew – again?'

'You did, Doc. But you didn't lose your bag. Crown or one of his girls lifted it, or snagged it when it sat loose beside you. And then I . . . I, Doc, lifted it from Crown's hip pocket. Yes, and kept that secret when Rixende and Crown came in demanding it this morning.

'Spar, my boy, I am deeply in your debt,' Doc said. 'More than you can know. Another three-star, please. Ah, nectar. Spar, ask any reward of me, and if it lies merely within the realm of the first transfinite infinity, I will grant it.'

To his own surprise, Spar began to shake – with excitement. Pulling himself forward halfway across the bar, he whispered hoarsely, 'Give me good eyes, Doc!' adding impulsively, 'and teeth!'

After what seemed a long while, Doc said in a dreamy, sorrowful voice, 'In the Old Days, that would have been easy. They'd perfected eye transplants. They could regenerate cranial nerves, and sometimes restore scanning power to an injured cerebrum. While transplanting tooth buds from a stillborn was intern's play. But now . . . Oh, I might be able to do what you ask in an uncomfortable, antique, inorganic fashion, but . . .' He broke off on a note that spoke of the misery of life and the uselessness of all effort.

'These Old Days,' one brewo said from the corner of his mouth to the brewo next to him. 'Witch talk!'

'Witch-smitch!' the second brewo replied in like fashion. 'The flesh mechanic's only senile. He dreams all four days, not just Sleepday.'

The third brewo whistled against the evil eye a tune like the wind.

Spar tugged at the long-armed sleeve of Doc's black jumper. 'Doc, you promised. I want to see sharp, bite sharp!'

Doc laid his shrunken hand commiseratingly on Spar's forearm. 'Spar,' he said softly, 'seeing sharply would only make you very unhappy. Believe me, I *know*. Life's easier to bear when things are blurred, just as it's best when thoughts are blurred by brew or mist. And while there are people in Windrush who yearn to bite sharply, you are not their kind. Another three-star, if you please.'

'I quit moonmist this morning, Doc,' Spar said somewhat proudly as he handed over the fresh pouch.

Doc answered with sad smile, 'Many quit moonmist every Workday morning and change their minds when Playday comes around.'

'Not me, Doc! Besides,' Spar argued, 'Keeper and Crown and his girls and even Suzy all see sharply, and they aren't unhappy.'

'I'll tell you a secret, Spar,' Doc replied. 'Keeper and Crown and the girls are all zombies. Yes, even Crown with his cunning and power. To them Windrush is the universe.'

'It isn't, Doc?'

Ignoring the interruption, Doc continued, 'But you wouldn't be like that, Spar. You'd want to know more. And that would make you far unhappier than you are.'

'I don't care, Doc,' Spar said. He repeated accusingly, 'You promised.'

The grey blurs of Doc's eyes almost vanished as he frowned in thought. Then he said, 'How would this be, Spar? I know moonmist brings pain and sufferings as well as easings and joys. But suppose that every Workday morning and Loafday noon I should bring you a tiny pill that would give you all the good effects of moonmist and none of the bad. I've one in this bag. Try it now and see. And every Playday night I would bring you without fail another sort of pill that would make you sleep soundly with never a nightmare. Much better than eyes and teeth. Think it over.'

As Spar considered that, Kim drifted up. He eyed Doc with his close-set green blurs. 'Resspectfful greetingss, ssir,' he hissed. 'Name izz Kim.'

Doc answered, 'The same to you, sir. May mice be ever abundant.' He softly stroked the cat, beginning with Kim's chin and chest. The dreaminess returned to his voice. 'In the Old Days, all cats talked, not just a few sports. The entire feline tribe. And many dogs, too – pardon me, Kim. While as for dolphins and whales and apes . . .'

Spar said eagerly, 'Answer me one question, Doc. If your pills give happiness without hangover, why do you always drink moonbrew yourself and sometimes spike it with moonmist?'

'Because for me—' Doc began and then broke off with a grin. 'You've trapped me, Spar. I never thought you used your mind. Very well, on your own mind be it. Come to my office this Loafday – you know the way? Good! – and we'll see what we can do about your eyes and teeth. And now a double pouch for the corridor.'

He paid in bright coins, thrust the big squunchy three-star in a big pocket, said, 'See you, Spar. So long, Kim,' and tugged himself towards the green hatch, zig-zagging.

'Ffarewell, ssir,' Kim hissed after him.

Spar held out the small black bag. 'You forgot it again, Doc.'

As Doc returned with a weary curse and pocketed it, the scarlet hatch unzipped and Keeper swam out. He looked in a good humour now and whistled the tune of 'I'll Marry the Man on the Bridge' as he began to study certain rounds on scrip-till and moonbrew valves, but when Doc was gone he asked Spar suspiciously, 'What was that you handed the old geezer?'

'His purse,' Spar replied easily. 'He forgot it now.' He shook his loosely fisted hand and it chinked. 'Doc paid in coins, Keeper.' Keeper took them eagerly. 'Back to sweeping, Spar.'

As Spar dived towards the scarlet hatch to take up larboard tubes, Suzy emerged and passed him with face averted. She sidled up to the bar and unsmilingly snatched the pouch of moonmist Keeper offered her with mock courtliness.

Spar felt a brief rage on her behalf, but it was hard for him to keep him mind on anything but his coming appointment with Doc. When Workday night fell swiftly as a hurled knife, he was hardly aware of it and felt none of his customary unease. Keeper turned on full all of the lights in the Bat Rack. They shone brightly while beyond the translucent walls there was a milky churning.

Business picked up a little. Suzy made off with the first likely mark. Keeper called Spar to take over the torus, while he himself got a much-erased sheet of paper and holding it to a clipboard held against his bent knees, wrote on it laboriously, as if he were thinking out each word, perhaps each letter, often wetting his pencil in his mouth. He became so absorbed in his difficult task that without realizing he drifted off towards the black below hatch, rotating over and over. The paper got dirtier and dirtier with his scrawlings and smudgings, new erasures, saliva and sweat.

The short night passed more swiftly than Spar dared hope, so that the sudden glare of Loafday dawn startled him. Most of the customers made off to take their siestas.

Spar wondered what excuse to give Keeper for leaving the Bat Rack, but the problem was solved for him. Keeper folded the grimy sheet, and sealed it with hot tape. 'Take this to the Bridge, loafer, to the Exec. Wait.' He took the repacked, orange bag from its nook and pulled on the cords to make sure they were drawn tight. 'On your way deliver this at Crown's Hole. With all courtesy and subservience, Spar! Now, on the jump!'

Spar slid the sealed message into his only pocket with working zipper and drew that tight. Then he dived slowly towards the aft hatch, where he almost collided with Kim. Recalling Keeper's talk of getting rid of the cat, he caught hold of him around the slim furry chest under the forelegs and gently thrust him inside his slopsuit, whispering, 'You'll take a trip with me, little Kim.' The cat set his claws in the thin material and steadied himself.

For Spar, the corridor was a narrow cylinder ending in mist either way and decorated by lengthwise blurs of green and red. He guided himself chiefly by touch and memory, this time remembering that he must pull himself against the light wind hand-over-hand along the centreline. After curving past the larger cylinders of the fore-and-aft gangways, the corridor straightened. Twice he worked his way around centrally slung fans whirring so softly that he recognized them chiefly by the increase in breeze before passing them and the slight suction after.

Soon he began to smell oil and green stuff growing. With a shiver he passed a black round that was the elastic-curtained door to Hold Three's big chewer. He met no one – odd even for Loafday. Finally he saw the green of the Gardens of Apollo and beyond it a huge black screen, in which hovered towards the aft side a small, smokey-orange circle that always filled Spar with inexplicable sadness and fear. He wondered in how many black screens that doleful circle was portrayed, especially in the starboard end of Windrush. He had seen it in several.

So close to the gardens that he could make out wavering green shoots and the silhouette of a floating farmer, the corridor right-angled below. Two dozen pulls along the line and he floated by an open hatch, which both memory for distance and the strong scent of musky, mixed perfumes told him was the entry to Crown's Hole. Peering in, he could see the intermelting black and silver spirals of the decor of the great globular room. Directly opposite the hatch was another large black screen with red-mottled dun disc placed similarly off centre.

From under Spar's chin, Kim hissed very softly, but urgently, 'Sstop! Ssilencce, on your liffe!' The cat had poked his head out of the slopsuit's neck. His ears tickled Spar's throat. Spar was getting used to Kim's melodrama, and in any case the warning was hardly needed. He had just seen the half-dozen floating naked bodies and would have held still if only from embarrassment. Not that Spar could see genitals any more than ears at the distance. But he could see that save for hair, each body was of one texture: one very dark brown and the other – five or was it four? no, five – fair. He didn't recognize the two with platinum and golden hair, who also happened to be the two palest. He wondered which was Crown's new girl, name of Almodie. He was relieved that none of the bodies were touching.

There was a glint of metal by the golden-haired girl, and he could just discern the red blur of a slender, five-forked tube which went from the metal to the five other faces. It seemed strange that even with a girl to play bartender, Crown should have moonbrew served in such plebeian fashion in his palatial Hole. Of course the tube might carry moonwine, or even moonmist.

Or was Crown planning to open a rival bar to the Bat Rack? A poor time, these days, and a worse location, he mused as he tried to think of what to do with the orange bag.

'Sslink offf!' Kim urged still more softly.

Spar's fingers found a snap-ring by the hatch. With the faintest of clicks he secured it around the draw-cords of the pouch and then pulled back the way he had come.

But faint as the click had been, there was a response from Crown's Hole – a very deep, long growl.

Spar pulled faster at the centreline. As he rounded the corner leading inboard, he looked back.

Jutting out from Crown's hatch was a big, prick-eared head narrower than a man's and darker even than Crown's.

The growl was repeated.

It was ridiculous he should be so frightened of Hellhound, Spar told himself as he jerked himself and his passenger along. Why, Crown sometimes even brought the big dog to the Bat Rack.

Perhaps it was the Hellhound never growled in the Bat Rack, only talked in a hundred or so monosyllables.

Besides, the dog couldn't pull himself along the centreline at any speed. He lacked sharp claws. Though he might be able to bound forward, caroming from one side of the corridor to another.

This time the centre-slit black curtains of the big chewer made Spar veer violently. He was a fine one – going to get new eyes today and frightened as a child!

'Why did you try to scare me back there, Kim?' he asked angrily.

'I ssaw shsheer evil, isssiot!'

'You saw five folk sucking moonbrew. And a harmless dog. This time you're the fool, Kim, you're the idiot!'

Kim shut up, drawing in his head, and refused to say another word. Spar remembered about the vanity and touchiness of all cats. But by now he had other worries. What if the orange bag were stolen by a passerby before Crown noticed it? And if Crown did find it, wouldn't he know Spar, forever Keeper's errand-boy, had been peering? That all this should happen on the most important day of his life!! His verbal victory over Kim was small consolation.

Also, although the platinum-haired girl had interested him most of the two strange ones, something began to bother him about the girl who'd been playing bartender, the one with golden hair like Suzy's, but much slimmer and paler – he had the feeling he'd seen her before. And something about her had frightened him.

When he reached the central gangways, he was tempted to go to Doc's office before the Bridge. But he wanted to be able to relax at Doc's and take as much time as needed, knowing all errands were done.

Reluctantly he entered the windy violet gangway and dived at a fore angle for the first empty space on the central gang-line, so that his palms were only burned a little before he had firm hold of it and was being sped fore at about the same speed as the wind. Keeper was a miser, not to buy him handgloves, let along footgloves! – but he had to pay sharp attention to passing the shroud-slung roller bearings that kept the thick, moving line centred in the big corridor. It was an easy trick to catch hold of the line ahead of the bearings and then get one's other hand out of the way, but it demanded watchfulness.

There were few figures travelling on the line and fewer still being blown along the corridor. He overtook a doubled up one tumbling over and over and crying out in an old cracked voice, 'Jacob's Ladder, Tree of Life, Marriage Lines . . .'

He passed the squeeze in the gangway marking the division between the Third and Second Holds without being stopped by the guard there and then he almost missed the big blue corridor leading aloft. Again he slightly burned his palms making the transfer from one moving gang-line to another. His fretfulness increased.

'Sspar, you isssiot—?' Kim began.

'Ssh! – we're in officers' territory,' Spar cut him off, glad to have that excuse for once more putting down the impudent cat. And true enough, the blue spaces of Windrush always did fill him with awe and dread.

Almost too soon to suit him, he found himself swinging from the gang-line to a stationary monkey jungle of tubular metal just below the deck of the Bridge. He worked his way to the aloftmost bars and floated there, waiting to be spoken to.

Much metal, in many strange shapes, gleamed in the Bridge, and there were irregularly pulsing rainbow surfaces, the closest of which sometimes seemed ranks and files of tiny lights going on and off – red, green, all colours. Aloft of everything was an endless velvet-black expanse very faintly blotched by churning, milky glintings.

Among the metal objects and the rainbows floated figures all clad in the midnight blue of officers. They sometimes gestured to each other, but never spoke a word. To Spar, each of their movements was freighted with profound significance. These were the gods of Windrush, who guided everything, if there were gods at all. He felt reduced in importance to a mouse, which would be chased off chittering if it once broke silence.

After a particularly tense flurry of gesture, there came a brief distant roar and a familiar creaking and crackling. Spar was amazed, yet at the same time realized he should have known that the Captain, the Navigator, and the rest were responsible for the familiar diurnal phenomena.

It also marked Loafday noon. Spar began to fret. His errands were taking too long. He began to lift his hand tentatively towards each passing figure in midnight blue.

None took the least note of him.

Finally he whispered, 'Kim—?'

The cat did not reply. He could hear a purring that might be a snore. He gently shook the cat. 'Kim, let's talk.'

'Shshut offf! I ssleep! Ssh!' Kim resettled himself and his claws and recommenced his purring snore – whether natural or feigned, Spar could not tell. He felt very despondent.

The lunths crept by. He grew desperate and weary. He must not miss his appointment with Doc! He was nerving himself to move farther aloft and speak, when he heard a pleasant 'Hello, grandpa, what's on your mind?'

Spar realized that he had been raising his hand automatically and that a person as dark-skinned as Crown, but clad in midnight blue, had at last taken notice. He unzipped the note and handed it over. 'For the Exec.'

'That's my department.' A trilled crackle – fingernail slitting the note? A larger crackle – note being opened. A brief wait. Then, 'Who's Keeper?'

'Owner of the Bat Rack, sir. I work there.'

'Bat Rack?'

'A moonbrew mansion. Once called the Happy Torus, I've been told. In the Old Days, Wine Mess Three, Doc told me.'

'Hmmm. Well, what's all this mean, gramps? And what's your name?'

Spar stared miserably at the dark-mottled grey square. 'I can't read, sir. Name's Spar.'

'Hmmm. Seen any . . . er . . . supernatural beings in the Bat Rack?'

'Only in my dreams, sir.'

'Mmmm. Well, we'll have a look in. If you recognize me, don't let on. I'm Ensign Drake, by the way. Who's your passenger, grandpa?'

'Only my cat, Ensign,' Spar breathed in alarm.

'Well, take the black shaft down.' Spar began to move

across the monkey jungle in the direction pointed out by the blue arm-blur.

'And next time remember animals aren't allowed on the Bridge.'

As Spar travelled below, his warm relief that Ensign Drake had seemed quite human and compassionate was mixed with anxiety as to whether he still had time to visit Doc. He almost missed the shift to the gang-line grinding aft in the dark red main-drag. The corpse light brightening into the false dawn of late afternoon bothered him. Once more he passed the tumbling bent figure, this time croaking, 'Trinity, Trellis, Wheat Ear . . .'

He was fighting down the urge to give up his visit to Doc and pull home to the Bat Rack, when he noticed he had passed the second squeeze and was in Hold Four with the passageway to Doc's coming up. He dived off, checked himself on a shroud and began the hand-drag to Doc's office, as far larboard as Crown's Hole was starboard.

He passed two figures clumsy on the line, their breaths malty in anticipation of Playday. Spar worried that Doc might have closed his office. He smelled soil and greenery again, from the Gardens of Diana.

The hatch was shut, but when Spar pressed the bulb, it unzipped after three honks, and the white-haloed grey eyed face peered out.

'I'd just about given up on you, Spar.'

'I'm sorry, Doc. I had to—'

'No matter. Come in, come in, Hello, Kim – take a look around if you want.'

Kim crawled out, pushed off from Spar's chest, and soon was engaged in a typical cat's tour of inspection.

And there was a great deal to inspect, as even Spar could see. Every shroud in Doc's office seemed to have objects clipped along its entire length. There were blobs large and small, gleaming and dull, light and dark, translucent and solid. They were silhouetted aginst a wall of the corpse-light Spar feared, but had no time to think of now. At one end was a band of even brighter light.

'Careful, Kim!' Spar called to the cat as he landed against a shroud and began to paw his way from blob to blob.

'He's all right,' Doc said. 'Let's have a look at you, Spar. Keep your eyes open.'

Doc's hands held Spar's head. The grey eyes and leathery face came so close they were one blur.

'Keep them open, I said. Yes, I know you have to blink them, that's all right. Just as I thought. The lenses are dissolved. You've suffered the side-effect which one in ten do who are infected with the Lethean rickettsia.'

'Styx ricks, Doc?'

'That's right, though the mob's got hold of the wrong river in the Underworld. But we've all had it. We've all drunk the water of Lethe. Though sometimes when we grow very old we begin to remember the beginning. Don't squirm.'

'Hey, Doc, is it because I've had the Styx ricks I can't remember anything back before the Bat Rack?'

'It could be. How long have you been at the Rack?'

'I don't know, Doc. Forever.'

'Before I found the place, anyhow. Then the Rumdum closed here in Four. But that's only a starth ago.'

'But I'm awful old, Doc. Why don't I start remembering?'

'You're not old, Spar. You're just bald and toothless and etched by moonmist and your muscles have shrivelled. Yes, and your mind has shrivelled too. Now open your mouth.'

One of Doc's hands went to the back of Spar's neck. The other probed. 'Your gums are tough, anyhow. That'll make it easier.'

Spar wanted to tell about the salt water, but when Doc finally took his hand out of Spar's mouth, it was to say, 'Now open wide as you can.'

Doc pushed into his mouth something big as a handbag and hot. 'Now bite down hard.'

Spar felt as if he had bitten fire. He tried to open his mouth, but hands on his head and jaw held it closed. Involuntarily he kicked and clawed air. His eyes filled with tears.

'Stop writhing! Breathe through your nose. It's not that hot. Not hot enough to blister, anyhow.'

Spar doubted that, but after a bit decided it wasn't quite hot enough to bake his brain through the roof of his mouth. Besides he didn't want to show Doc his cowardice. He held still. He blinked several times and the general blur became the blurs of Doc's face and the cluttered room silhouetted by the corpse-glare. He tried to smile, but his lips were already stretched wider than their muscles could ever have done. That hurt too; he realized now that the heat was abating a little.

Doc was grinning for him. 'Well, you would ask an old drunkard to use techniques he'd only read about. To make it up to you, I'll give you teeth sharp enough to sever shrouds. Kim, please get away from that bag.'

The black blur of the cat was pushing off from a black blur twice his length. Spar mumbled disapprovingly at Kim through his nose and made motions. The larger blur was shaped like Doc's little bag, but bigger than a hundred of them. It must be massive too, for in reaction to Kim's push it had bent the shroud to which it was attached and – the point – the shroud was very slow in straightening.

'That bag contains my treasure, Spar,' Doc explained, and when Spar lifted his eyebrows twice to signal another question, went on, 'No, not coin and gold and jewels, but a second transfinite infinitude – sleep and dreams and nightmares for every soul in a thousand Windrushes.' He glanced at his wrist. 'Time enough now. Open your mouth.' Spar obeyed, though it cost him new pain.

Doc withdrew what Spar had bitten on, wrapped it in gleam, and clipped it to the nearest shroud. Then he looked in Spar's mouth again.

'I guess I did make it a bit too hot,' he said. He found a small pouch, set it to Spar's lips, and squeezed it. A mist filled Spar's mouth and all pain vanished.

Doc tucked the pouch in Spar's pocket. 'If the pain returns, use it again.'

But before Spar could thank Doc, the latter had pressed a tube to his eye. 'Look, Spar, what do you see?'

Spar cried out, he couldn't help it, and jerked his eye away.

'What's wrong, Spar?'

'Doc, you gave me a dream,' Spar said hoarsely. 'You won't tell anyone, will you? And it tickled.'

'What was the dream like?' Doc asked eagerly.

'Just a picture, Doc. The picture of a goat with the tail of a fish. Doc, I saw the fish's . . .' His mind groped, '. . . scales! Everything had . . . edges! Doc, is *that* what they mean when they talk about seeing sharply?'

'Of course, Spar. This is good. It means there's no cerebral or retinal damage. I'll have no trouble making up field glasses – that is, if there's nothing seriously wrong with my antique pair. So you still see things sharp-edged in dreams – that's natural enough. But why were you afraid of telling?'

'Afraid of being accused of witchcraft, Doc. I thought seeing things like that was clairvoyance. The tube tickled my eye a little.'

'Isotopes and insanity! It's supposed to tickle. Let's try the other eye.'

Again Spar wanted to cry out, but he restrained himself, and this time he had no impulse to jerk his eye away, although there was again the faint tickling. The picture was that of a slim girl. He could tell she was female because of her general shape. But he could see her edges. He could see . . . details.

For instances, her eyes weren't mist-bounded coloured ovals. They had points at both ends, which were china-white . . . triangles. And the pale violet round between the triangles had a tiny black round at its centre.

She had silvery hair, yet she looked young, he thought, though it was hard to judge such matter when you could see edges. She made him think of the platinum-haired girl he'd glimpsed in Crown's Hole.

She wore a long, gleaming white dress, which left her shoulders bare, but either art or some unknown force had drawn her hair and her dress towards her feet. In her dress it made . . . folds.

'What's her name Doc? Almodie?'

'No. Virgo. The Virgin. You can see her edges?'

'Yes, Doc. Sharp. I get it! – like a knife. And the goat-fish?'

'Capricorn,' Doc answered, removing the tube from Spar's eye.

'Doc, I know Capricorn and Virgo are the names of lunths, terranths, sunths, and starths, but I never knew they had pictures. I never knew they *were* anything.'

'You— Of course, you've never seen watches, or stars, let alone the constellations of the zodiac.'

Spar was about to ask what all *those* were, but then he saw that the corpse-light was all gone, although the ribbon of brighter light had grown very wide.

'At least in this stretch of your memory,' Doc added. 'I should have your new eyes and teeth ready next Loafday. Come earlier if you can manage. I may see you before that at the Bat Rack, Playday night or earlier.'

'Great, Doc, but now I've got to haul. Come on, Kim! Sometimes business heavies up Loafday night, Doc, like it was Playday night come at the wrong end. Jump in, Kim.'

'Sure you can make it back to the Bat Rack all right, Spar? It'll be dark before you get there.'

'Course I can, Doc.'

But when night fell, like a heavy hood jerked down over his head, halfway down the first passageway, he would have gone back to ask Doc to guide him except he feared Kim's contempt, even though the cat still wasn't talking. He pulled ahead rapidly, though the few running lights hardly let him see the centreline.

The fore gangway was even worse – completely empty and its lights dim and flickering. Seeing blurs bothered him now that he knew what seeing sharp was like. He was beginning to sweat and shake and cramp from his withdrawal from alcohol and his thoughts were a tumult. He wondered if *any* of the weird things that had happened since meeting Kim were real or dream. Kim's refusal – or inability? – to talk any more was disquieting. He began seeing the misty rims of blurs that vanished when he looked straight towards them. He remembered Keeper and the brewos talking about vamps and witches.

Then instead of waiting for the Bat Rack's green hatch, he dived off into the passageway leading to the aft one. This passageway had no lights at all. Out of it he thought he could hear Hellhound growling, but couldn't be sure because the big chewer was grinding. He was scrabbling with panic when he entered the Bat Rack through the dark red hatch, remembering barely in time to avoid the new glue.

The place was jumping with light and excitement and dancing figures, and Keeper at once began to shout abuse at him. He dived into the torus and began taking orders and serving automatically, working entirely by touch and voice, because withdrawal now had his vision swimming – a spinning blur of blurs.

After a while that got better, but his nerves got worse. Only the unceasing work kept him going – and shut out Keeper's abuse – but he was getting too tired to work at all. As Playday dawned, with the crowd around the torus getting thicker all the while, he snatched a pouch of moonmist and set it to his lips.

Claws dug his chest. 'Isssiot! Sssot! Ssslave of fffear!'

Spar almost went into convulsions, but put back the moonmist. Kim came out of the slopsuit and pushed off contemptuously, circled the bar and talked to various of the drinkers, soon became a conversation piece. Keeper started to boast about him and quit serving. Spar worked on and on and on through sobriety more nightmarish than any drunk he could recall. And far, far longer.

Suzy came in with a mark and touched Spar's hand when he served her dark to her. It helped.

He thought he recognized a voice from below. It came from a kinky-haired, slopsuited brewo he didn't know. But then he heard the man again and thought he was Ensign Drake. There were several brewos he didn't recognize.

The place started really jumping. Keeper upped the music. Singly or in pairs, somersaulting dancers bounded back and forth between shrouds. Others toed a shroud and shimmied. A girl in black did splits on one. A girl in white dived through the torus. Keeper put it on her boyfriend's check. Brewos tried to sing.

Spar heard Kim recite:

'Izz a cat.
Killzz a rat.
Grreetss each guy,
Thin or ffat.
Saay dolls, hi!'

Playday night fell. The pace got hotter. Doc didn't come. But Crown did. Dancers parted and a whole section of drinkers made way aloft for him and his girls and Hellhound, so that they had a third of the torus to themselves, with no one below in that third either. To Spar's surprise they all took coffee except the dog, who when asked by Crown, responded, 'Bloody Mary,' drawing out the words in such deep tones that they were little more than a low 'Bluh-Muh' growl.

'Iss that sspeech, I assk you?' Kim commented from the other side of the torus. Drunks around him choked down chuckles.

Spar served the pouched coffee piping hot with felt holders and mixed Hellhound's drink in a self-squeezing syringe with sipping tube. He was very groggy and for the moment more afraid for Kim than himself. The face blurs tended to swim, but he could distinguish Rixende by her black hair, Phanette and Doucette by their matching red-blonde hair and oddly red-mottled fair skins, while Almodie *was* the platinum-haired one, yet she looked horribly right between the dark brown, purple-vested blur to one side of her and the blacked, narrower, prick-eared silhouette to the other.

Spar heard Crown whisper to her, 'Ask Keeper to show you the talking cat.' The whisper was very low and Spar wouldn't have heard it except that Crown's voice had a strange excited vibrancy Spar had never known in it before.

'But won't they fight then? – I mean Hellhound,' she answered in a voice that sent silver tendrils around Spar's heart. He yearned to see her face through Doc's tube. She would look like Virgo, only more beautiful. Yet, Crown's girl, she could be no virgin. It was a strange and horrible world. Her eyes *were* violet. But he was sick of blurs. Almodie sounded very frightened, yet she continued, 'Please don't, Crown.' Spar's heart was captured.

'But that's the whole idea, baby. And nobody don'ts us. We thought we'd schooled you to that. We'd teach you another lesson here, except tonight we smell his fuzz – lots of it, Keeper! – our new lady wishes to hear your cat talk. Bring it over.'

'I really don't . . .' Almodie began and went no further.

Kim came floating across the torus while keeper was shouting in the opposite direction. The cat checked himself against a slender shroud and looked straight at Crown. 'Yesss?'

'Keeper, shut that junk off.' The music died abruptly. Voices rose, then died abruptly too. 'Well, cat, talk.'

'Shshall ssing insstead,' Kim announced and began an eerie caterwauling that had a pattern but was not Spar's idea of music.

'It's an abstraction,' Almodie breathed delightedly. 'Listen, Crown, that was a diminished seventh.'

'A demented third, I'd say,' Phanette commented from the other side.

Crown signed them to be quiet.

Kim finished with a high trill. He slowly looked around at his baffled audience and then began to groom his shoulder.

Crown gripped a ridge of the torus with his left hand and said evenly, 'Since you will not talk to us, will you talk to our dog?'

Kim stared at Hellhound sucking his Bloody Mary. His eyes widened, their pupils slitted, his lips writhed back from needlelike fans.

He hissed, 'Schschweinhund!'

Hellhound launched himself, hind paws against the palm of Crown's left hand, which threw him forward towards the left, where Kim was dodging. But the cat switched directions, rebounding hindwards from the next shroud. The dog's white-jagged jaws snapped sideways a foot from their mark as his great-chested black body hurtled past.

Hellhound landed with four paws in the middle of a fat drunk, who puffed out his wind barely before his swallow, but the dog took off instantly on reverse course. Kim bounced back and forth between shrouds. This time hair flew when jaws snapped, but also a rigidly spread paw slashed.

Crown grabbed Hellhound by his studded collar, restraining him from another dive. He touched the dog below the eye and smelled his fingers. 'That'll be enough, boy,' he said. 'Can't go around killing musical geniuses.' His hand dropped from his nose to below the torus and came up loosely fisted. 'Well, cat, you've talked with our dog. Have you a word for us?'

'Yesss!' Kim drifted to the shroud nearest Crown's face. Spar pushed off to grab him back, while Almondie gazed at Crown's fist and edged a hand towards it.

Kim loudly hissed, 'Hellzzz ssspawn! Fffiend!'

Both Spar and Almodie were too late. From between two of Crown's fisted fingers a needle-stream jetted and struck Kim in the open mouth.

After what seemed to Spar a long time, his hand interrupted the stream. Its back burned acutely.

Kim seemed to collapse into himself, then launched himself away from Crown, towards the dark, open-jawed.

Crown said, 'That's mace, an antique weapon like Greek fire, but well-known to our folks. The perfect answer to a witch cat.'

Spar sprang at Crown, grappled his chest, tried to butt his jaw. They moved away from the torus at half the speed with which Spar had sprung.

Crown got his head aside. Spar closed his gums on Crown's throat. There was a *snick*. Spar felt wind on his bare back. Then a cold triangle pressed his flesh over his kidneys. Spar opened his jaws and floated limp. Crown chuckled.

A blue fuzz-glare, held by a brewo, made everyone in the Bat Rack look more corpse-like than larboard light. A voice commanded, 'Okay, folks, break it up. Go home. We're closing the place.'

Sleepday dawned, drowning the fuzz-glare. The cold

triangle left Spar's back. There was another *snick*. Saying, 'Bye-bye, baby,' Crown pushed off through the white glare towards four women's faces and one dog's. Phanette's and Doucette's faintly red-mottled ones were close beside Hellhound's, as if they might be holding his collar.

Spar sobbed and began to hunt for Kim. After a while Suzy came to help him. The Bat Rack emptied. Spar and Suzy cornered Kim. Spar grasped the cat around the chest. Kim's forelegs embraced his wrist, claws pricking. Spar got out the pouch Doc had given him and shoved its mouth between Kim's jaws. The claws dug keep. Taking no note of that, Spar gently sprayed. Gradually the claws came out and Kim relaxed. Spar hugged him gently. Suzy bound up Spar's wounded wrist.

Keeper came up followed by two brewos, one of them Ensign Drake, who said, 'My partner and I will watch today by the aft and starboard hatches.' Beyond them the Bat Rack was empty.

Spar said, 'Crown has a knife.' Drake nodded.

Suzy touched Spar's hand and said, 'Keeper, I want to stay here tonight. I'm scared.'

Keeper said, 'I can offer you a shroud.'

Drake and his mate dived slowly toward their posts.

Suzy squeezed Spar's hand. He said, rather heavily, 'I can offer you my shroud, Suzy.'

Keeper laughed and after looking towards the Bridge men, whispered, 'I can offer you mine, which, unlike Spar, I own. And moonmist. Otherwise, the passageways.'

Suzy sighed, paused then went off with him.

Spar miserably made his way to the fore corner. Had Suzy expected him to fight Keeper? The sad thing was that he no longer wanted her, except as a friend. He loved Crown's new girl. Which was sad too.

He was very tired. Even the thought of new eyes tomorrow

didn't interest him. He clipped his ankle to a shroud and tied a rag over his eyes. He gently clasped Kim, who had not spoken. He was asleep at once.

He dreamed of Almodie. She looked like Virgo, even to the white dress. She held Kim, who looked sleek as polished black leather. She was coming towards him smiling. She kept coming without getting closer.

Much later – he thought – he woke in the grip of withdrawal. He sweat and shook, but those were minor. His nerves were jumping. Any moment, he was sure, they would twitch all his muscles into a stabbing spasm of sinew-snapping agony. His thoughts were moving so fast he could hardly begin to understand one in ten. It was like speeding through a curving, ill-lit passageway ten times faster than the main drag. If he touched a wall, he would forget even what little Spar knew, forget he was Spar. All around him black shrouds whipped in perpetual sine curves.

Kim was no longer by him. He tore the rag from his eyes. It was dark as before. Sleepday night. But his body stopped speeding and his thoughts slowed. His nerves still crackled, and he still saw the black snakes whipping, but he knew them for illusion. He even made out the dim glows of three running lights.

Then he saw two figures floating towards him. He could barely make out their eye-blurs, green in the smaller, violet in the other, whose face was spreadingly haloed by silvery glints. She was pale and whiteness floated around her. And instead of a smile, he could see the white horizontal blur of bared teeth. Kim's teeth too were bared.

Suddenly he remembered the golden-haired girl who he'd thought was playing bartender in Crown's Hole. She was Suzy's onetime friend Sweetheart, snatched last Sleepday by vamps.

He screamed, which in Spar was a hoarse, retching bellow,

and scrabbled at his clipped ankle.

The figures vanished. Below, he thought.

Lights came on. Someone dived and shook Spar's shoulder. 'What happened, gramps?'

Spar gibbered while he thought what to tell Drake. He loved Almodie and Kim. He said, 'Had a nightmare. Vamps attacked me.'

'Description?'

'An old lady and a . . . a . . . little dog.'

The other officer dived in. 'The black hatch is open.'

Drake said, 'Keeper told us that was always locked. Follow through, Fenner.' As the other dived below, 'You're sure this was a nightmare, gramps? A *little* dog? And an *old* woman?'

Spar said, 'Yes,' and Drake dived after his comrade, out through the black hatch.

Workday dawned. Spar felt sick and confused, but he set about his usual routine. He tried to talk to Kim, but the cat was as silent as yesterday afternoon. Keeper bullied and found many tasks – the place was a mess from Playday. Suzy got away quickly. She didn't want to talk about Sweetheart or anything else. Drake and Fenner didn't come back.

Spar swept and Kim patrolled, out of touch. In the afternoon Crown came in and talked with Keeper while Spar and Kim were out of earshot. The mightn't have been there for all notice Crown took of them.

Spar wondered about what he had seen last night. It might really have been a dream, he decided. He was no longer impressed by his memory-identification of Sweetheart. Stupid of him to have thought that Almodie and Kim, dream or reality, were vamps. Doc had said vamps were superstitions. But he didn't think much. He still had withdrawal symptoms, only less violent.

When Loafday dawned, Keeper gave Spar permission to

leave the Bat Rack without his usual prying questions. Spar looked around for Kim, but couldn't see his black blob. Besides, he didn't really want to take the cat.

He went straight to Doc's office. The passageways weren't as lonely as last Loafday. For a third time he passed the bent figure croaking, 'Seagull, Kestrel, Cathedral . . .'

Doc's hatch was unzipped, but Doc wasn't there. Kim waited a long while, uneasy in the corpse-light. It wasn't like Doc to leave his office unzipped and unattended. And he hadn't turned up at the Bat Rack last night, as he'd half promised.

Finally Spar began to look around. One of the first things he noticed was that the big black bag, which Doc had said contained his treasure, was missing.

Then he noticed that the gleaming pliofilm bag in which Doc had put the mould of Spar's gums, now held something different. He unclipped it from its shroud. There were two items in it.

He cut a finger on the first, which was half circle, half pink and half gleaming. He felt out its shape more cautiously then, ignoring the tiny red blobs welling from his fingers. It had irregular depressions in its pink top and bottom. He put it in his mouth. His gums mated with the depressions. He opened his mouth, then closed it, careful to keep his tongue back. There was a *snick* and a dull *click*. He had teeth!

His hands were shaking, not just from withdrawal, as he felt the second time.

It was two thick rounds joined by a short bar and with a thicker long bar ending in a semicircle going back from each.

He thrust a finger into one of the rounds. It tickled, just as the tube had tickled his eyes, only more intensely, almost painfully.

Hands shaking worse than ever, he fitted the contraption to his face. The semicircles went around his ears, the rounds circled his eyes, not closely enough to tickle.

He could see sharply! *Everything* had edges, even his spread-fingered hands and the . . . clot of blood on one finger. He cried out – a low, wondering wail – and scanned the office. At first the scores and dozens of sharp-edged objects, each as distinct as the pictures of Capricorn and Virgo had been, were too much for him. He closed his eyes.

When his breathing was a little evener and his shaking less, he opened them cautiously and began to inspect the objects clipped to the shrouds. Each one was a wonder. He didn't know the purpose of half of them. Some of them with which he was familiar by use of blurred sight startled him greatly in their appearance – a comb, a brush, a book with pages (that infinitude of ranked black marks), a wrist watch, the tiny pictures around the circular margin of Capricorn and Virgo, and of the Bull and the Fishes, and so on, and the narrow bars radiating from the centre and swinging swiftly or slowly or not at all – and pointing to the signs of the zodiac.

Before he knew it, he was at the corpse-glow wall. He faced it with a new courage, though it forced from his lips another wondering wail.

The corpse-glow didn't come from everywhere, though it took up the central quarter of his field of vision. His fingers touched taut, transparent pliofilm. What he saw beyond – a great way beyond, he began to think – was utter blackness with a great many tiny . . . points of bright light in it. Points were even harder to believe in than edges, he had to believe what he saw.

But centrally, looking much bigger than all the blackness, was a vast corpse-white round pocked with faint circles and scored by bright lines and mottled with slightly darker areas.

It didn't look as if it were wired for electricity, and it certainly didn't look afire. After a while Spar got the weird idea that its light was reflected from something much brighter *behind* Windrush.

It was infinitely strange to think of so much *space* around Windrush. Like thinking of a reality containing reality.

And if Windrush were between the hypothetical brighter light and the pocked white round, its shadow ought to be on the latter. Unless Windrush were almost infinitely small. Really these speculations were utterly too fantastic to deal with.

Yet could anything be too fantastic? Werewolves, witches, points, edges, size and space beyond any but the most insane belief.

When he had first looked at the corpse-white object, it had been round. And he had heard and felt creakings of Loafday noon, without being conscious of it at the time. But now the round had its fore edge evenly sliced off, so that it was lopsided. Spar wondered if the hypothetical incandescence behind Windrush were moving, or the white round rotating, or Windrush itself revolving around the white round. Such thoughts, especially the last, were dizzying almost beyond endurance.

He made for the open door, wondering if he should zip it behind him, decided not to. The passageway was another amazement, going off and off and off, and narrowing as it went. Its walls bore . . . arrows, the red pointing to larboard, the way from which he'd come, the green pointing starboard, the way he was going. The arrows were what he'd always seen as dash-shaped blurs. As he pulled himself along the strangely definite dragline, the passageway stayed the same diameter, all the way to the violet main drag.

He wanted to jerk himself as fast as the green arrows to the starboard end of Windrush to verify the hypothetical incandescence and see the details of the orange-dun round that always depressed him.

But he decided he ought first to report Doc's disappearance

to the Bridge. He might find Drake there. And report the loss of Doc's treasure too, he reminded himself.

Passing faces fascinated him. Such a welter of noses and ears! He overtook the croaking, bent shape. It was that of an old woman whose nose almost met her chin. She was doing something twitchy with her fingers to two narrow sticks and a roll of slender, fuzzy line. He impulsively dived off the dragline and caught hold of her, whirling them around.

'What are you doing, grandma?' he asked.

She puffed with anger, 'Knitting,' she answered indignantly.

'What are the words you keep saying?'

'Names of knitting patterns,' she replied, jerking loose from him and blowing on. 'Sand Dunes, Lightning, Soldiers Marching . . .'

He started to swim for the dragline, then saw he was already at the blue shaft leading aloft. He grabbed hold of its speeding centreline, not minding the burn, and speeded to the Bridge.

When he got there, he saw there was a multitude of stars aloft. The oblong rainbows were all banks of multi-coloured lights winking on and off. But the silent officers – they looked very old, their faces stared as if they were sleep-swimming, their gestured orders were mechanical, he wondered if they knew where Windrush was going – or anything at all, beyond the Bridge of Windrush.

A dark young officer with tightly curly hair floated to him. It wasn't until he spoke that Spar knew he was Ensign Drake.

'Hello, gramps. Say, you look younger. What are those things around your eyes?'

'Field glasses. They help me see sharp.'

'But fieldglasses have tubes. They're a sort of binocular telescope.'

Spar shrugged and told about the disappearance of Doc

and his big, black treasure bag.

'But you say he drank a lot and he told you his treasures were dreams? Sounds like he was wacky and wandered off to do his drinking somewhere else.'

'But Doc was a regular drinker. He always came to the Bat Rack.'

'Well, I'll do what I can. Say, I've been pulled off the Bat Rack investigation. I think that character Crown got at someone higher up. The old ones are easy to get at – not so much greed as going by custom, taking the easiest course. Fenner and I never did find the old woman and the little dog, or any female and animal . . . or anything.'

Spar told about Crown's earlier attempt to steal Doc's little black bag.

'So you think the two cases might be connected. Well, as I say, I'll do what I can.'

Spar went back to the Bat Rack. It was very strange to see Keeper's face in details. It looked old and its pink target centre was a big red nose criss-crossed by veins. His brown eyes were not so much curious as avid. He asked about the things around Spar's eyes. Spar decided it wouldn't be wise to tell Keeper about seeing sharply.

'They're a new kind of costume jewellery, Keeper. Blasted Earth, I don't have any hair on my head, ought to have something.'

'Language, Spar! It's like a drunk to spend precious scrip on such a grotesque bauble.'

Spar neither reminded Keeper that all the scrip he'd earned at the Bat Rack amounted to no more than a wad as big as his thumb-joint, nor that he'd quit drinking. Nor did he tell him about his teeth, but kept them hidden behind his lips.

Kim was nowhere in sight. Keeper shrugged. 'Gone off somewhere. You know the way of strays, Spar.'

Yes, thought Spar, this one's stayed put too long.

He kept being amazed that he could see *all* of the Bat Rack sharply. It was an octahedron criss-crossed by shrouds and made up of two pyramids put together square base to square base. The apexes of the pyramids were the violet fore and dark red aft corners. The four other corners were the starboard green, the black below, the larboard scarlet, and the blue aloft, if you named them from aft in the way the hands of a watch move.

Suzy drifted in early Playday. Spar was shocked by her blowsy appearance and bloodshot eyes. But he was touched by her signs of affection and he felt the strong friendship between them. Twice when Keeper wasn't looking he switched her nearly empty pouch of dark for a full one. She told him that, yes, she'd once known Sweetheart and that, yes, she'd heard people say Mable had seen Sweetheart snatched by vamps.

Business was slow for Playday. There were no strange brewos. Hoping against fearful, gut-level certainty, Spar kept waiting for Doc to come in zig-zagging along the ratlines and comment on the new gadgets he'd given Spar and spout about the Old Days and his strange philosophy.

Playday night Crown came in with his girls, all except Almodie. Doucette said she'd had a headache and stayed at the Hole. Once again, all of them ordered coffee, though to Spar all of them seemed high.

Spar covertly studied their faces. Though nervous and alive, they all had something in their stares akin to those he'd seen in most of the officers on the Bridge. Doc had said they were all zombies. It was interesting to find out that Phanette's and Doucette's red-mottled appearance was due to . . . freckles, tiny reddish star-clusters on their white skins.

'Where's that famous talking cat?' Crown asked Spar.

Spar shrugged. Keeper said. 'Strayed. For which I'm glad. Don't want a little feline who makes fights like last night.'

Keeping his yellow-brown irised eyes on Spar, Crown said, 'We believe it was that fight last Playday gave Almodie her headache, so she didn't want to come back tonight. We'll tell her you got rid of the witch cat.'

'I'd have got rid of the beast if Spar hadn't,' Keeper put in. 'So you think it was a witch cat, coroner?'

'We're certain. What's that stuff on Spar's face?'

'A new sort of cheap eye-jewellery, coroner, such as attracts drinks.'

Spar got the feeling that this conversation had been pre-arranged, that there was a new agreement between Crown and Keeper. But he just shrugged again. Suzy was looking angry, but she said nothing.

Yet she stayed behind again after the Bat Rack closed. Keeper put no claim on her, though he leered knowingly before disappearing with a yawn and a stretch through the scarlet hatch. Spar checked that all six hatches were locked and shut off the lights, though that made no difference in the morning glare, before returning to Suzy, who had gone to his sleeping shroud.

Suzy asked, 'You didn't get rid of Kim?'

Spar answered, 'No, he just strayed, as Keeper said at first. I don't know where Kim is.'

Suzy smiled and put her arms around him. 'I think your new eye-things are beautiful,' she said.

Spar said, 'Suzy, did you know that Windrush isn't the Universe? That it's a ship going through space around a white round marked with circles, a round much bigger than all Windrush?'

Suzy replied, 'I know Windrush is sometimes called the Ship. I've seen that round – in pictures. Forget all wild thoughts, Spar, and lose yourself in me.'

Spar did so, chiefly from friendship. He forgot to clip his ankle to the shroud. Suzy's body didn't attract him. He was thinking of Almodie.

When it was over, Suzy slept. Spar put the rag around his eyes and tried to do the same. He was troubled by withdrawal symptoms only a little less bad than last Sleepday's. Because of that little, he didn't go to the torus for a pouch of moonmist. But then there was a sharp jab in his back, as if a muscle had spasmed there, and the symptoms got much worse. He convulsed, once, twice, then just as the agony became unbearable, blanked out.

Spar woke, his head throbbing, to discover that he was not only clipped, but lashed to his shroud, his wrists stretched in one direction, his ankles in the other, his hands and his feet both numb. His nose rubbed the shroud.

Light made his eyelids red. He opened them a little at a time and saw Hellhound poised with bent hind legs against the next shroud. He could see Hellhound's great stabbing teeth very clearly. If he had opened his eyes a little more swiftly, Hellhound would have dived at his throat.

He rubbed his sharp metal teeth together. At least he had more than gums to meet an attack on his face.

Beyond Hellhound he saw black and transparent spirals. He realized he was in Crown's Hole. Evidently the last jab in his back had been the injection of a drug.

But Crown had not taken away his eye jewellery, nor noted his teeth. He had thought of Spar as old Eyeless Toothless.

Between Hellhound and the spirals, he saw Doc lashed to a shroud and his big black bag clipped next to him. Doc was gagged. Evidently he had tried to cry out. Spar decided not to. Doc's grey eyes were open and Spar thought Doc was looking at him.

Very slowly Spar moved his numb fingers on top of the knot lashing his wrists to the shroud and slowly contracted all his muscles and pulled. The knot slid down the shroud a millimetre. So long as he did something slowly enough,

Hellhound could not see it. He repeated this action at intervals.

Even more slowly he swung his face to the left. He saw nothing more than that the hatch to the corridor was zipped shut, and that beyond the dog and Doc, between the black spirals, was an empty and unfurnished cabin whose whole starboard side was stars. The hatch to that cabin was open, with its black-striped emergency hatch wavering beside it.

With equal slowness he swung his face to the right, past Doc and past Hellhound, who was eagerly watching him for signs of life or waking. He had pulled down the knot on his wrists two centimetres.

The first thing he saw was a transparent oblong. In it were more stars and, by its aft edge, the smoky orange round. At last he could see more clearly. The smoke was on top, the orange underneath and irregularly placed. The whole was about as big as Spar's palm could have covered, if he had been able to stretch out his arm to full length. As he watched, he saw a bright flash in one of the orange areas. The flash was short, then it turned to a tiny black round pushing out through the smoke. More than ever, Spar felt sadness.

Below the transparency, Spar saw a horrible tableau. Suzy was strapped to a bright metal rack guyed by shrouds. She was very pale and her eyes were closed. From the side of her neck, went a red sipping-tube which forked into five branches. Four of the branches went into the red mouths of Crown, Rixende, Phanette, and Doucette. The fifth was shut by a small metal clip, and beyond it Almodie floated cowering, hands over her eyes.

Crown said softly, 'We want it all. Strip her, Rixie.'

Rixende clipped shut the end of her tube and swam to Suzy. Spar expected her to remove the blue culottes and bra, but instead she simply began to massage one of Suzy's legs, pressing always from ankle towards waist, driving her remaining blood nearer her neck.

Crown removed his sipping tube from his lips long enough to say, 'Ahhh, good to the last drop.' Then he had mouthed the blood that spurted out in the interval and had the tube in place again.

Phanette and Doucette convulsed with soundless giggles.

Almodie peered between her parted fingers, out of her mass of platinum hair, then scissored them shut again.

After a while Crown said, 'That's all we'll get. Phan and Doucie, feed her to the big chewer. If you meet anyone in the passageway, pretend she's drunk. Afterwards we'll get Doc to dose us high, and give him a little brew if he behaves, then we'll drink Spar.'

Spar had his wrist knot more than halfway to his teeth. Hellhound kept watching eagerly for movement, unable to see movement that slow. Slaver made tiny grey globules beside his fangs.

Phanette and Doucette opened the hatch and steered Suzy's dead body through it.

Embracing Rixende, Crown said expansively towards Doc, 'Well, isn't it the right thing, old man? Nature bloody in tooth and claw, a wise one said. They've poisoned everything there.' He pointed towards the smoky orange round sliding out of sight. 'They're still fighting, but they'll soon all be dead. So death should be the rule too for this gimcrack, so-called survival ship. Remember they are aboard her. When we've drunk the blood of everyone aboard Windrush, including their blood, we'll drink our own, if our own isn't theirs.'

Spar thought, Crown thinks too much in they's. The knot was close to his teeth. He heard the big chewer start to grind.

In the empty next cabin, Spar saw Drake and Fenner, clad once more as brewos, swimming towards the open hatch.

But Crown saw them too. 'Get 'em, Hellhound,' he

directed, pointing. 'It's our command.'

The big black dog bulleted from his shroud through the open hatch. Drake pointed something at him. The dog went limp.

Chuckling softly, Crown took by one tip a swastika with curved, gleaming, razor-sharp blades and sent it off spinning. It curved past Spar and Doc, went through the open hatch, missed Drake and Fenner – and Hellhound – and struck the wall of stars.

There was a rush of wind, then the emergency hatch smacked shut. Spar saw Drake, Fenner, and Hellhound, wavery through the transparent pliofilm, spew blood, bloat, burst bloodily open. The empty cabin they had been in disappeared. Windrush had a new wall and Crown's Hole was distorted.

Far beyond, growing ever tinier, the swastika spun towards the stars.

Phanette and Doucette came back. 'We fed in Suzy. Someone was coming, so we beat it.' The big chewer stopped grinding.

Spar bit cleanly through his wrist lashings and immediately doubled over to bite his ankles loose.

Crown dived at him. Pausing to draw knives, the four girls did the same.

Phanette, Doucette, and Rixende went limp. Spar had the impression that small black balls had glanced from their skulls.

There wasn't time to bite his feet loose, so he straightened. Crown hit his chest as Almodie hit his feet.

Crown and Spar giant-swung around the shroud. Then Almodie had cut Spar's ankles loose. As they spun off along the tangent, Spar tried to knee Crown in the groin, but Crown twisted and evaded the blow as they moved towards the inboard wall.

There was the *snick* of Crown's knife unfolding. Spar saw the the dark wrist and grabbed it. He butted at Crown's jaw. Crown evaded. Spar set his teeth in Crown's neck and bit.

Blood covered Spar's face, spurted over it. He spat out a hunk of flesh. Crown convulsed. Spar fought off the knife. Crown went limp. That the pressure in a man should work against him.

Spar shook the blood from his face. Through its beads, he saw Keeper and Kim side by side. Almodie was clutching his ankles. Phanette, Doucette, Rixende floated.

Keeper said proudly, 'I shot them with my gun for drunks. I knocked them out. Now I'll cut their throats, if you wish.'

Spar said, 'No more throat-cutting. No more blood.' Shaking off Almodie's hands he took off for Doc, picking up Doucette's floating knife by the way.

He slashed Doc's lashings and cut the gag from his face.

Meanwhile Kim hissed, 'Sstole and ssecreted Keeper's sscrip from the boxx. Ashshured him you sstole it, Sspar. You and Ssuzzy. Sso he came. Keeper izz a shshlemiel.'

Keeper said, 'I saw Suzy's foot going into the big chewer. I knew it by its anklet of hearts. After that I had the courage to kill Crown or anyone. I loved Suzy.'

Doc cleared his throat and croaked, 'Moonmist.' Spar found a triple pouch and Doc sucked it all. Doc said, 'Crown spoke the truth. Windrush is a plastic survival ship from Earth. Earth—' He motioned towards the dull orange round disappearing aft in the window '—poisoned herself with smog pollution and with nuclear war. She spent gold for war, plastic for survival. Best forgotten. Windrush went mad. Understandably. Even without the Lethean ricksettia, or Styx ricks, as you call it. Thought Windrush was the cosmos. Crown kidnapped me to get my drugs, kept me alive to know the doses.'

Spar looked at Keeper. 'Clean up here,' he ordered. 'Feed Crown to the big chewer.'

Almodie pulled herself from Spar's ankles to his waist.
'There was a second survival ship. Circumluna. When
Windrush went mad, my father and mother – and you – were
sent here, to investigate and cure. But my father died and you
got Styx ricks. My mother died just before I was given to
Crown. She sent you Kim.'

Kim hissed, 'My fforebear came from Circumluna to
Windrush, too. Great grandmother. Taught me ffigures for
Windrushsh . . . Radiuss from moon-ccentre, 2,500 miles.
Period, ssixx hours – sso, the sshort dayss. A terranth izz the
time it takess Earth to move through a consstellation, and sso
on.'

Doc said, 'So, Spar, you're the only one who remembers
without cynicism. You'll have to take over. It's all yours,
Spar.'

Spar had to agree.

Catch That Zeppelin!

This year on a trip to New York City to visit my son, who is a
social historian at a leading municipal university there, I had a
very unsettling experience. At black moments, of which at my
age I have quite a few, it still makes me distrust profoundly
those absolute boundaries in Space and Time which are our
sole protection against Chaos, and fear that my mind – no, my
entire individual existence – may at any moment at all and
without any warning whatsoever be blown by a sudden gust
of Cosmic Wind to an entirely different spot in a Universe of
Infinite Possibilities. Or, rather, into another Universe
altogether. And that my mind and individuality will be
changed to fit.

But at other moments, which are still in the majority, I
believe that my unsettling experience was only one of those
remarkably vivid waking dreams to which old people become
increasingly susceptible, generally waking dreams about the
past, and especially waking dreams about a past in which at
some crucial point one made an entirely different and braver
choice than one actually did, or in which the whole world
made such a decision, with a completely different future
resulting. Golden glowing might-have-beens nag increasingly at the minds of some older people.

In line with this interpretation I must admit that my whole
unsettling experience was structured very much like a dream.
It began with startling flashes of a changed world. It
continued into a longer period when I completely accepted
the changed world and delighted in it and, despite fleeting
quivers of uneasiness, wished I could bask in its glow forever.

And it ended in horrors, or nightmares, which I hate to mention, let alone discuss, until I must.

Opposing this dream notion, there are times when I am completely convinced that what happened to me in Manhattan and in a certain famous building there was no dream at all, but absolutely real, and that I did indeed visit another Time Stream.

Finally, I must point out that what I am about to tell you I am necessarily describing in retrospect, highly aware of several transitions involved and, whether I want to or not, commenting on them and making deductions that never once occurred to me at the time.

No, at the time it happened to me – and now at this moment of writing I am convinced that it did happen and was absolutely real – one instant simply succeeded another in the most natural way possible. I questioned nothing.

As to why it all happened to me, and what particular mechanism was involved, well, I am convinced that every man and woman has rare brief moments of extreme sensitivity, or rather vulnerability, when his mind and entire being may be blown by the Change Winds to Somewhere Else. And then, by what I call the Law of the Conservation of Reality, blown back again.

I was walking down Broadway somewhere near 34th Street. It was a chilly day, sunny despite the smog – a bracing day – and I suddenly began to stride along more briskly than is my cautious habit, throwing my feet ahead of me with a faint suggestion of the goose step. I also threw back my shoulders and took deep breaths, ignoring the fumes which tickled my nostrils. Beside me, traffic growled and snarled, rising at times to a machine-gun rata-tat-tat. While pedestrians were scuttling about with that desperate ratlike urgency characteristic of all big American cities, but which reaches its ultimate in New York. I cheerfully ignored that too. I even smiled at the sight of a ragged bum and a fur-coated grey-haired society lady both independently dodging across the street through the hurtling traffic with a cool practised skill one sees only in America's biggest metropolis.

Just then I noticed a dark, wide shadow athwart the street ahead of me. It could not be that of a cloud, for it did not move. I craned my neck sharply and looked straight up like the veriest yokel, a regular *Hans-Kopf-in-die-Luft* (Hans-Head-in-the-Air, a German figure of comedy).

My gaze had to climb up the giddy 102 storeys of the tallest building in the world, the Empire State. My gaze was strangely accompanied by the vision of a gigantic, long-fanged ape making the same ascent with a beautiful girl in one paw – oh, yes, I was recollecting the charming American fantasy film *King Kong*, or as they name it in Sweden, *Kong King*.

And then my gaze clambered higher still, up the 222-foot sturdy tower, to the top of which was moored the nose of the vast, breathtakingly beautiful, streamlined, silvery shape which was making the shadow.

Now here is a most important point. I was not at the time in the least startled by what I saw. I knew at once that it was simply the bow section of the German Zeppelin *Ostwald*, named for the great German pioneer of physical chemistry and electro-chemistry, and queen of the mighty passenger and light-freight fleet luxury airliners working out of Berlin, Baden-Baden, and Bremerhaven. That matchless Armada of Peace, each titanic airship named for a world-famous German scientist – the *Mach*, the *Nernst*, the *Humboldt*, the *Fritz Haber*, the French-named *Antoine Henri Becquerel*, the American-named *Edison*, the Polish-named *Sklodowska*, the American-Polish *T. Sklodowska Edison*, and even the Jewish-named *Einstein!* The great humanitarian navy in which I held a not unimportant position as international sales consultant and *Fachman* – I mean expert. My chest swelled with justified pride at this *edel* – noble – achievement of *der Vaterland*.

I knew also without any mind-searching or suprise that the length of the *Ostwald* was more than one half the 1,472-foot height of the Empire State Building plus its mooring tower, thick enough to hold an elevator. And my heart swelled again with the thought that the Berlin *Zeppelinturm* (dirigible tower) was only a few metres less high. Germany, I told myself, need not strain for mere numerical records – her sweeping scientific and technical achievements speak for themselves to the entire planet.

All this literally took little more than a second, and I never broke my snappy stride. As my gaze descended, I cheerfully hummed under my breath *Deutschland, Deutschland über Alles*.

The Broadway I saw was utterly transformed, though at the time this seemed every bit as natural as the serene presence of the *Ostwald* high overhead, vast ellipsoid held aloft by helium. Silvery electric trucks and buses and private cars innumerable purred along far more evenly and quietly, and almost as swiftly, as had the noisy, stenchful, jerky gasoline-powered vehicles only moments before, though to me now the latter were completely forgotten. About two blocks ahead, an occasional gleaming electric car smoothly swung into the wide silver arch of a quick-battery-change station, while others emerged from under the arch to rejoin the almost dreamlike stream of traffic.

The air I gratefully inhaled was fresh and clean, without a trace of smog.

The somewhat fewer pedestrians around me still moved quite swiftly, but with a dignity and courtesy largely absent before, with the numerous blackamoors among them quite as well dressed and exuding the same quiet confidence as the Caucasians.

The only slightly jarring note was struck by a tall, pale, rather emaciated man in black dress and with unmistakably Hebraic features. His sombre clothing was somewhat shabby, though well kept, and his thin shoulders were hunched. I got the impression he had been looking closely at me, and then instantly glancing away as my eyes sought his. For some reason I recalled what my son had told me about the City College of New York – CCNY – being referred to surreptitiously and jokingly as Christian College Now Yiddish. I couldn't help chuckling a bit at that witticism, though I am glad to say it was a genial little guffaw rather than a malicious snicker. Germany in her well-known tolerance and noble-mindedness has completely outgrown her old, disfiguring anti-Semitism – after all, we must admit in all fairness that perhaps a third of our great men are Jews or carry Jewish genes, Haber and Einstein among them – despite what dark and, yes, wicked memories may lurk in the subconscious minds of oldsters like myself and occasionally briefly surface into awareness like submarines bent on ship murder.

My happily self-satisfied mood immediately reasserted itself, and with a smart, almost military gesture I brushed to either side with a thumbnail the short, horizontal black moustache which decorates my upper lip, and I automatically swept back into place the thick comma of black hair (I confess I dye it) which tends to fall down across my forehead.

I stole another glance up at the *Ostwald*, which made me think of the matchless amenities of that wondrous deluxe airliner: the softly purring motors that powered its propellers – electric motors, naturally, energized by banks of lightweight TSE batteries and as safe as its helium; the Grand Corridor running the length of the passenger deck from the Bow Observatory to the stern's like-windowed Games Room, which becomes the Grand Ballroom at night; the other peerless room letting off that corridor – the *Gesellschaftsraum der Kapitan* (Captain's Lounge) with its dark woodwork, manly cigar smoke and *Damentische* (Tables for Ladies), the Premier Dining Room with its linen napery and silver-plated aluminium dining service, the Ladies' Retiring Room always set out profusely with fresh flowers, the Schwartzwald bar, the gaming casino with its roulette, baccarat, chemmy, blackjack (*vingt-et-un*), its tables for skat and bridge and dominoes and sixty-six, its chess tables presided over by the delightfully eccentric world's champion Nimzowitch, who would defeat you blindfold, but always brilliantly, simultaneously or one at a time, in charmingly baroque brief games for only two gold pieces per person per game (one gold piece to nutsy Nimzy, one to the DLG), and the supremely luxurious staterooms with costly veneers of mahogony over balsa; the hosts of attentive stewards, either as short and skinny as jockeys or else actual dwarfs, both types chosen to save weight; and the titanium elevator rising through the countless bags of helium to the two-decked Zenith Observatory, the sun deck wind-screened but roofless to let in the ever-changing clouds, the mysterious fog, the rays of the stars and good old Sol, and all the heavens. Ah, where else on land or sea could you buy such high living?

I called to mind in detail the single cabin which was always mine when I sailed on the *Ostwald – meine Stammkabine*. I visualized the Grand Corridor thronged with wealthy passengers in evening dress, the handsome officers, the unobtrusive ever-attentive stewards, the gleam of white shirt fronts, the glow of bare shoulders, the muted dazzle of jewels, the music of conversation like string quartets, the lilting low laughter that travelled along.

Exactly on time I did a neat *'Links, marschieren!'* ('To the left, march!') and passed through the impressive portals of the Empire State and across its towering lobby to the mutedly silver-glowing date: 6 May 1937 and the time of day: 1.07 pm. Good! – since the *Ostwald* did not cast off until the tick of 3 pm, I would be left plenty of time for a leisurely lunch and good talk with my son, if he had remembered to meet me – and there was actually no doubt of that, since he is the most considerate and orderly minded of sons, a real German mentality, though I say it myself.

I headed for the express bank, enjoying my passage through the clusters of high-class people who thronged the lobby without any unseemly crowding, and placed myself before the doors designated 'Dirigible Departure Lounge' and in briefer German '*Zum Zeppelin*'.

The elevator hostess was an attractive Japanese girl in skirt of dull silver with the DLG, Double Eagle and Dirigible insignia of the German Airship Union emblazoned in small on the left breast of her mutedly silver jacket. I noted with unvoiced approval that she appeared to have an excellent command of both German and English and was uniformly courteous to the passengers in her smiling but unemotional Nipponese fashion, which is so like our German scientific precision of speech, though without the latter's warm underlying passion. How good that our two federations, at opposite sides of the globe, have strong commercial and behavioural ties!

My fellow passengers in the lift, chiefly Americans and Germans, were of the finest type, very well dressed – except that just as the doors were about to close, there pressed in my doleful Jew in black. He seemed ill at ease, perhaps because of his shabby clothing. I was surprised, but made a point of being particularly polite towards him, giving him a slight bow and brief but friendly smile, while flashing my eyes. Jews have as much right to the acme of luxury travel as any other people on the planet, if they have the money – and most of them do.

During our uninterrupted and infinitely smooth passage upward, I touched my outside left breast pocket to reassure myself that my ticket – first class on the *Ostwald!* – and my papers were there. But actually I got far more reassurance and even secret joy from the feel and thought of the documents in my tightly zippered inside left breast pocket: the signed preliminary agreements that would launch America herself into the manufacture of passenger Zeppelins. Modern Germany is always generous in sharing her great technical achievements with responsible sister nations, supremely confident that the genius of her scientists and engineers will continue to keep her well ahead of all other lands; and after all, the genius of two Americans, father and son, had made vital though indirect contributions to the development of safe airship travel (and not forgetting the part played by the Polish-born wife of the one and the mother of the other).

The obtaining of those documents had been the chief and official reason for my trip to New York City, though I had been able to combine it most pleasurably with a long overdue visit with my son, the social historian, and with his charming wife.

These happy reflections were cut short by the jarless arrival of our elevator at its lofty terminus on the 100th floor. The journey old love-smitten King Kong had made only after exhausting exertion we had accomplished effortlessly. The silvery doors spread wide. My fellow passengers hung back for a moment in awe and perhaps a little trepidation at the thought of the awesome journey ahead of them, and I – seasoned airship traveller that I am – was the first to step out, favouring with a smile and nod of approval my pert yet cool Japanese fellow employee of the lower echelons.

Hardly sparing a glance towards the great, fleckless window confronting the doors and showing a matchless view of Manhattan from an elevation of 1,250 feet minus two storeys, I briskly turned, not right to the portals of the Departure Lounge and tower elevator, but left to those of the superb German restaurant *Krahenest* (Crow's Nest).

I passed between the flanking three-foot-high bronze statuettes of Thomas Edison and Maria Sklodowska Edison niched in one wall and those of Count von Zeppelin and Thomas Sklodowska Edison facing them from the other, and entered the select precincts of the finest German dining place outside the Fatherland. I paused while my eyes travelled searchingly around the room with its restful, dark wood panelling deeply carved with beautiful representations of the Black Forest and its grotesque supernatural denizens – kobolds, elves, gnomes, dryads (tastefully sexy) and the like. They interest me since I am what Americans call a Sunday painter, though almost my sole subject matter is zeppelins seen against blue sky and airy, soaring clouds.

The *Oberkellner* came hurrying towards me with menu tucked under his left elbow and saying, '*Mein Herr!* Charmed to see you once more! I have a perfect table-for-one with porthole looking out across the Hudson.'

But just then a youthful figure rose springily from behind a table set against the far wall, and a dear and familiar voice rang out to me with '*Hier, Papa!*'

'*Nein, Herr Ober,*' I smilingly told the head waiter as I walked past him, '*heute hab ich ein Gesellschafter. Mein Sohn.*'

I confidently made my way between tables occupied by well-dressed folk, both white and black.

My son wrung my hand with fierce family affection, though we had last parted only that morning. He insisted that I take the wide, dark, leather-upholstered seat against the wall, which gave me a fine view of the entire restaurant, while he took the facing chair.

'Because during this meal I wish to look only on you, Papa,' he assured me with manly tenderness. 'And we have at least an hour and a half together, Papa – I have checked your luggage through, and it is likely already aboard the *Ostwald*.' Thoughtful, dependable boy!

'And now, Papa, what shall it be?' he continued after we had settled ourselves. 'I see that today's special is *Sauerbraten mit Spatzel* and sweet-sour red cabbage. But there is also *Praprikahuhn* and—'

'Leave the chicken to flaunt her paprika in lonely red splendour today,' I interrupted him. '*Sauerbraten* sounds fine.'

Ordered by my Herr Ober, the aged wine waiter had already approached our table. I was about to give him directions when my son took upon himself that task with an authority and a hostfulness that warmed my heart. He scanned the wine menu rapidly but thoroughly.

'The Zinfandel 1933,' he ordered with decision, though glancing my way to see if I concurred with his judgement. I smiled and nodded.

'And perhaps *ein Tropfchen Schnapps* to begin with?' he suggested.

'A brandy? – yes!' I replied. 'And not just a drop, either. Make it a double. It is not every day I lunch with that distinguished scholar, my son.'

'Oh, Papa,' he protested, dropping his eyes and almost blushing. Then firmly to the bent-backed, white-haired wine waiter, '*Schnapps also. Doppel.*' The old waiter nodded his approval and hurried off.

We gazed at each other fondly for a few blissful seconds. Then I said, 'Now tell me more fully about your achievements as a social historian on an exchange professorship in the New World. I know we have spoken about this several times, but only rather briefly and generally when various of your friends were present, or at least your lovely wife. Now I would like a more leisurely man-to-man account of your great work. Incidentally, do you find the scholarly apparatus – books, *und so weiter* (et cetera) – of the Municipal Universities of New York City adequate to your needs after having enjoyed those of Baden-Baden University and the institutions of higher learning in the German Federation?'

'In some respects they are lacking,' he admitted. 'However, for my purposes they have proved completely adequate.' Then once more he dropped his eyes and almost blushed. 'But, Papa, you praise my small efforts far too highly.' He lowered his voice. 'They do not compare with the victory for international industrial relations you yourself have won in a fortnight.'

'All in a day's work for the DLG,' I said self-deprecatingly, though once again lightly touching my left chest to establish contact with those most important documents safely stowed in my inside left breast pocket. 'But now, no more polite fencing!' I went on briskly. 'Tell me about those "small efforts", as you modestly refer to them.'

His eyes met mine. 'Well, Papa,' he began in suddenly matter-of-fact fashion, 'all my work these last two years has been increasingly dominated by a firm awareness of the fragility of the underpinnings of the good world-society we enjoy today. If certain historically minute key-events, or cusps, in only the past one hundred years had been decided differently – if another course had been chosen than the one that was – then the whole world might now be plunged in wars and worse horrors than we ever dream of. It is a chilling insight, but it bulks continually larger in my entire work, my every paper.'

I felt the thrilling touch of inspiration. At that moment the wine waiter arrived with our double brandies in small goblets of cut glass. I wove the interruption into the fabric of my inspiration. 'Let us drink then to what you name your chilling insight,' I said. '*Prosit!*'

The bite and spreading warmth of the excellent *schnapps* quickened my inspiration further. 'I believe I understand exactly what you're getting at . . .' I told my son. I set down my half-emptied goblet and pointed at something over my son's shoulder.

He turned his head around, and after one glance back at my pointing finger, which intentionally waggled a tiny bit from side to side, he realized that I was not indicating the entry of the *Krahenest*, but the four sizeable bronze statuettes flanking it.

'For instance,' I said, 'if Thomas Edison and Maria Sklodowska had not married, and especially if they had not had their supergenius son, then Edison's knowledge of electricity and hers of radium and other radioactives might never have been joined. There might never have been developed the fabulous T. S. Edison battery, which is the prime mover of all today's surface and air traffic. Those pioneering electric trucks introduced by the *Saturday Evening Post* in Philadelphia might have remained an expensive freak. And the gas helium might never have been produced industrially to supplement earth's meagre subterranean supply.'

My son's eyes brightened with the flame of pure scholarship. 'Papa,' he said eagerly, 'you are a genius yourself! You have precisely hit on what is perhaps the most important of those cusp-events I referred to. I am at this moment finishing the necessary research for a long paper on it. Do you know, Papa, that I have firmly established by researching Paris records that there was in 1894 a close personal relationship between Maria Sklodowska and her fellow radium researcher Pierre Curie, and that she might well have become Madame Curie – or perhaps Madame Becquerel, for he too was in that work – if the dashing and brilliant Edison had not most opportunely arrived in Paris in December 1894 to sweep her off her feet and carry her off to the New World to even greater achievements?

'And just think, Papa,' he went on, his eyes aflame, 'what might have happened if their son's battery had not been invented – the most difficult technical achievement, hedged by all sorts of seeming scientific impossibilities, in the entire millennium-long history of industry. Why, Henry Ford might have manufactured automobiles powered by steam or by exploding natural gas or conceivably even vaporized liquid gasoline, rather than the mass-produced electric cars which have been such a boon to mankind everywhere – not our smokeless cars, but cars spouting all sorts of noxious fumes to pollute the environment.'

Cars powered by the danger-fraught combustion of vaporized liquid gasoline! – it almost made me shudder and certainly it was a fantastic thought, yet not altogether beyond the bounds of possibility, I had to admit.

Just then I noticed my gloomy, black-clad Jew sitting only two tables away from us, though how he got himself into the exclusive *Krahenest* was a wonder. Strange that I had missed his entry – probably immediately after my own, while I had eyes only for my son. His presence somehow threw a dark though only momentary shadow over my bright mood. Let him get some good German food inside him and some fine German wine, I thought generously – it will fill that empty belly of his and even put a bit of a good German smile into those sunken Yiddish cheeks! I combed my little moustache with my thumbnail and swept the errant lock of hair off my forehead.

Meanwhile my son was saying, 'Also, Father, if electric transport had not been developed, and if during the last decade relations between Germany and the United States had not been so good, then we might never have got from the wells in Texas the supply of natural helium our Zeppelins desperately needed during the brief but vital period before we had put the artificial creation of helium on to an industrial footing. My researchers at Washington have revealed that there was a strong movement in the US military to ban the sale of helium to any other nation, Germany in particular. Only the powerful influence of Edison, Ford, and a few other key Americans, instantly brought to bear, prevented that stupid injunction. Yet if it had gone through, Germany might have been forced to use hydrogen instead of helium to float her passenger dirigibles. That was another crucial cusp.'

'A hydrogen-supported Zeppelin – ridiculous! Such an airship would be a floating bomb, ready to be touched off by the slightest spark,' I protested.

'Not ridiculous, Father,' my son calmly contradicted me, shaking his head. 'Pardon me for trespassing in your field, but there is an inescapable imperative about certain industrial developments. If there is not a safe road of advance, then a dangerous one will invariably be taken. You must admit, Father, that the development of commercial airships was in its early stages a most perilous adventure. During the 1920s there were the dreadful wrecks of the American dirigibles *Roma, Shenandoah*, which broke in two, *Akron*, and *Macon*, the British *R-38*, which also broke apart in the air, and *R-101*, the French *Dixmude*, which disappeared in the Mediterranean, Mussolini's *Italia*, which crashed trying to reach the North Pole, and the Russian *Maxim Gorky*, struck down by a plane, with a total loss of no fewer than 350 crew members for the nine accidents. If that had been followed by the explosions of two or three hydrogen Zeppelins, world industry might well have abandoned forever the attempt to create passenger airships and turned instead to the development of large propeller-driven heavier-than-air craft.'

Monster aeroplanes, in danger every moment of crash from

engine failure, competing with good old unsinkable Zeppelins? – impossible, at least at first thought. I shook my head, but not with as much conviction as I might have wished. My son's suggestion was really a valid one.

Besides, he had all his facts at his fingertips and was complete master of his subject, as I also had to allow. Those nine fearful airship disasters he mentioned had indeed occurred, as I knew well, and might have tipped the scale in favour of long-distance passenger and troop-carrying aeroplanes, had it not been for helium, the T. S. Edison battery, and German genius.

Fortunately I was able to dump from my mind these uncomfortable speculations and immerse myself in admiration of my son's multisided scholarship. That boy was a wonder! – a real chip off the old block, and, yes, a bit more.

'And now, Dolfy,' he went on, using my nickname (I did not mind), 'may I turn to an entirely different topic? Or rather to a very different example of my hypothesis of historical cusps?'

I nodded mutely. My mouth was busily full with fine *Sauerbraten* and those lovely, tiny German dumplings, while my nostrils enjoyed the unique aroma of sweet-sour red cabbage. I had been so engrossed in my son's revelations that I had not consciously noted our luncheon being served. I swallowed, took a slug of the good, red Zinfandel, and said, 'Please go on.'

'It's about the consequences of the American Civil War, Father,' he said surprisingly. 'Did you know that in the decade after that bloody conflict, there was a very real danger that the whole cause of Negro freedom and rights – for which the war was fought, whatever they say – might well have been completely smashed? The fine work of Abraham Lincoln, Thaddeus Stevens, Charles Sumner, the Freedmen's Bureau, and the Union League Clubs put to naught? And even the Ku

Klux Klan underground allowed free reign rather than being sternly repressed? Yes, Father, my thoroughgoing researchings - have convinced me such things might easily have happened, resulting in some sort of re-enslavement of the Blacks, with the whole war to be refought at an indefinite future date, or at any rate Reconstruction brought to a dead halt for many decades – with what disastrous effects on the American character, turning its deep simple faith in freedom to hypocrisy, it is impossible to exaggerate. I have published a sizeable paper on this subject in the *Journal of Civil War Studies.*'

I nodded sombrely. Quite a bit of this new subject matter of his was *terra incognita* to me; yet I knew enough of American history to realize he had made a cogent point. More than ever before, I was impressed by his multifaceted learning – he was indubitably a figure in the great tradition of German scholarship, a profound thinker, broad and deep. How fortunate to be his father. Not for the first time, but perhaps with the greatest sincerity yet, I thanked God and the Laws of Nature that I had early moved my family from Braunau, Austria, where I had been born in 1899, to Baden-Baden where he had grown up in the ambience of the great new university on the edge of the Black Forest and only 150 kilometers from Count Zeppelin's dirigible factory in Wurttemberg, at Friedrichshafen on Lake Constance.

I raised my glass of *Kirschwasser* to him in a solemn, silent toast – we had somehow got to that stage in our meal – and downed a sip of the potent, fiery, white cherry brandy.

He leaned towards me and said, 'I might as well tell you, Dolf, that my big book, at once popular and scholarly, my *Meisterwerk*, to be titled *If Things Had Gone Wrong*, or perhaps *If Things Had Turned for the Worse*, will deal solely – though illuminated by dozens of diverse examples – with my theory of historical cusps, a highly speculative concept but firmly footed in fact.' He glanced at his wristwatch, muttered, 'Yes, there's still time for it. So now—' His face grew grave, his voice clear though small – 'I will venture to tell you about one more cusp, the most disputable and yet most crucial of them all.' He paused. 'I warn you, dear Dolf, that this cusp may cause you pain.'

'I doubt that,' I told him indulgently. 'Anyhow, go ahead.'

'Very well. In November of 1918, when the British had broken the Hindenburg Line and the weary German Army was defiantly dug in along the Rhine, and just before the Allies, under Marshal Foch, launched the final crushing drive which would cut a bloody swath across the heartland to Berlin—'

I understood his warning at once. Memories flamed in my mind like the sudden blinding flares of the battlefield with their deafening thunder. The company I had commanded had been among the most desperately defiant of those he mentioned, heroically nerved for a last-ditch resistance. And then Foch had delivered that last vast blow, and we had fallen back and back and back before the overwhelming numbers of our enemies with their field guns and tanks and armoured cars innumerable and above all their huge aerial armadas of De Haviland and Handley-Page and other big bombers escorted by insect-buzzing fleets of Spads and other fighters shooting to bits our last Fokkers and Pfalzes and visiting on Germany a destruction greater far than our Zeps had worked on England. Back, back, back, endlessly reeling and regrouping, across the devastated German countryside, a dozen times decimated yet still defiant until the end came at last amid the ruins of Berlin, and the most bold among us had to admit we were beaten and we surrendered unconditionally—

These vivid, fiery recollections came to me almost instantaneously.

I heard my son continuing, 'At that cusp moment in November 1918, Dolf, there existed a very strong possibility – I have established this beyond question – that an immediate armistice would be offered and signed, and the war ended inconclusively. President Wilson was wavering, the French were very tired, and so on.

'And if that had happened in actuality – harken closely to me now, Dolf – then the German temper entering the decade of the 1920s would have been entirely different. She would have felt she had not been really licked, and there would inevitably have been a secret recrudescence of pan-German militarism. German scientific humanism would not have won its total victory over the Germany of the – yes! – Huns.

'As for the Allies, self-tricked out of the complete victory which lay within their grasp, they would in the long run have treated Germany far less generously than they did after their lust for revenge had been sated by that last drive to Berlin. The League of Nations would not have become the strong instrument for world peace that it is today; it might well have been repudiated by America and certainly secretly detested by Germans. Old wounds would not have healed because, paradoxically, they would not have been deep enough.

'There, I've had my say. I hope it hasn't bothered you too badly, Dolf.'

I let out a gusty sigh. Then my wincing frown was replaced by a brow serene. I said very deliberately, 'Not one bit, my son, though you have certainly touched my old wounds to the quick. Yet I feel in my bones that your interpretation is completely valid. Rumours of an armistice were indeed running like wildfire through our troops in that black autumn of 1918. And I know only too well that if there had been an armistice at that time, then officers like myself would have believed that the German soldier had never really been defeated, only betrayed by his leaders and by red incendiaries, and we would have begun to conspire endlessly for a resumption of the war under happier circumstances. My son, let us drink to your amazing cusps.'

Our tiny glasses touched with a delicate ting, and the last drops went down of biting, faintly bitter *Kirschwasser*. I buttered a thin slice of pumpernickel and nibbled it – always good to finish off a meal with bread. I was suddenly filled with an immeasurable content. It was a golden moment, which I would have been happy to have go on forever, while I listened to my son's wise words and fed my satisfaction in him. Yes, indeed, it was a golden nugget of pause in the terrible rush of time – the enriching conversation, the peerless food and drink, the darkly pleasant surroundings—

At that moment I chanced to look at my discordant Jew two tables away. For some weird reason he was glaring at me with naked hate, though he instantly dropped his gaze—

But even that strange and disquieting event did not disrupt my mood of golden tranquillity, which I sought to prolong by saying in summation, 'My dear son, this has been the most exciting though eerie lunch I have ever enjoyed. Your remarkable cusps have opened to me a fabulous world in which I can nevertheless utterly believe. A horridly fascinating world of sizzling hydrogen Zeppelins, of countless evil-smelling gasoline cars built by Ford instead of his electrics, of re-enslaved American blackamoors, of Madame Becquerels or Curies, a world without the T. S. Edison battery and even T. S. himself, a world in which German scientists are sinister pariahs instead of tolerant, humanitarian, great-souled leaders of world thought, a world in which a mateless old Edison tinkers forever at a powerful storage battery he cannot perfect, a world in which Woodrow Wilson doesn't insist on Germany being admitted at once to the League of Nations, a world of festering hatreds reeling towards a second and worse world war. Oh, altogether an incredible world, yet one in

which you have momentarily made me believe, to the extent
that I do actually have the fear that time will suddenly shift
gears and we will be plunged into that bad dream world, and
our real world will become a dream—'

I suddenly chanced to see the face of my watch—

At the same time my son looked at his own left wrist—

'Dolf,' he said, springing up in agitation, 'I do hope that
with my stupid chatter I haven't made you miss—'

I had sprung up too—

'No, no, my son,' I heard myself say in a fluttering voice,
'but it's true I have little time in which to catch the *Ostwald.
Auf Wiedersehn, mein Sohn, auf Weidersehn!*'

And with that I was hastening, indeed almost running, or
else sweeping through the air like a ghost – leaving him
behind to settle our reckoning – across a room that seemed to
waver with my feverish agitation, alternately darkening and
brightening like an electric bulb with its fine tungsten
filament about to fly to powder and wink out forever—

Inside my head a voice was saying in a calm yet death-knell
tones, 'The lights of Europe are going out. I do not think they
will be rekindled in my generation—'

Suddenly the only important thing in the world for me was
to catch the *Ostwald*, get aboard her before she unmoored.
That and only that would reassure me that I was in my
rightful world. I would touch and feel the *Ostwald*, not just
talk about her—

As I dashed between the four bronze figures, they seemed
to hunch down and become deformed, while their faces
became those of grotesque, aged witches – four evil kobolds
leering up at me with a horrid knowledge bright in their
eyes—

While behind me I glimpsed in pursuit a tall, black, white-
faced figure, skeletally lean—

The strangely short corridor ahead of me had a blank end –

the Departure Lounge wasn't there—

I instantly jerked open the narrow door to the stairs and darted nimbly up them as if I were a young man again and not forty-eight years old—

On the third sharp turn I risked a glance behind and down—

Hardly a flight behind me, taking great pursuing leaps, was my dreadful Jew—

I tore open the door to the 102nd floor. There at last, only a few feet away, was the silver door I sought of the final elevator and softly glowing above it the words, '*Zum Zeppelin*'. At last I would be shot aloft to the *Ostwald* and reality.

But the sign began to blink as the *Krahenest* had, while across the door was pasted askew a white cardboard sign which read 'Out of Order'.

I threw myself at the door and scrabbled at it, squeezing my eyes several times to make my vision come clear. When I finally fully opened them the cardboard sign was gone.

But the silver door was gone too, and the words above it forever. I was scrabbling at seamless pale plaster.

There was a touch on my elbow. I spun around.

'Excuse me, sir, but you seem troubled,' my Jew said solicitously. 'Is there anything I can do?'

I shook my head, but whether in negation or rejection or to clear it, I don't know. 'I'm looking for the *Ostwald*,' I gasped, only now realizing I'd winded myself on the stairs. 'For the Zeppelin,' I explained when he looked puzzled.

I may be wrong, but it seemed to me that a look of secret glee flashed deep in his eyes, though his general sympathetic expression remained unchanged.

'Oh, the Zeppelin,' he said in a voice that seemed to me to have become sugary in its solicitude. 'You must mean the *Hindenburg*.'

Hindenburg? – I asked myself. There was no Zeppelin

named *Hindenburg*. Or was there? Could it be that I was mistaken about such a simple and, one would think, immutable matter? My mind had been getting very foggy the last minute or two. Desperately I tried to assure myself that I was indeed myself and in my right world. My lips worked and I muttered to myself, *Bin Adolf Hitler, Zeppelin Fachman . . .*

'But the *Hindenburg* doesn't land here, in any case,' my Jew was telling me, 'though I think some vague intention once was voiced about topping the Empire State with a mooring mast for dirigibles. Perhaps you saw some news story and assumed—'

His face fell, or he made it seem to fall. The sugary solicitude in his voice became unendurable as he told me, 'But apparently you can't have heard today's tragic news. Oh, I do hope you weren't seeking the *Hindenburg* so as to meet some beloved family member or close friend. Brace yourself, sir. Only hours ago, coming in for her landing at Lakehurst, New Jersey, the *Hindenburg* caught fire and burned up entire in a matter of seconds. Thirty or forty at least of her passengers and crew were burned alive. Oh, steady yourself, sir.'

'But the *Hindenburg* – I mean the *Ostwald!* – couldn't burn like that,' I protested. 'She's a helium Zeppelin.'

He shook his head. 'Oh, no. I'm no scientist, but I know the *Hindenburg* was filled with hydrogen – a wholly typical bit of reckless German risk-running. At least we've never sold helium to the Nazis, thank God.'

I stared at him, wavering my face from side to side in feeble denial.

While he stared back at me with obviously a new thought in mind.

'Excuse me once again,' he said, 'but I believe I heard you start to say something about Adolf Hitler. I suppose you know that you bear a certain resemblance to that execrable dictator. If I were you, sir, I'd shave my moustache.'

I felt a wave of fury at this inexplicable remark with all its baffling references, yet withal a remark delivered in the unmistakeable tones of an insult. And then all my surroundings momentarily reddened and flickered, and I felt a tremendous wrench in the inmost core of my being, the sort of wrench one might experience in transiting timelessly from one universe into another parallel to it. Briefly I became a man still named Adolf Hitler, same as the Nazi dictator and almost the same age, a German-American born in Chicago, who had never visited Germany or spoke German, whose friends teased him about his chance resemblance to the other Hitler, and who used stubbornly to say, 'No, I won't change my name! Let that *Fuehrer* bastard across the Atlantic change his! Ever hear about the British Winston Churchill writing the American Winston Churchill, who wrote *The Crisis* and other novels, and suggesting he change his name to avoid confusion, since the Englishman had done some writing too? The American wrote back it was a good idea, but since he was three years older, he was senior and so the Britisher should change *his* name. That's exactly how I feel about that son of a bitch Hitler.'

The Jew still stared at me sneeringly, I started to tell him off, but then I was lost in a second weird, wrenching transition. The first had been directly from one parallel universe to another. The second was also in time – I aged fourteen or fifteen years in a single infinite instant while transiting from 1937 (where I had been born in 1889 and was forty-eight) to 1973 (where I had been born in 1910 and was sixty-three). My name changed back to my truly own (but what is that?), and I no longer looked one bit like Adolf Hitler the Nazi dictator (or dirigible expert?), and I had a married son who was a sort of social historian in a New York City municipal university, and he had many brilliant theories, but none of historical cusps.

And the Jew – I mean the tall, thin man in black with possibly Semitic features – was gone. I looked around and around but there was no one there.

I touched my outside left breast pocket, then my hand darted trembling underneath. There was no zipper on the pocket inside and no precious documents, only a couple of grimy envelopes with notes I'd scribbled on them in pencil.

I don't know how I got out of the Empire State Building. Presumably by elevator. Though all my memory holds for that period is a persistent image of King Kong tumbling down from its top like a ridiculous yet poignantly pitiable giant teddy bear.

I do recollect walking in a sort of trance for what seemed hours through a Manhattan stinking with monoxide and carcinogens innumerable, half waking from time to time (usually while crossing streets that snarled, not purred) and then relapsing into trance. There were big dogs.

When I at last fully came to myself, I was walking down a twilit Hudson Street at the north end of Greenwich Village. My gaze was fixed on a distant and unremarkable pale-grey square of building top. I guessed it must be that of the World Trade Centre, 1,350 feet tall.

And then it was blotted out by the grinning face of my son, the professor.

'Justin!' I said.

'Fritz!' he said. 'We'd begun to worry a bit. Where did you get off to, anyhow? Not that it's a damn bit of my business. If you had an assignation with a go-go girl, you needn't tell me.'

'Thanks,' I said. 'I do feel tired, I must admit, and somewhat cold. But no, I was just looking at some of my old stamping grounds,' I told him, 'and taking longer than I realized. Manhattan's changed during my years on the West Coast, but not all that much.'

'It's getting chilly,' he said. 'Let's stop in that place ahead with the black front. It's the White Horse. Dylan Thomas used to drink there. He's supposed to have scribbled a poem on the wall of the can, only they painted it over. But it has the authentic sawdust.'

'Good,' I said, 'only we'll make mine coffee, not ale. Or if I can't get coffee, then cola.'

I am not really a *Prosit!*-type person.

Gonna Roll the Bones

Suddenly Joe Slattermill knew for sure he'd have to get out quick or else blow his top and knock out with the shrapnel of his skull the props and patches holding up his decaying home, that was like a house of big wooden and plaster and wallpaper cards except for the huge fireplace and ovens and chimneys across the kitchen from him.

Those were stone-solid enough, though. The fireplace was chin-high, at least twice that long, and filled from end to end with roaring flames. Above were the square doors of the ovens in a row – his Wife baked for part of their living. Above the ovens was the wall-long mantelpiece, too high for his Mother to reach or Mr Guts to jump any more, set with all sorts of ancestral curios, but any of them that weren't stone or glass or china had been so dried and darkened by decades of heat that they looked like nothing but shrunken human heads and black golf balls. At one end were clustered his Wife's square gin bottles. Above the mantelpiece hung one old chromo, so high and so darkened by soot and grease that you couldn't tell whether the swirls and fat cigar shape were a whaleback steamer ploughing through a hurricane or a spaceship plunging through a storm of light-driven dust motes.

As soon as Joe curled his toes inside his boots, his Mother knew what he was up to. 'Going bumming,' she mumbled with conviction. 'Pants pockets full of cartwheels of house money, too, to spend on sin.' And she went back to munching the long shreds she stripped fumblingly with her right hand off the turkey carcass set close to the terrible heat, her left hand ready to fend off Mr Guts, who stared at her yellow-eyed, gaunt-flanked, with long mangy tail a-twitch. In her dirty dress, streaky as the turkey's sides, Joe's Mother looked like a bent brown bag and her fingers were lumpy twigs.

Joe's Wife knew as soon or sooner, for she smiled thin-eyed at him over her shoulder from where she towered at the centremost oven. Before she closed its door, Joe glimpsed that she was baking two long, flat, narrow, fluted loaves and one high, round-domed one. She was thin as death and disease in her violet wrapper. Without looking, she reached out a yard-long, skinny arm for the nearest gin bottle and downed a warm slug and smiled again. And without a word spoken, Joe knew she'd said, 'You're going out and gamble and get drunk and lay a floozy and come home and beat me and go to jail for it,' and he had a flash of the last time he'd been in the dark gritty cell and she'd come by moonlight, which showed the green and yellow lumps on her narrow skull where he'd hit her, to whisper to him through the tiny window in the back and slip him half a pint through the bars.

And Joe knew for certain that this time it would be that bad and worse, but just the same he heaved up himself and his heavy, muffledly clanking pockets and shuffled straight to the door, muttering, 'Guess I'll roll the bones, up the pike a stretch and back,' swinging his bent, knobbly-elbowed arms like paddle-wheels to make a little joke about his words.

When he stepped outside, he held the door open a hand's breadth behind him for several seconds. When he finally closed it, a feeling of deep misery struck him. Earlier years, Mr Guts would have come streaking along to seek fights and females on the roofs and fences, but now the big tom was content to stay at home and hiss by the fire and snatch for turkey and dodge a broom, quarrelling and comforting with two housebound women. Nothing had followed Joe to the door but his Mother's chomping and her gasping breaths and the clink of the gin bottle going back on the mantel and the creaking of the floorboards under his feet.

The night was upside-down deep among the frosty stars. A few of them seemed to move, like the white hot jets of spaceships. Down below it looked as if the whole town of Ironmine had blown or buttoned out the light and gone to sleep, leaving the streets and spaces to the equally unseen breezes and ghosts. But Joe was still in the hemisphere of the musty dry odour of the worm-eaten carpenty behind him, and as he felt and heard the dry grass of the lawn brush his calves, it occurred to him that something deep down inside him had for years been planning things so that he and the house and his Wife and Mother and Mr Guts would all come to an end together. Why the kitchen heat hadn't touched off the tindery place ages ago was a physical miracle.

Hunching his shoulders, Joe stepped out, not up to the pike, but down the dirt road that led past Cypress Hollow Cemetery to Night Town.

The breezes were gentle, but unusually restless and variable tonight, like leprechaun squalls. Beyond the drunken, whitewashed cemetery fence dim in the starlight, they rustled the scraggy trees of Cypress Hollow and made it seem they were stroking their beards of Spanish moss. Joe sensed that the ghosts were just as restless as the breezes, uncertain where and whom to haunt, or whether to take the night off, drifting together in sorrowfully lecherous companionship. While among the trees the red-green vampire lights pulsed faintly and irregularly, like sick fireflies or a plague-stricken space fleet. The feeling of deep misery stuck with Joe and deepened and he was tempted to turn aside and curl up in any convenient tomb or around some half-toppled headboard and cheat his Wife and the other three behind him out of a shared doom. He thought: Gonna roll the bones, gonna roll 'em up and go to sleep. But while he was deciding, he got past the sagged-open gate and the rest of the delirious fence and Shantyville too.

At first Night Town seemed dead as the rest of Ironmine, but then he noticed a faint glow, sick as the vampire lights but more feverish, and with it a jumping music, tiny at first as a jazz for jitterbugging ants. He stepped along the springy sidewalk, wistfully remembering the days when the spring was all in his own legs and he'd bound into a fight like a bobcat or a Martian sand-spider. God, it had been years now since he had fought a real fight, or felt *the power*. Gradually the midget music got raucous as a bunnyhug for grizzly bears and loud as a polka for elephants, while the glow became a riot of gas flares and flambeaux and corpse-blue mercury tubes and jiggling pink neon ones that all jeered at the stars where the spaceships roved. Next thing, he was facing a three-storey false front flaring everywhere like a devil's rainbow, with a pale blue topping of St. Elmo's fire. There were wide swinging doors in the centre of it, spilling light above and below. Above the doorway, golden calcium light scrawled over and over again, with wild curlicues and flourishes, 'The Bone-yard', while a fiendish red kept printing out, 'Gambling'.

So the new place they'd all been talking about for so long had opened at last! For the first time that night, Joe Slattermill felt a stirring of real life in him and the faintest caress of excitement.

Gonna roll the bones, he thought.

He dusted off his blue-green work clothes with big, careless swipes and slapped his pockets to hear the clank. Then he threw back his shoulders and grinned his lips sneeringly and pushed through the swinging doors as if giving the foe the straight-armed heel of his palm.

Inside, the Boneyard seemed to cover the area of a township and the bar looked as long as the railroad tracks. Round pools of light on the green poker tables alternated with hour-glass shapes of exciting gloom, through which drink girls and change girls moved like white-legged witches. By the jazz-stand in the distance, belly dancers made *their* white hour-glass shapes. The gamblers were thick and hunched down as mushrooms, all bald from agonizing over the fall of a card or a die or the dive of an ivory ball, while the Scarlet Women were like fields of poinsettia.

The calls of the croupiers and the slaps of dealt cards were as softly yet fatefully staccato as the rustle and beat of the jazz drums. Every tight-locked atom of the place was controllably jumping. Even the dust motes jigged tensely in the cones of light.

Joe's excitement climbed and he felt it sift through him, like a breeze that heralds a gale, the faintest breath of a confidence which he knew could become a tornado. All thoughts of his house and Wife and Mother dropped out of his mind, while Mr Guts remained only as a crazy young tom walking stiff-legged around the rim of his consciousness. Joe's own leg muscles twitched in sympathy and he felt them grow supplely strong.

He coolly and searchingly looked the place over, his hand going out like it didn't belong to him to separate a drink from a passing, gently bobbing tray. Finally his gaze settled on what he judged to be the Number One Crap Table. All the Big Mushrooms seemed to be there, bald as the rest but standing tall as toadstools. Then through a gap in them Joe saw on the other side of the table a figure still taller, but dressed in a long dark coat with collar turned up and a dark slouch hat pulled low, so that only a triangle of white face showed. A suspicion and a hope rose in Joe and he headed straight for the gap in the Big Mushrooms.

As he got nearer, the white-legged and shiny-topped drifters eddying out of his way, his suspicion received confirmation after confirmation and his hope budded and

swelled. Back from one end of the table was the fattest man
he'd ever seen, with a long cigar and a silver vest and a gold tie
clasp at least eight inches wide that just said in thick script,
'Mr Bones'. Back a little from the other end was the nakedest
change-girl yet and the only one he'd seen whose tray, slung
from her bare shoulders and indenting her belly just below
her breasts, was stacked with gold in gleaming little towers
and with jet-black chips. While the dice-girl, skinnier and
taller and longer armed than his Wife even, didn't seem to be
wearing much but a pair of long white gloves. She was all
right if you went for the type that isn't much more than pale
skin over bones with breasts like china doorknobs.

Beside each gambler was a high round table for his chips.
The one by the gap was empty. Snapping his fingers at the
nearest silver change-girl, Joe traded all his greasy dollars for
an equal number of pale chips and tweaked her left nipple for
luck. She playfully snapped her teeth towards his fingers.

Not hurrying but not wasting any time, he advanced and
carelessly dropped his modest stacks on the empty table and
took his place in the gap. He noted that the second Big
Mushroom on his right had the dice. His heart but no other
part of him gave an extra jump. Then he steadily lifted his
eyes and looked straight across the table.

The coat was a shimmering elegant pillar of black satin with
jet buttons, the upturned collar of fine dull plush black as the
darkest cellar, as was the slouch hat with the down-turned
brim and for band only a thin braid of black horsehair. The
arms of the coat were long, lesser satin pillars, ending in slim,
long-fingered hands that moved swiftly when they did, but
held each position of rest with a statue's poise.

Joe still couldn't see much of the face except for the smooth
lower forehead with never a bead or trickle of sweat – the
eyebrows were like straight snippets of the hat's braid – and
gaunt, aristocratic cheeks and narrow but somewhat flat nose.

The complexion of the face wasn't as white as Joe had first judged. There was a faint touch of brown in it, like ivory that's just begun to age, or Venusian soapstone. Another glance at the hands confirmed this.

Behind the man in black was a knot of just about the flashiest and nastiest customers, male or female, Joe had ever seen. He knew from one look that each bediamonded, pomaded bully had a belly gun beneath the flap of his flowered vest and a blackjack in his hip pocket, and each snake-eyed sporting girl a stiletto in her garter and a pearl-handled silver-plated derringer under the sequinned silk in the hollow between her jutting breasts.

Yet at the same time Joe knew they were just trimmings. It was the man in black, their master, who was the deadly one, the kind of man you knew at a glance you couldn't touch and live. If without asking you merely laid a finger on his sleeve, no matter how lightly and respectfully, an ivory hand would move faster than thought and you'd be stabbed or shot. Or maybe just the touch would kill you, as if every black article of his clothing were charged from his ivory skin outwards with a high-voltage, high-amperage ivory electricity. Joe looked at the shadowed face again and decided he wouldn't care to try it.

For it was the eyes that were the most impressive feature. All great gamblers have dark-shadowed, deep-set eyes. But this one's eyes were sunk so deep you couldn't even be sure you were getting a gleam of them. They were inscrutability incarnate. They were unfathomable. They were like black holes.

But all this didn't disappoint Joe one bit, though it did terrify him considerably. On the contrary, it made him exult. His first suspicion was completely confirmed and his hope spread into full flower.

This must be one of those really big gamblers who hit

Ironmine only once in a decade at most, come from the Big City on one of the river boats that ranged the watery dark like luxurious comets, spouting long thick tails of sparks from their sequoia-tall stacks with top foliage of curvy-snipped sheet iron. Or like silver space-liners with dozens of jewel-flamed jets, their portholes a-twinkle like ranks of marshalled asteroids.

For that matter, maybe some of those really big gamblers actually came from other planets where the night-time pace was hotter and the sporting life a delirium of risk and delight.

Yes, this was the kind of man Joe had always yearned to pit his skill against. He felt *the power* begin to tingle in his rock-still fingers, just a little.

Joe lowered his gaze to the crap table. It was almost as wide as a man is tall, at least twice as long, unusually deep, and lined with black, not green, felt, so that it looked like a giant's coffin. There was something familiar about its shape which he couldn't place. Its bottom, though not its sides or ends, had a twinkling iridescence, as if it had been lightly sprinkled with very tiny diamonds. As Joe lowered his gaze all the way and looked directly down, his eyes barely over the table, he got the crazy notion that it went all the way down through the world, so that the diamonds were the stars on the other side, visible despite the sunlight there, just as Joe was always able to see the stars by day up the shaft of the mine he worked in, and so that if a cleaned-out gambler, dizzy with defeat, toppled forward into it, he'd fall forever, towards the bottom-most bottom, be it Hell or some black galaxy. Joe's thoughts swirled and he felt the cold, hard-fingered clutch of fear at his crotch. Someone was crooning beside him, 'Come on, Big Dick.'

Then the dice, which had meanwhile passed to the Big Mushroom immediately on his right, came to rest near the table's centre, contradicting and wiping out Joe's vision. But instantly there was another oddity to absorb him. The ivory dice were large and unusually round-cornered with dark red spots that gleamed like real rubies, but the spots were arranged in such a way that each face looked like a miniature skull. For instance, the seven thrown just now, by which the Big Mushroom to his right had lost his point, which had been ten, consisted of a two with the spots evenly spaced towards one side, like eyes, instead of towards opposite corners, and of a five with the same red eye-spots but also a central red nose and two spots close together below that to make teeth.

The long, skinny, white-gloved arm of the dice-girl snaked out like an albino cobra and scooped up the dice and whisked them on to the rim of the table right in front of Joe. He inhaled silently, picked up a single chip from his table and started to lay it beside the dice, then realized that wasn't the way things were done here, and put it back. He would have liked to examine the chip more closely, though. It was curiously lightweight and pale tan, about the colour of cream with a shot of coffee in it, and it had embossed on its surface a symbol he could feel, though not see. He didn't know what the symbol was, that would have taken more feeling. Yet its touch had been very good, setting the power tingling full blast in his shooting hand.

Joe looked casually yet swiftly at the faces around the table, not missing the Big Gambler across from him, and said quietly, 'Roll a penny,' meaning of course one pale chip, or a dollar.

There was a hiss of indignation from all the Big Mushrooms and the moonface of big-bellied Mr Bones grew purple as he started forward to summon his bouncers.

The Big Gambler raised a black-satined forearm and sculptured hand, palm down. Instantly Mr Bones froze and the hissing stopped faster than that of a meteor prick in self-sealing space steel. Then in a whispery, cultured voice, without the faintest hint of derision, the man in black said, 'Get on him, gamblers.'

Here, Joe thought, was the final confirmation of his suspicion, had it been needed. The really great gamblers were perfect gentlemen and generous to the poor.

With only the tiny, respectful hint of a guffaw, one of the Big Mushrooms called to Joe, 'You're faded.'

Joe picked up the ruby-featured dice.

Now ever since he had first caught two eggs on one plate, won all the marbles in Ironmine, and juggled six alphabet blocks so they finally fell in a row on the rug spelling 'Mother', Joe Slattermill had been almost incredibly deft at precision throwing. In the mine he could carom a rock off a wall of ore to crack a rat's skull fifty feet away in the dark and he sometimes amused himself by tossing little fragments of rock back into the holes from which they had fallen, so that they stuck there, perfectly fitted in, for at least a second. Sometimes, by fast tossing, he could fit seven or eight fragments into the hole from which they had fallen, like putting together a puzzle block. If he could ever have got into space, Joe would undoubtedly have been able to pilot six Moon-skimmers at once and do figure eights through Saturn's rings blindfold.

Now the only real difference between precision-tossing rocks or alphabet blocks and dice is that you have to bounce the latter off the end wall of the crap table, and that just made it a more interesting test of skill for Joe.

Rattling the dice now, he felt the power in his fingers and palm as never before.

He made a swift low roll, so that the bones ended up exactly in front of the white-gloved dice-girl. His natural seven was made up, as he'd intended, of a four and a three. In red-spot features they were like the five, except that both had only one tooth and the three had no nose. Sort of baby-faced skulls. He had won a penny – that is, a dollar.

'Roll two cents,' said Joe Slattermill.

This time, for variety, he made his natural with an eleven. The six was like the five, except that it had three teeth, the best-looking skull of the lot.

'Roll a nickel less one.'

Two Big Mushrooms divided that bet with a covert smirk at each other.

Now Joe rolled a three and an ace. His point was four. The ace, with its single spot off centre towards a side, still somehow looked like a skull – maybe of a Lilliputian Cyclops.

He took a while making his point, once absent-mindedly rolling three successive tens the hard way. He wanted to watch the dice-girl scoop up the cubes. Each time it seemed to him that her snake-swift fingers went under the dice while they were still flat on the felt. Finally he decided it couldn't be an illusion. Although the dice couldn't penetrate the felt, her white-gloved fingers somehow could, dipping in a flash through the black, diamond-sparkling material as if it wasn't there.

Right away the thought of a crap-table-size hole through the earth came back to Joe. This would mean that the dice were rolling and lying on a perfectly transparent flat surface, impenetrable for them but nothing else. Or maybe it was only the dice-girl's hands that could penetrate the surface, which would turn into a mere fantasy Joe's earlier vision of a cleaned-out gambler taking the Big Dive down that dreadful shaft, which made the deepest mine a mere pin dent.

Joe decided he had to know which was true. Unless absolutely unavoidable, he didn't want to take the chance of being troubled by vertigo at some crucial stage of the game.

He made a few more meaningless throws, from time to time crooning for realism, 'Come on, Little Joe.' Finally he settled on his plan. When he did at last make his point – the hard way, with two twos – he caromed the dice off the far corner so that they landed exactly in front of him. Then, after a minimum pause for his throw to be seen by the table, he shot his left hand down under the cubes, just a flicker ahead of the dice-girl's strike, and snatched them up.

Wow! Joe had never had a harder time in his life making his face and manner conceal what his body felt, not even when the wasp had stung him on the neck just when he had been for the first time putting his hand under the skirt of his prudish, fickle, demanding Wife-to-be. His fingers and the back of his hand were in as much agony as if he'd stuck them into a blast furnace. No wonder the dice-girl wore white gloves. They must be asbestos. And a good thing he hadn't used his shooting hand, he thought as he ruefully watched the blisters rise.

He remembered he'd been taught in school what Twenty-Mile Mine also demonstrated: that the earth was fearfully hot under its crust. The crap-size-table hole must pipe up that heat, so that any gambler taking the Big Dive would fry before he'd fallen a furlong and come out less than a cinder in China.

As if his blistered hand weren't bad enough, the Big Mushrooms were all hissing at him again and Mr Bones had purpled once more and was opening his melon-sized mouth to shout for his bouncers.

Once again a lift of the Big Gambler's hand saved Joe. The whispery, gentle voice called, 'Tell him, Mr Bones.'

The latter roared towards Joe, 'No gambler may pick up the dice he or any other gambler has shot. Only my dice-girl may do that. Rule of the house!'

Joe snapped Mr Bones the barest nod. He said coolly, 'Rolling a dime less two,' and when that still peewee bet was covered, he shot Phoebe for his point and then fooled around for quite a while, throwing anything but a five or a seven, until the throbbing in his left hand should fade and all his nerves fell rock-solid again. There had never been the slightest alteration in the power in his right hand; he felt that strong as ever, or stronger.

Midway of this interlude, the Big Gambler bowed slightly but respectfully towards Joe, hooding those unfathomable eye sockets, before turning around to take a long black cigarette from his prettiest and evilest-looking sporting girl. Courtesy in the smallest matters, Joe thought, another mark of the master devotee of games of chance. The Big Gambler sure had himself a flash crew, all right, though in idly looking them over again as he rolled, Joe noted one bummer towards the back who didn't fit in – a raggedy-elegant chap with the elflocked hair and staring eyes and TB-spotted cheeks of a poet.

As he watched the smoke trickling up from under the black slouch hat, he decided that either the lights across the table had dimmed or else the Big Gambler's complexion was yet a shade darker than he'd thought at first. Or it might even be – wild fantasy – that the Big Gambler's skin was slowly darkening tonight, like a meerschaum pipe being smoked a mile a second. That was almost funny to think of – there was enough heat in this place, all right, to darken meerschaum, as Joe knew from sad experience, but so far as he was aware it was all under the table.

None of Joe's thoughts, either familiar or admiring, about the Big Gambler decreased in the slightest degree his certainty of the supreme menace of the man in black and his conviction that it would be death to touch him. And if any doubts had stirred in Joe's mind, they would have been squelched by the chilling incident which next occurred.

The Big Gambler had just taken into his arms his prettiest-evilest sporting girl and was running an aristocratic hand across her haunch with perfect gentility, when the poet chap, green-eyed from jealousy and lovesickness, came leaping forward like a wild-cat and aimed a long gleaming dagger at the black satin back.

Joe couldn't see how the blow could miss, but without taking his genteel right hand off the sporting girl's plush rear end, the Big Gambler shot out his left arm like a steel spring straightening. Joe couldn't tell whether he stabbed the poet chap in the throat, or judo-chopped him there, or gave him the Martian double-finger, or just touched him, but anyhow the fellow stopped as dead as if he'd been shot by a silent elephant gun or an invisible ray pistol and he slammed down on the floor. A couple of darkies came running up to drag off the body and nobody paid the least attention, such episodes apparently being taken for granted at The Boneyard.

It gave Joe quite a turn and he almost shot Phoebe before he intended to.

But by now waves of pain had stopped running up his left arm and his nerves were like metal-wrapped new guitar strings, so three rolls later he shot a five, making his point, and set in to clean out the table.

He rolled nine successive naturals, seven sevens and two elevens, pyramiding his first wager of a single chip to a stake of over four thousand dollars. None of the Big Mushrooms had dropped out yet, but some of them were beginning to look worried and a couple were sweating. The Big Gambler still hadn't covered any part of Joe's bets, but he seemed to be following the play with interest from the cavernous depths of his eye sockets.

Then Joe got a devilish thought. Nobody could beat him tonight, he knew, but if he held on to the dice until the table was cleaned out, he'd never get a chance to see the Big Gambler exercise *his* skill, and he was truly curious about that. Besides, he thought, he ought to return courtesy for courtesy and have a crack at being a gentleman himself.

'Pulling out forty-one dollars less a nickel,' he announced.

'Rolling a penny.'

This time there wasn't any hissing and Mr Bones's moonface didn't cloud over. But Joe was conscious that the Big Gambler was staring at him disappointedly, or sorrowfully, or maybe just speculatively.

Joe immediately crapped out by throwing boxcars, rather pleased to see the two best-looking skulls grinning ruby-toothed side by side, and the dice passed to the Big Mushroom on his left.

'Knew when his streak was over,' he heard another Big Mushroom mutter with grudging admiration.

The play worked rather rapidly around the table, nobody getting very hot and the stakes never more than medium high. 'Shoot a fin.' 'Rolling a sawbuck.' 'An Andrew Jackson.' 'Rolling thirty bucks.' Now and then Joe covered part of a bet, winning more than he lost. He had over seven thousand dollars, real money, before the bones got around to the Big Gambler.

That one held the dice for a long moment on his statue-steady palm while he looked at them reflectively, though not the hint of a furrow appeared in his almost brownish forehead down which never a bead of sweat trickled. He murmured, 'Rolling a double sawbuck,' and when he had been faded, he closed his fingers, lightly rattled the cubes – the sound was like big seeds inside a small gourd only half dry – and negligently cast the dice towards the end of the table.

It was a throw like none Joe had ever seen before at any crap table. The dice travelled flat through the air without turning over, struck the exact juncture of the table's end and bottom, and stopped there dead, showing a natural seven.

Joe was distinctly disappointed. On one of his own throws he was used to calculating something like, 'Launch three-up, five north, two and a half rolls in the air, hit on the six-five-three corner, three-quarter roll and one-quarter side-twist right, hit end on the one-two edge, one-half reverse roll and three-quarter side-twist left, land on five face, roll over twice, come up two,' and that would be for just one of the dice, and a really commonplace throw, without extra bounces.

By comparison, the technique of the Big Gambler had been ridiculously, absymally, horrifyingly simple. Joe could have duplicated it with the greatest ease, of course. It was no more than an elementary form of his old pastime of throwing fallen rocks back into their holes. But Joe had never once thought of pulling such a babyish trick at the crap table. It would make the whole thing too easy and destroy the beauty of the game.

Another reason Joe had never used the trick was that he'd never dreamed he'd be able to get away with it. By all the rules he'd ever heard of, it was a most questionable throw. There was the possibility that one of the other die hadn't completely reached the end of the table, or lay a wee bit cocked against the end. Besides, he reminded himself, weren't both dice supposed to rebound off the end, if only for a fraction of an inch?

However, as far as Joe's very sharp eyes could see, both dice lay perfectly flat and sprang up against the end wall. Moreover, everyone else at the table seemed to accept the throw, the dice-girl had scooped up the cubes, and the Big Mushrooms who had faded the man in black were paying off. As far as the rebound business went, well, The Boneyard appeared to put a slightly different interpretation on that rule, and Joe believed in never questioning House Rules except in dire extremity – both his Mother and Wife had long since taught him it was the least troublesome way.

Besides, there hadn't been any of his own money riding on that roll.

In a voice like wind through Cypress Hollow or on Mars, the Big Gambler announced, 'Roll a century.' It was the biggest bet yet tonight, ten thousand dollars, and the way the

Big Gambler said it made it seem something more than that. A hush fell on The Boneyard, they put the mutes on the jazz horns, the croupiers' calls became more confidential, the cards fell softlier, even the roulette balls seemed to be trying to make less noise as they rattled into their cells. The crowd around the Number One Crap Table quietly thickened. The Big Gambler's flash boys and girls formed a double semicircle around him, ensuring him lots of elbow room.

That century bet, Joe realized, was thirty bucks more than his own entire pile. Three or four of the Big Mushrooms had to signal each other before they'd agree how to fade it.

The Big Gambler shot another natural seven with exactly the same flat, stop-dead throw.

He bet another century and did it again.

And again.

And again.

Joe was getting mighty concerned and pretty indignant too. It seemed unjust that the Big Gambler should be winning such huge bets with such machine-like, utterly unromantic rolls. Why, you couldn't even call them rolls, the dice never turned over an iota, in the air or after. It was the sort of thing you'd expect from a robot, and a very dully programmed robot at that. Joe hadn't risked any of his own chips fading the Big Gambler, of course, but if things went on like this he'd have to. Two of the Big Mushrooms had already retired sweatingly from the table, confessing defeat, and no one had taken their places. Pretty soon there'd be a bet the remaining Big Mushrooms couldn't entirely cover between them, and then he'd have to risk some of his own chips or else pull out of the game himself – and he couldn't do that, not with the power surging in his right hand like chained lightning.

Joe waited and waited for someone else to question one of the big Gambler's shots, but no one did. He realized that, despite his efforts to look imperturbable, his face was slowly reddening.

With a little lift of his left hand, the Big Gambler stopped the dice-girl as she was about to snatch at the cubes. The eyes that were like black wells directed themselves at Joe, who forced himself to look back into them steadily. He still couldn't catch the faintest gleam in them. All at once he felt the lightest touch-on-neck of a dreadful suspicion.

With the utmost civility and amiability, the Big Gambler whispered, 'I believe that the fine shooter across from me has doubts about the validity of my last throw, though he is too much of a gentleman to voice them. Lottie, the card test.'

The wraith-tall, ivory dice-girl plucked a playing card from below the table and with a venomous flash of her little white teeth spun it low across the table through the air at Joe. He caught the whirling pasteboard and examined it briefly. It was the thinnest, stiffest, flattest, shiniest playing card Joe had ever handled. It was also the Joker, if that meant anything. He spun it back lazily into her hand and she slid it very gently, letting it descend by its own weight, down the end wall against which the two dice lay. It came to rest in the tiny hollow their rounded edges made against the black felt. She deftly moved it about without force, demonstrating that there was no space between either of the cubes and the table's end at any point.

'Satisfied?' the Big Gambler asked. Rather against his will Joe nodded. The Big Gambler bowed to him. The dice-girl smirked her short, thin lips and drew herself up, flaunting her white-china-doorknob breasts at Joe.

Casually, almost with an air of boredom, the Big Gambler returned to his routine of shooting a century and making a natural seven. The Big Mushrooms wilted fast and one by one tottered away from the table. A particularly pink-faced Toadstool was brought some extra cash by a gasping runner, but it was no help, he only lost the additional centuries. While the stacks of pale and black chips beside the Big Gambler grew skyscraper-tall.

Joe got more and more furious and frightened. He watched like a hawk or spy satellite the dice nestling against the end wall, but never could spot justification for calling for another card test, or nerve himself to question the House Rules at this late date. It was maddening, in fact insanitizing, to know that if only he could get the cubes once more he could shoot circles around that black pillar of sporting aristocracy. He damned himself a googelplex of ways for the idiotic, conceited, suicidal impulse that had led him to let go of the bones when he'd had them.

To make matter worse, the Big Gambler had taken to gazing steadily at Joe with those eyes like coal mines. Now he made three rolls running without even glancing at the dice or the end wall, as far as Joe could tell. Why, he was getting as bad as Joe's Wife or Mother – watching, watching, watching Joe.

But the constant staring of those eyes that were not eyes was mostly throwing a terrific scare into him. Supernatural terror added itself to his certainty of the deadliness of the Big Gambler. Just who, Joe kept asking himself, had he got into a game with tonight? There was curiosity and there was dread – a dreadful curiosity as strong as his desire to get the bones and win. His hair rose and he was all over goose bumps, though the power was still pulsing in his hand liked a braked locomotive or a rocket wanting to lift from the pad.

At the same time the Big Gambler stayed just that – a black satin-coated, slouch-hatted elegance, suave, courtly, lethal. In fact, almost the worst thing about the spot Joe found himself in was that, after admiring the Big Gambler's perfect sportsmanship all night, he must now be disenchanted by his machine-like throwing and try to catch him out on any technicality he could.

The remorseless mowing down of the Big Mushrooms

went on. The empty spaces outnumbered the Toadstools. Soon there were only three left.

The Boneyard had grown still as Cypress Hollow or the Moon. The jazz had stopped and the gay laughter and the shuffle of feet and the squeak of goosed girls and the clink of drinks and coins. Everybody seemed to be gathered around the Number One Crap Table, rank on silent rank.

Joe was racked by watchfulness, sense of injustice, self-contempt, wild hopes, curiosity and dread. Especially the last two.

The complexion of the Big Gambler, as much as you could see of it, continued to darken. For one wild moment Joe found himself wondering if he'd got into a game with a nigger, maybe a witchcraft-drenched Voodoo Man whose white make-up was wearing off.

Pretty soon there came a century wager which the two remaining Big Mushrooms couldn't fade between them. Joe had to make up a sawbuck from his miserably tiny pile or get out of the game. After a moment's agonizing hesitation, he did the former.

And lost ten.

The two Big Mushrooms reeled back into the hushed crowd.

Pit-black eyes bored into Joe. A whisper: 'Rolling your pile.'

Joe felt well up in him that shameful impulse to confess himself licked and run home. At least his six thousand dollars would make a hit with his Wife and Ma.

But he just couldn't bear to think of the crowd's laughter, or the thought of living with himself knowing that he'd had a final chance, however slim, to challenge the Big Gambler and passed it up.

He nodded.

The Big Gambler shot, Joe leaned out over and down the

table, forgetting his vertigo, as he followed the throw with eagle or space-telescope eyes.

'Satisfied?'

Joe knew he ought to say, 'Yes,' and slink off with head held as high as he could manage. It was the gentlemanly thing to do. But then he reminded himself that he wasn't a gentleman, but just a dirty, working-stiff miner with a talent for precision hurling.

He also knew that it was probably very dangerous for him to say anything but 'Yes', surrounded as he was by enemies and strangers. But then he asked himself what right had he, a miserable, mortal, homebound failure, to worry about danger.

Besides, one of the ruby-grinning dice looked just the tiniest hair out of line with the other.

It was the biggest effort yet of Joe's life, but he swallowed and managed to say, 'No. Lottie, the card test.'

The dice-girl fairly snarled and reared up and back as if she were going to spit in his eyes, and Joe had a feeling her spit was cobra venom. But the Big Gambler lifted a finger at her in reproof and she skimmed the card at Joe, yet so low and viciously that it disappeared under the black felt for an instant before flying up into Joe's hand.

It was hot to the touch and singed a pale brown all over, though otherwise unimpaired. Joe gulped and spun it back high.

Sneering poisoned daggers at him, Lottie let it glide down the end wall . . . and after a moment's hesitation, it slithered behind the die Joe had suspected.

A bow and then the whisper: 'You have sharp eyes, sir. Undoubtedly that die failed to reach the wall. My sincerest apologies and . . . your dice, sir.'

Seeing the cubes sitting on the black rim in front of him almost gave Joe apoplexy. All the feelings racking him,

including his curiosity, rose to an almost unbelievable pitch of
intensity, and when he'd said, 'Rolling my pile,' and the Big
Gambler had replied, 'You're faded,' he yielded to an
uncontrollable impulse and cast the two dice straight at the
Big Gamblers ungleaming midnight eyes.

They went right through into the Big Gambler's skull and
bounced around inside there, rattling like big seeds in a big
gourd not quite yet dry.

Throwing out a hand, palm back, to either side, to indicate
that none of his boys and girls or anyone else must make a
reprisal on Joe, the Big Gambler dryly gargled the two cubical
bones, then spat them out so that they landed in the centre of
the table, the one die flat, the other leaning against it.

'Cocked dice, sir,' he whispered as graciously as if no
indignity whatever had been done him. 'Roll again.'

Joe shook the dice reflectively, getting over the shock. After
a little bit he decided that though he could now guess the Big
Gambler's real name, he'd still give him a run for his money.

A little corner of Joe's mind wondered how a live skeleton
hung together. Did the bones still have gristle and thews,
were they wired, was it done with force-fields, or was each
bone a calcium magnet clinging to the next? – this tying in
somehow with the generation of the deadly ivory electricity.

In the great hush of The Boneyard, someone cleared his
throat, a Scarlet Woman tittered hysterically, a coin fell from
the nakedest change-girl's tray with a golden clink and rolled
musically across the floor.

'Silence,' the Big Gambler commanded and in a movement
almost too fast to follow whipped a hand inside the bosom of
his coat and out to the crap table's rim in front of him. A
short-barrelled silver revolver lay softly gleaming there.
'Next creature, from the humblest nigger night-girl to you,
Mr Bones, who utters a sound while my worthy opponent
rolls, gets a bullet in the head.'

Joe gave him a courtly bow back, it felt funny, and then decided to start his run with a natural seven made up of an ace and a six. He rolled and this time the Big Gambler, judging from the movements of his skull, closely followed the course of the cubes with his eyes that weren't there.

The dice landed, rolled over, and lay still. Incredulously, Joe realized that for the first time in his crap-shooting life he'd made a mistake. Or else there was a power in the Big Gambler's gaze greater than that in his own right hand. The six cube had come down okay, but the ace had taken an extra half roll and come down six too.

'End of the game,' Mr Bones boomed sepulchrally.

The Big Gambler raised a brown skeletal hand. 'Not necessarily,' he whispered. His black eyepits aimed themselves at Joe like the mouths of siege guns. 'Joe Slattermill, you still have something of value to wager, if you wish. Your life.'

At that a giggling and a hysterical tittering and a guffawing and a braying and a shrieking burst uncontrollably out of the whole Boneyard. Mr Bones summed up the sentiments when he bellowed over the rest of the racket, 'Now what use or value is there in the life of a bummer like Joe Slattermill? Not two cents, ordinary money.'

The Big Gambler laid a hand on the revolver gleaming before him and all the laughter died.

'I have a use for it,' the Big Gambler whispered. 'Joe Slattermill, on my part I will venture all my winnings of tonight, and throw in the world and everything in it for a side bet. You will wager your life, and on the side your soul. You to roll the dice. What's your pleasure?'

Joe Slattermill quailed, but then the drama of the situation took hold of him. He thought it over and realized he certainly wasn't going to give up being stage centre in a spectacle like this to go home broke to his Wife and Mother and decaying house and the dispirited Mr Guts. Maybe, he told himself encouragingly, there wasn't a power in the Big Gambler's gaze, maybe Joe had just made his one and only crap-shooting error. Besides, he was more inclined to accept Mr Bones's assessment of the value of his life than the Big Gamblers.

'It's a bet,' he said.

'Lottie, give him the dice.'

Joe concentrated his mind as never before, the power tingled triumphantly in his hand, and he made his throw.

The dice never hit the felt. They went swooping down, then up, in a crazy curve far out over the end of the table, and then came streaking back like tiny red-glinting meteors towards the face of the Big Gambler, where they suddenly nested and hung in his black eye sockets, each with the single red gleam of an ace showing.

Snake eyes.

The whisper, as those red-glinting dice-eyes stared mockingly at him: 'Joe Slattermill, you've crapped out.'

Using thumb and middle finger – or bone rather – of either hand, the Big Gambler removed the dice from his eye sockets and dropped them in Lottie's white-gloved hand.

'Yes, you've crapped out, Joe Slattermill,' he went on tranquilly. 'And now you can shoot yourself' – he touched the silver gun – 'or cut your throat' – he whipped a gold-handled bowie knife out of his coat and laid it beside the revolver – 'or poison yourself' – the two weapons were joined by a small black bottle with white skull and crossbones on it – 'or Miss Flossie here can kiss you to death.' He drew forward beside him his prettiest, evilist-looking sporting girl. She preened herself and flounced her short violet skirt and gave Joe a provocative, hungry look, lifting her carmine upper lip to show her long white canines.

'Or else,' the Big Gambler added, nodding significantly towards the black-bottomed crap table, 'you can take the Big Dive.'

Joe said evenly, 'I'll take the Big Dive.'

He put his right foot on his empty chip table, his left on the black rim, fell forward . . . and suddenly kicking off from the rim, launched himself in a tiger spring straight across the crap table at the Big Gambler's throat, solacing himself with the thought that certainly the poet chap hadn't seemed to suffer long.

As he flashed across the exact centre of the table he got an instant photograph of what really lay below, but his brain had no time to develop that snapshot, for the next instant he was ploughing into the Big Gambler.

Stiffened brownpalm edge caught him in the temple with a lighting-like judo chop . . . and the brown fingers or bones flew all apart like puff paste. Joe's left hand went through the Big Gambler's chest as if there was nothing there but black satin coat, while his right hand, straight-armedly clawing at the slouch-hatted skull, crunched it to pieces. Next instant Joe was sprawled on the floor with some black clothes and brown fragments.

He was on his feet in a flash and snatching at the Big Gambler's tall stacks. He had time for one left-handed grab. He couldn't see any gold or silver or any black chips, so he stuffed his left pants pocket with a handful of the pale chips and ran.

Then the whole population of The Boneyard was on him and after him. Teeth, knives and brass knuckles flashed. He was punched, clawed, kicked, tripped and stamped on with spike heels. A gold-plated trumpet with a bloodshot-eyed black face behind it bopped him on the head. He got a white flash of the golden change-girl and made a grab for her, but she got away. Someone tried to mash a lighted cigar in his eye. Lottie, writhing and flailing like a white boa constrictor, almost got a simultaneous strangle hold and scissors on him. From a squat wide-mouth bottle Flossie, snarling like a feline fiend threw what smelt like acid past his face. Mr Bones peppered shots around him from the silver revolver. He was stabbed at, gouged, rabbit-punched, scragmauled, slugged, kneed, bitten, bearhugged, butted, beaten and had his toes trampled.

But somehow none of the blows or grabs had much real force. It was like fighting ghosts. In the end it turned out that the whole population of The Boneyard, working together, had just a little more strength than Joe. He felt himself being lifted by a multitude of hands and pitched out through the swinging door so that he thudded down on his rear end on the board sidewalk. Even that didn't hurt much. It was more like a kick of encouragement.

He took a deep breath and felt himself over and worked his bones. He didn't seem to have suffered any serious damages. He stood up and looked around. The Boneyard was dark and silent as the grave, or the planet Pluto, or all the rest of Ironmine. As his eyes got accustomed to the starlight and occasional roving spaceship-gleam, he saw a padlocked sheet-iron door where the swinging ones had been.

He found he was chewing on something crusty he'd somehow carried in his right hand all the way through the final fracas. Mighty tasty, like the bread his Wife baked for best customers. At that instant his brain developed the photograph it had taken when he had glanced down as he flashed across the centre of the crap table. It was a thin wall of flames moving sideways across the table and just beyond the flames the faces of his Wife, Mother, and Mr Guts, all looking very surprised. He realized that what he was chewing was a fragment of the Big Gambler's skull, and he remembered the shape of the three loaves his Wife had started to bake when he left the house. And he understood the magic she'd made to let him get a little ways away and feel half a man, and then come diving home with his fingers burned.

He spat out what was in his mouth and pegged the rest of the bit of giant-popover skull across the street.

He fished in his left pocket. Most of the pale poker chips had been mashed in the fight, but he found a whole one and explored its surface with its fingertips. The symbol embossed on it was a cross. He lifted it to his lips and took a bite. It tasted delicate, but delicious. He ate it and felt his strength revive. He patted his bulging left pocket. At least he'd start out well provisioned.

Then he turned and headed straight for home, but he took the long way, around the world.

Belsen Express

George Simister watched the blue flames writhe beautifully in the grate, like dancing girls drenched with alchohol and set afire, and congratulated himself on having survived well through the middle of the twentieth century without getting involved in military service, world-saving, or any activities that interfered with the earning and enjoyment of money.

Outside rain dripped, a storm snarled as the city from the outskirts, and sudden gusts of wind produced in the chimney a sound like the mourning of doves. Simister shimmied himself a fraction of an inch deeper in his easy chair and took a slow sip of diluted scotch – he was sensitive to most cheaper liquors. Simister's physiology was on the delicate side; during his childhood certain tastes and odours, playing on an elusive heart weakness, had been known to make him faint.

The outspread newspaper started to slip from his knee. He detained it, let his glance rove across the next page, noted a headline about an uprising in Prague like that in Hungary in 1956 and murmured 'Damn Slavs', noted another about border fighting around Israel and muttered, 'Damn Jews', and let the paper go. He took another sip of his drink, yawned, and watched a virginal blue flame flutter frightenedly the length of the log before it turned to a white smoke ghost. There was a sharp *knock-knock*.

Simister jumped and then got up and hurried tight-lipped to the front door. Lately some of the neighbourhood children had been trying to annoy him, probably because his was the most respectable and best-kept house on the block. Doorbell ringing, obscene sprayed scrawls, that sort of thing. And hardly children – young rowdies rather, who need rough handling and a trip to the police station. He was really angry by the time he reached the door and swung it wide. There was nothing but a big wet empty darkness. A chilly draught spattered a couple of cold drops on him. Maybe the noise had come from the fire. He shut the door and started back to the living room, but a small pile of books untidily nested in wrapping paper on the hall table caught his eye and he grimaced.

They constituted a blotchily addressed parcel which the postman had delivered by mistake a few mornings ago. Simister could probably have deciphered the address, for it was clearly on this street, and rectified the postman's error, but he did not choose to abet the activities of illiterates with leaky pens. And the delivery must have been a mistake for the top book was titled *The Scourge of the Swastika* and the other two had similar titles, and Simister had an acute distate for books that insisted on digging up that satisfactorily buried historical incident known as Nazi Germany.

The reason for this distaste was a deeply hidden fear that George Simister shared with millions, but that he had never revealed even to his wife. It was a quite unrealistic and now completely anachronistic fear of the Gestapo.

It had begun years before the Second World War, with the first small reports from Germany of minority persecutions and organized hoodlumism – the sense of something reaching out across the dark Atlantic to threaten his life, his security, and his confidence that he would never have to suffer pain except in a hospital.

Of course it had never got close to Simister, but it had exercised an evil tyranny over his imagination. There was one nightmarish series of scenes that had slowly grown in his mind and then kept bothering him for a long time. It began with a thunderous knocking, of boots and rifle butts rather than fists, and a shouted demand: 'Open up! It's the Gestapo.' Next he would find himself in a stream of frantic people being driven towards a portal where a division was made between those reprieved and those slated for immediate extinction. Last he would be inside a closed motor van jammed so tightly with people that it was impossible to move. After a long time the van would stop, but the motor would keep running, and from the floor, leisurely seeking the crevices between the packed bodies, the entrapped exhaust fumes would begin to mount.

Now in the shadowy hall the same horrid movie had a belated showing. Simister shook his head sharply, as if he could shake the scenes out, reminding himself that the Gestapo was dead and done with for more than ten years. He felt the angry impulse to throw in the fire the books responsible for the return of his waking nightmare. But he remembered that books are hard to burn. He stared at them uneasily, excited by thoughts of torture and confinement, concentration and death camps, but knowing the nasty aftermath they left in his mind. Again he felt the sudden impulse, this time to bundle the books together and throw them in the trash can. But that would mean getting wet, it could wait until tomorrow. He put the screen in front of the fire, which had died and was smoking like a crematory, and went up to bed.

Some hours later he awoke with the memory of a thunderous knocking.

He started up, exclaiming, 'Those damned kids!' The drawn shades seemed abnormally dark – probably they'd thrown a stone through a street lamp.

He put one foot on the chilly floor. It was now profoundly still. The storm had gone off like a roving cat. Simister strained his ears. Beside him his wife breathed with irritating evenness. He wanted to wake her and explain about the young delinquents. It was criminal that they were permitted to roam the streets at this hour. Girls with them too, likely as not.

The knocking was not repeated. Simister listened for footsteps going away, or for the creaking of boards that would betray a lurking presence on the porch.

After a while he began to wonder if the knocking might not have been part of a dream, or perhaps a final rumble of actual thunder. He lay down and pulled the blankets up to his neck. Eventually his muscles relaxed and he got to sleep.

At breakfast he told his wife about it.

'George, it may have been burglars,' she said.

'Don't be stupid, Joan. Burglars don't knock. If it was anything it was those damned kids.'

'Whatever it was, I wish you'd put a bigger bolt on the front door.'

'Nonsense. If I'd known you were going to act this way I wouldn't have said anything. I told you it was probably just the thunder.'

But next night at about the same hour it happened again.

This time there could be little question of dreaming. The knocking still reverberated in his ears. And there had been words mixed with it, some sort of yapping in a foreign language. Probably the children of some of those European refugees who had settled in the neighbourhood.

Last night they'd fooled him by keeping perfectly still after banging on the door, but tonight he knew what to do. He tiptoed across the bedroom and went down the stairs rapidly, but quietly because of his bare feet. In the hall he snatched up something to hit them with, then in one motion unlocked and jerked open the door.

There was no one.

He stood looking at the darkness. He was puzzled as to how they could have got away so quickly and silently. He shut the door and switched on the light. Then he felt the thing in his hand. It was one of those books. With a feeling of disgust he dropped it on the others. He must remember to throw them out first thing tomorrow.

But he overslept and had to rush. The feeling of disgust or annoyance, or something akin, must have lingered, however, for he found himself sensitive to things he wouldn't ordinarily have noticed. People especially. The swollen-handed man seemed deliberately surly as he counted Simister's pennies and handed him the paper. The tight-lipped woman at the gate hesitated suspiciously, as if he were trying to pass of a last month's ticket.

And when he was hurrying up the stairs in response to an approaching rumble, he brushed against a little man in an oversize coat and received in return a glance that give him a positive shock.

Simister vaguely remembered having seen the little man several times before. He had the thin nose, narrow-set eyes and receding chin that is by a stretch of the imagination described as 'rat-faced'. In the movies he'd have played a stool pigeon. The flapping overcoat was rather comic.

But there seemed to be something at once so venomous and sly, so time-bidingly vindictive, in the glance he gave Simister that the latter was taken aback and almost missed the train.

He just managed to squeeze through the automatically closing door of the smoker after the barest squint at the sign to assure himself that the train was an express. His heart was pounding in a way that another time would have worried him, but now he was immersed in a savage pleasure at having thwarted the man in the oversize coat. The latter hadn't hurried fast enough and Simister had made no effort to hold open the door for him.

As a smooth surge of electric power sent them gliding away from the station Simister pushed his way from the vestibule into the car and snagged a strap. From the next one already swayed his chief commuting acquaintance, a beefy, suspiciously red-nosed, irritating man named Holstrom, now reading a folded newspaper one-handed. He shoved a headline in Simister's face. The latter knew what to expect.

'Atomic Weapons for West Germany,' he read tonelessly. Holstrom was always trying to get him into outworn arguments about totalitarianism, Nazi Germany, racial prejudice and the like. 'Well, what about it?'

Holstrom shrugged. 'It's a natural enough step, I suppose, but it started me thinking about the top Nazis and whether we really got all of them.'

'Of course,' Simister snapped.

'I'm not so sure,' Holstrom said. 'I imagine quite a few of them got away and are still hiding out somewhere.'

But Simister refused the bait. The question bored him. Who talked about the Nazis any more? For that matter, the whole trip this morning was boring; the smoker was overcrowded; and when they finally piled out at the downtown terminus, the rude jostling increased his irritation.

The crowd was approaching an iron fence that arbitrarily split the stream of hurrying people into two sections which reunited a few steps farther on. Beside the fence a new guard was standing, or perhaps Simister hadn't noticed him before. A cocky-looking young fellow with close-cropped blond hair and blue eyes.

Suddenly it occurred to Simister that he habitually passed to the right of the fence, but that this morning he was being edged over towards the left. This trifling circumstance, coming on top of everything else, made him boil. He deliberately pushed across the stream, despite angry murmurs and the hard stare of the guard.

He had intended to walk the rest of the way, but his anger made him forgetful and before he realized it he had climbed aboard a bus. He soon regretted it. The bus was even more crowded than the smoker and the standees were morose and lumpy in their heavy overcoats. He was tempted to get off and waste his fare, but he was trapped in the extreme rear and moreover shrank from giving the impression of a man who didn't know his own mind.

Soon another annoyance was added to the ones already plaguing him – a trace of exhaust fumes was seeping up from the motor at the rear. He immediately began to feel ill. He looked around indignantly, but the others did not seem to notice the odour, or else accepted it fatalistically.

In a couple of blocks the fumes had become so bad that Simister decided he must get off at the next stop. But as he started to push past her, a fat woman beside him gave him such a strangely apathetic stare that Simister, whose mind was perhaps a little clouded by nausea, felt almost hypnotized by it, so that it was several seconds before he recalled and carried out his intention.

Ridiculous, but the woman's face stuck in his mind all day.

In the evening he stopped at a hardware store. After supper his wife noticed him working in the front hall.

'Oh, you're putting on a bolt,' she said.

'Well, you asked me to, didn't you?'

'Yes, but I didn't think you'd do it.'

'I decided I might as well.' He gave the screw a final turn and stepped back to survey the job. 'Anything to give you a feeling of security.'

Then he remembered the stuff he had been meaning to throw out that morning. The hall table was bare.

'What did you do with them?' he asked.

'What?'

'Those fool books.'

'Oh, those. I wrapped them up again and gave them to the postman.'

'Now why did you do that? There wasn't any return address and I might have wanted to look at them.'

'But you said they weren't addressed to us and you hate all that war stuff.'

'I know, but—' he said and then stopped, hopeless at making her understand why he particularly wanted to feel he had got rid of that package himself, and by throwing it in the trash can. For that matter, he didn't quite understand his feelings himself. He began to poke around the hall.

'I did return the package,' his wife said sharply. 'I'm not losing my memory.'

'Oh, all right!' he said and started for bed.

That night no knocking awoke him, but rather a loud crashing and rending of wood along with a harsh metallic *ping* like a lock giving.

In a moment he was out of bed, his sleep-sodden nerves jangling with anger. Those hoodlums! Rowdy pranks were perhaps one thing, deliberate destruction of property certainly another. He was halfway down the stairs before it occurred to him that the sound he had heard had a distinctly menacing aspect. Juvenile delinquents who broke down doors would hardly panic at the appearance of an unarmed householder.

But just then he saw that the front door was intact.

Considerably puzzled and apprehensive, he searched the first floor and even ventured into the basement, racking his brains as to just what could have caused such a noise. The water heater? Weight of coal bursting a side of the bin? Those objects were intact. But perhaps the porch trellis giving way?

That last notion kept him peering out of the front window several moments. When he turned around there was someone behind him.

'I didn't mean to startle you,' his wife said. 'What's the matter, George?'

'I don't know. I thought I heard a sound. Something being smashed.'

He expected that would send her into one of her burglar panics, but instead she kept looking at him.

'Don't stand there all night,' he said. 'Come on to bed.'

'George, is something worrying you? Something you haven't told me about?'

'Of course not. Come on.'

Next morning Holstrom was on the platform when Simister got there and they exchanged guesses as to whether the dark rainclouds would burst before they got downtown. Simister noticed the man in the oversize coat loitering about, but he paid no attention to him.

Since it was a bank holiday there were empty seats in the smoker and he and Holstrom secured one. As usual the latter had his newspaper. Simister waited for him to start his ideological sniping – a little uneasily for once; usually he was secure in his prejudices, but this morning he felt strangely vulnerable.

It came. Holstrom shook his head. 'That's a bad business in Czechoslovakia. Maybe we were a little too hard on the Nazis.'

To his surprise Simister found himself replying with both nervous hypocrisy and uncharacteristic vehemence. 'Don't be ridiculous! Those rats deserved a lot worse than they got!'

As Holstrom turned towards him saying, 'Oh, so you've changed your mind about the Nazis,' Simister thought he heard someone just behind him say at the same time in a low, distinct, pitiless voice: 'I heard you.'

He glanced around quickly. Leaning forward a little, but with his face turned sharply away as if he had just become interested in something passing the window, was the man in the oversize coat.

'What's wrong?' Holstrom asked.

'What do you mean?'

'You've turned pale. You look sick.'

'I don't feel that way.'

'Sure? You know, at our age we've got to begin to watch out. Didn't you once tell me something about your heart?'

Simister managed to laugh that off, but when they parted just outside the train he was conscious that Holstrom was still eyeing him rather closely.

As he slowly walked through the terminus his face began to assume an abstracted look. In fact he was lost in thought to such a degree that when he approached the iron fence, he started to pass it on the left. Luckily the crowd was thin and he was able to cut across to the right without difficulty. The blond young guard looked at him closely – perhaps he remembered yesterday morning.

Simister had told himself that he wouldn't again under any circumstances take the bus, but when he got outside it was raining torrents. After a moment's hesitation he climbed aboard. It seemed even more crowded than yesterday, if that were possible, with more of the same miserable people, and the damp air made the exhaust odour particularly offensive.

The abstracted look clung to his face all day long. His secretary noticed, but did not comment. His wife did, however, when she found him poking around in the hall after supper.

'Are you still looking for that package, George?' Her tone was flat.

'Of course not,' he said quickly, shutting the table drawer he'd opened.

She waited. 'Are you sure you didn't order those books?'

'What gave you that idea?' he demanded. 'You know I didn't.'

'I'm glad,' she said. 'I looked through them. There were pictures. They were nasty.'

'You think I'm the sort of person who'd buy books for the sake of nasty pictures?'

'Of course not, dear, but I thought you might have seen them and they were what had depressed you.'

'Have I been depressed?'

'Yes. Your heart hasn't been bothering you, has it?'

'No.'

'Well, what is it then?'

'I don't know.' Then with considerable effort he said, 'I've been thinking about war and things.'

'War! No wonder you're depressed. You shouldn't think about things you don't like, especially when they aren't happening. What started you?'

'Oh, Holstrom keeps talking to me on the train.'

'Well, don't listen to him.'

'I won't.'

'Well, cheer up then.'

'I will.'

'And don't let anyone make you look at morbid pictures. There was one of some people who had been gassed in a motor van and then laid out—'

'Please, Joan! Is it any better to tell me about them than to have me look at them?'

'Of course not, dear. That was silly of me. But do cheer up.'

'Yes.'

The puzzled, uneasy look was still in her eyes as she watched him go down the front walk next morning. It was foolish, but she had the feeling that his grey suit was really black – and he had whimpered in his sleep. With a shiver at her fancy she stepped inside.

That morning George Simister created a minor disturbance in the smoker, it was remembered afterwards, though Holstrom did not witness the beginning of it. It seems that Simister had run to catch the express and had almost missed it, due to a collision with a small man in a large overcoat. Someone recalled that trifling prelude because of the amusing circumstance that the small man, although he had been thrown to his knees and the collision was chiefly Simister's fault, was still anxiously begging Simister's pardon after the latter had dashed on.

Simister just managed to squeeze through the closing door while taking a quick squint at the sign. It was then that his queer behaviour started. He instantly turned around and unsuccessfully tried to force his way out again, even inserting his hands in the crevice between the doorframe and the rubber edge of the sliding door and yanking violently.

Apparently as soon as he noticed the train was in motion, he turned away from the door, his face pale and set, and roughly pushed his way into the interior of the car.

There he made a beeline for the little box in the wall containing the identifying signs of the train and the miniature window which showed in reverse the one now in use, which read simply EXPRESS. He stared at it as if he couldn't believe his eyes and then started to turn the crank, exposing in turn all the other white signs on the roll of black cloth. He scanned each one intently, oblivious to the puzzled or outraged looks of those around him.

He had been through all the signs once and was starting through them again before the conductor noticed what was happening and came hurrying. Ignoring his expostulations, Simister asked him loudly if this was really the express. Upon receiving a curt affirmative, Simister went on to assert that he had in the moment of squeezing aboard glimpsed another sign in the window – and he mentioned a strange name. He seemed both very positive and very agitated about it, the conductor said. The latter asked Simister to spell the name. Simister haltingly compiled: 'B...E...L...S...E...N...' The conductor shook his head, then his eyes widened and he demanded, 'Say, are you trying to kid me? That was one of those Nazi death camps.' Simister slunk towards the other end of the car.

It was there that Holstrom saw him, looking 'as if he'd just got a terrible shock'. Holstrom was alarmed – and as it happened felt a special private guilt – but could hardly get a word out of him, though he made several attempts to start a conversation, choosing uncharacteristically neutral topics. Once, he remembered, Simister looked up and said, 'Do you suppose there are some things a man simply can't escape, no matter how quietly he lives or how carefully he plans?' But his face immediately showed he had realized there was at least one very obvious answer to this question, and Holstrom didn't know what to say. Another time he suddenly remarked, 'I wish we were like the British and didn't have standing in the buses,' but he subsided as quickly. As they neared the downtown terminus Simister seemed to brace up a little, but Holstrom was still worried about him to such a degree that he went out of his way to follow him through the terminus. 'I was afraid something would happen to him, I don't know what,' Holstrom said. 'I would have stayed right beside him except he seemed to resent my presence.'

Holstrom's private guilt, which intensified his anxiety and doubtless accounted for his feeling that Simister resented him, was due to the fact that ten days ago, cumulatively irritated by Simister's smug prejudices and blinkered narrow-mindedness, he had anonymously mailed him three books recounting with uncompromising realism and documentation some of the least pleasant aspects of the Nazi tyranny. Now he couldn't but feel they might have helped to shake Simister up in a way he hadn't intended, and he was ashamedly glad that he had been in such a condition when he sent the package that it had been addressed in a drunken scrawl. He never discussed the matter afterwards, except occasionally to make strangely feelingful remarks about 'what little things can unseat a spring in a man's clockworks!'

So, continuing Holstrom's story, he followed Simister at a distance as the latter dejectedly shuffled across the busy terminus. 'Terminus?' Holstrom once interrupted his story to remark. 'He's a god of endings, isn't he? – and of human rights. Does that mean anything?'

When Simister was nearing an iron fence a puzzling episode occurred. He was about to pass it to the right, when someone just ahead of him lurched or stumbled. Simister almost fell himself, veering towards the fence. A nearby guard reached out and in steadying him pulled him round the fence to the left.

Then, Holstrom maintains, Simister turned for a moment and Holstrom caught a glimpse of his face. There must have been something peculiarly frightening about that backward look, something perhaps that Holstrom cannot adequately describe, for he instantly forgot any idea of surveillance at a distance and made every effort to catch up.

But the crowd from another commuters' express enveloped Holstrom. When he got outside the terminus it was some moments before he spotted Simister in the midst of a group jamming their way aboard an already crowded bus across the street. This perplexed Holstrom, for he knew Simister didn't have to take the bus and he recalled his recent complaint.

Heavy traffic kept Holstrom from crossing. He says he shouted, but Simister did not seem to hear him. He got the impression that Simister was making feeble efforts to get out of the crowd that was forcing him on to the bus, but, 'They were all jammed together like cattle.'

The best testimony to Holstrom's anxiety about Simister is that as soon as the traffic thinned a trifle he darted across the street, skipping between the cars. But by then the bus had started. He was in time only for a whiff of particularly obnoxious exhaust fumes.

As soon as he got to his office he phoned Simister. He got Simister's secretary and what she had to say relieved his worries, which is ironic in view of what happened a little later.

What happened a little later is best described by the same girl. She said, 'I never saw him come in looking so cheerful, the old grouch – excuse me. But anyway he came in all smiles, like he'd just got some bad news about somebody else, and right away he started to talk and kid with everyone, so that it was awfully funny when that man called up worried about him. I guess maybe, now I think back, he did seem a bit shaken underneath, like a person who's just had a narrow squeak and is very thankful to be alive.

'Well, he kept it up all morning. Then just as he was throwing his head back to laugh at one of his own jokes, he grabbed his chest, let out an awful scream, doubled up and fell on the floor. Afterwards I couldn't believe he was dead, because his lips stayed so red and there were bright spots of colour on his cheeks, like rouge. Of course it was his heart, though you can't believe what a scare that stupid first doctor gave us when he came in and looked at him.'

Of course, as she said, it must have been Simister's heart, one way or the other. And it is undeniable that the doctor in question was an ancient, possibly incompetent dispenser of penicillin, morphine and snap diagnoses swifter than Charcot's. They only called him because his office was in the same building. When Simister's own doctor arrived and pronounced it heart failure, which was what they'd thought all along, everyone was much relieved and inclined to be severely critical of the first doctor for having said something that sent them all scurrying to open the windows.

For when the first doctor had come in, he had taken one look at Simister and rasped, 'Heart failure? Nonsense! Look at the colour of his face. Cherry red. That man died of carbon monoxide poisoning.'

The Big Time

One

When shall we three meet again
In thunder, lightning, or in rain?

When the hurlyburly's done.
When the battle's lost and won.
   –Macbeth

Enter Three Hussars

My name is Greta Forzane. Twenty-nine and a party girl would describe me. I was born in Chacago, of Scandinavian parents, but now I operate chiefly outside space and time – not in Heaven or Hell, if there are such places, but not in the cosmos or universe you know either.

I am not as romantically entrancing as the immortal film star who also bears my first name, but I have a rough-and-ready charm of my own. I need it, for my job is to nurse back to health and kid back to sanity Soldiers badly roughed up in the biggest war going. This war is the Change War, a war of time travellers – in fact, our private name for being in this war is being on the Big Time. Our Soldiers fight by going back to change the past, or even ahead to change the future, in ways to help our side win the final victory a billion or more years from now. A long killing business believe me.

You don't know about the Change War, but it's influencing your lives all the time and maybe you've had hints of it without realizing.

Have you ever worried about your memory, because it doesn't seem to be bringing you exactly the same picture of the past from one day to the next? Have you ever been afraid that your personality was changing because of forces beyond your knowledge or control? Have you ever felt sure that sudden death was about to jump you from nowhere? Have you ever been scared of Ghosts – not the story-book kind, but the billions of beings who were once so real and strong it's hard to believe they'll just sleep harmlessly forever? Have you ever wondered about those things you may call devils or Demons – spirits able to range through all time and space, through the hot hearts of stars and the cold skeleton of space between the galaxies? Have you ever thought that the whole universe might be a crazy, mixed-up dream? If you have, you've had hints of the Change War.

How I got recruited into the Change War, how it's conducted, what the two sides are, why you don't consciously know about it, what I really think about it – you'll learn in due course.

The place outside the cosmos where I and my pals do our nursing job I simply call the Place. A lot of my nursing consists of amusing and humanizing Soldiers fresh back from raids into time. In fact my formal title is Entertainer and I've got my silly side, as you'll find out.

My pals are two other gals and three guys from quite an assortment of times and places. We're a pretty good team, and with Sid bossing, we run a pretty good Recuperation Station, though we have our family troubles. But most of our troubles come slamming into the Place with the beat-up Soldiers, who've generally just been going through hell and want to raise some of their own. As a matter of fact, it was three newly arrived Soldiers who started this thing I'm going to tell you about, this thing that showed me so much about myself and everything.

When it started, I had been on the Big Time for a thousand sleeps and two thousand nightmares, and working in the Place for five hundred-one thousand. This two-nightmares routine every time you lay down your dizzy little head is rough, but you pretend to get used to it because being on the Big Time is supposed to be worth it.

The Place is midway in size and atmosphere between a large

nightclub where the Entertainers sleep in and a small Zeppelin hangar decorated for a party, though a Zeppelin is one thing we haven't had yet. You go out of the Place, but not often if you have any sense and if you are an Entertainer like me, into the cold light of a morning filled with anything from the earliest dinosaurs to the later spacemen, who look strangely similar except for size.

Solely on doctor's orders, I have been on cosmic leave six times since coming to work at the Place, meaning I have had six brief vacations, if you care to call them that, for believe me they are busman's holidays, considering what goes on in the Place all the time. The last one I spent in Renaissance Rome, where I got a crush on Cesare Borgia, but I got over it. Vacations are for the birds, anyway, because they have to be fitted by the Spiders into serious operations of the Change War, and you can imagine how restful that makes them.

'See those Soldiers changing the past? You stick along with them. Don't go too far up front, though, but don't wander off either. Relax and enjoy yourself.'

Ha! Now the kind of recuperation Soldiers get when they come to the Place is a horse of a far brighter colour, simply dazzling by comparison. Entertainment is our business and we give them a bang-up time and send them staggering happily back into action, though once in a great while something may happen to throw a wee shadow on the party.

I am dead in some ways, but don't let that bother you – I am lively enough in others. If you met me in the cosmos, you would be more apt to yak with me or try to pick me up than to ask a cop to do the same or a father to douse me with holy water, unless you are one of those hard-boiled reformer types. But you are not likely to meet me in the cosmos, because (bar Basin Street and the Prater) 15th Century Italy and Augustan Rome – until they spoiled it – are my favourite (Ha!) vacation spots and, as I have said, I stick as close to the Place as I can. It is really the nicest Place in the whole Change World. (Crisis! I even *think* of it capitalized!)

Anyhow, when this thing started, I was twiddling my thumbs on the couch nearest the piano and thinking it was too late to do my fingernails and whosoever came in probably wouldn't notice them anyway.

The Place was jumpy like it always is on an approach and the grey velvet of the Void around us was curdled with the uneasy lights you see when you close your eyes in the dark.

Sid was tuning the Maintainers for the pickup and the right shoulder of his gold-worked grey doublet was streaked where he'd been wiping his face on it with quick ducks of his head.

Beauregard was leaning as close as he could over Sid's other shoulder, one white-trousered knee neatly indenting the rose plush of the control divan, and he wasn't missing a single flicker of Sid's old fingers on the dials; Beau's co-pilot besides piano player. Beau's face had that dead blank look it must have had when every double eagle he owned and more he didn't were riding on the next card to be turned in the gambling saloon on one of those wedding-cake Mississippi steamboats.

Doc was soused as usual, sitting at the bar with his top hat pushed back and his knitted shawl pulled around him, his wide eyes seeing whatever horrors a life in Nazi-occupied Czarist Russia can add to being a drunk Demon in the Change World.

Maud, who is the Old Girl, and Lili – the New Girl, of course – were telling the big beads of their identical pearl necklaces.

You might say that all us Entertainers were a bit edgy; being Demons doesn't automatically make us brave.

The the red telltale on the Major Maintainer went out and the Door began to darken in the Void facing Sid and Beau, and I felt Change Winds blowing hard and my heart missed a couple of beats, and the next thing three Soldiers had stepped out of the cosmos and into the Place, their first three steps hitting the floor hard as they changed times and weights.

They were dressed as officers of hussars, as we'd been advised, and – praise the Bonny Dew! – I saw that the first of them was Erich, my own dear little commandant, the pride of the von Hohenwalds and the Terror of the Snakes. Behind him was some hard-faced Roman or other, and beside Erich and shouldering into him as they stamped forward was a new boy, blond, with a face like a Greek god who's just been touring a Christian hell.

They were uniformed exactly alike in black – shakos, fur-edged pelisses, boots, and so forth – with white skull emblems on the shakos. The only difference between them was that Erich had a Caller on his wrist and the New Boy had a gauntleted glove on his left hand and was clenching the mate in it, his right hand being bare like both of Erich's and the Roman's.

'You've made it, lads, hearts of gold,' Sid boomed at them, and Beau twitched a smile and murmured something courtly and Maud began to chant, 'Shut the Door!' and the New Girl copied her and I joined in because the Change Winds do blow like crazy when the Door is open, even though it can't ever be shut tight enough to keep them from leaking through.

'Shut it before it blows wrinkles in our faces,' Maud called in her gamin voice to break the ice, looking like a skinny teenager in the tight, knee-length frock she'd copied from the New Girl.

But the three Soldiers weren't paying attention. The Roman – I remembered his name was Mark – was blundering forward stiffly as if there was something wrong with his eyes, while Erich and the New Boy were yelling at each other about a kid and Einstein and a summer palace and a bloody glove and the Snakes having booby-trapped St Petersburg. Erich had that taut, sadistic smile he gets when he wants to hit me.

The New Boy was in a tearing rage. 'Why'd you pull us out so bloody fast? We fair chewed the Nevsky Prospekt to pieces galloping away.'

'Didn't you feel their stun guns, *Dummkopf*, when they sprung the trap – too soon, *Gott sie Dank*?' Erich demanded.

'I did,' the New Boy told him. 'Not enough to numb a cat. Why didn't you show us action?'

'Shut up. I'm your leader. I'll show you action enough.'

'You won't. You're a filthy Nazi coward.'

'*Weibischer Engländer!*'

'Bloody Hun!'

'*Schlange!*'

The blond lad knew enough German to understand that last crack. He threw back his sable-edged pelisse to clear his sword arm and he swung away from Erich, which bumped him into Beau. At the first sign of the quarrel, Beau had raised himself from the divan as quickly and silently as a – no, I won't use that word – and slithered over to them.

'Sirs, you forget yourselves,' he said sharply, off balance, supporting himself on the New Boy's upraised arm. 'This is Sidney Lessingham's Place of Entertainment and Recuperation. There are ladies—'

With a contemptuous snarl, the New Boy shoved him off and snatched with his bare hand for his sabre. Beau reeled against the divan, it caught him in the shins and he fell towards the Maintainers. Sid whisked them out of the way as if they were a couple of beach radios – simply nothing in the Place is nailed down – and had them back on the coffee table before Beau hit the floor. Meanwhile, Erich had his sabre out and had parried the New Boy's first wild slash and lunged in return, and I heard the scream of steel and the rutch of his boot on the diamond-studded pavement.

Beau rolled over and came up pulling from the ruffles of his shirt bosom a derringer I knew was some other weapon in disguise – a stun gun or even an Atropos. Besides scaring me damp for Erich and everybody, that brought me up short: us Entertainers' nerves must be getting as naked as the Soldiers', probably starting when the Spiders cancelled all cosmic leaves twenty sleeps back.

Sid shot Beau his look of command, rapped out, 'I'll handle this, you whoreson firebrand,' and turned to the Minor Maintainer. I noticed that the telltale on the Major was glowing a reassuring red again, and I found a moment to thank Mamma Devi that the Door was shut.

Maud was jumping up and down cheering I don't know which – nor did she, I bet – and the New Girl was white and I saw that the sabres were working more businesslike. Erich's flicked, flicked, flicked again and came away from the blond lad's cheek spilling a couple of red drops. The blond lad lunged fiercely, Erich jumped back, and the next moment they were both floating helplessly in the air, twisting like they had cramps.

I realized quick enough that Sid had shut off gravity in the Door and Stores sectors of the Place, leaving the rest of us firm on our feet in the Refresher and Surgery sectors. The Place has sectional gravity to suit our Extraterrestrial buddies – those crazy ETs sometimes come whooping in for recuperation in very mixed batches.

From his central position, Side called out, kindly enough but taking no nonsense, 'All right, lads, you've had your fun. Now sheathe those swords.'

For a second or so, the two black hussars drifted and contorted. Erich laughed harshly and neatly obeyed – the commandant is used to free fall. The blond lad stopped writhing, hesitated while he glared upside down at Erich and managed to get his sabre into its scabbard, although he turned a slow somersault doing it. Then Sid switched on the gravity, slow enough so they wouldn't get sprained landing.

Erich laughed, lightly this time, and stepped out briskly

towards us. He stopped to clap the New Boy firmly on the shoulder and look him in the face.

'So, now you get a good scar,' he said.

The other didn't pull away, but he didn't look up and Erich came on. Sid was hurrying after the New Boy, and as he passed Erich, he wagged a finger at him and gaily said, 'You rogue.' Next thing I was giving Erich my 'Man, you're home' hug and he was kissing me and cracking my ribs and saying, '*Liebchen! Doppchen!*' – which was fine with me because I do love him and I'm a good lover and as much a Doubleganger as he is.

We had just pulled back from each other to get a breath – his blue eyes looked so sweet in his worn face – when there was a thud behind us. With the snapping of the tension, Doc had fallen off his bar stool and his top hat was over his eyes. As we turned to chuckle at him, Maud squeaked and we saw that the Roman had walked straight up against the Void and was marching along there steadily without gaining a foot, like it does happen, his black uniform melting into that inside-your-head grey.

Maud and Beau rushed over to fish him back, which can be tricky. The thin gambler was all courtly efficiency again. Sid supervised from a distance.

'What's wrong with him?' I asked Erich.

He shrugged. 'Overdue for Change Shock. And he was nearest the stun guns. His horse almost threw him. *Mein Gott*, you should have seen St Petersburg, *Liebchen*: the Nevsky Prospekt, the canals flying by like reception carpets of blue sky, a cavalry troop in blue and gold that blundered across our escape, fine women in furs and ostrich plumes, a monk with a big tripod and head under a hood – it gave me the horrors seeing all those Zombies flashing past and staring at me in that sick unawakened way they have, and knowing that some of them, say the photographer, might be Snakes.'

Our side in the Change War is the Spiders, the other side is the Snakes, though all of us – Spider and Snakes alike – are Doublegangers and Demons too, because we're cut out of our lifelines in the cosmos. Your lifeline is all of you from birth to death. We're Doublegangers because we can operate both in the cosmos and outside of it, and Demons because we act reasonably alive while doing so – which the Ghosts don't. Entertainers and Soldiers are all Demon-Doublegangers, whichever side they're on – though they say the Snake Places are simply ghastly. Zombies are dead people whose lifelines lie in the so-called past.

'What were you doing in St Petersburg before the ambush?' I asked Erich. 'That is, if you can talk about it.'

'Why not? We were kidnapping the infant Einstein back from the snakes in 1883. Yes, the Snakes got him, *Liebchen*, only a few sleeps back, endangering the West's whole victory over Russia—'

'—which gave your dear little Hitler the world on a platter for fifty years and got me loved to death by your sterling troops in the Liberation of Chicago—'

'—but which leads to the ultimate victory of the Spiders and the West over the Snakes and Communism, *Liebchen*, remember that. Anyway, our counter-snatch didn't work. The Snakes had guards posted – most unusual and we weren't armed. The whole thing was a great mess. No wonder Bruce lost his head – not that it excuses him.'

'The New Boy?' I asked. Sid hadn't got to him and he was still standing with hooded eyes where Erich had left him, a dark pillar of shame and rage.

'*Ja*, a lieutenant from World War One. An Englishman.'

'I gathered that,' I told Erich. 'Is he really effeminate?'

'*Weibischer*?' He smiled. 'I had to call him something when he said I was a coward. He'll make a fine Soldier – only needs a little more shaping.'

'You men are so original when you spat.' I lowered my voice. 'But you shouldn't have gone on and called him a

Snake, Erich mine.'

'*Schlange*?' The smile got crooked. 'Who knows – about any of us? As St Petersburg showed me, the Snakes' spies are getting cleverer than ours.' The blue eyes didn't look sweet now. 'Are you *Liebchen*, really nothing more than a good loyal spider?'

'Erich!'

'All right, I went too far – with Bruce and with you too. We're all hacked over these days riding with one leg over the breaking edge.'

Maud and Beau were supporting the Roman to a couch, Maud taking most of his weight with Sid still supervising and the New Boy still sulking by himself. The New Girl should have been with him, of course, but I couldn't see her anywhere and I decided she was probably having a nervous breakdown in the Refresher the little jerk.

'The Roman looks pretty bad, Erich,' I said.

'Ah Mark's tough. Got virtue, as his people say. And our little starship girl will bring him back to life if anybody can and if . . .'

' . . . you call this living,' I filled in dutifully.

He was right. Maud had fifty-odd years of psycho-medical experience, 23rd Century at that. It should have been Doc's job, but that was fifty drunks back.

'Maud and Mark, that will be an interesting experiment,' Erich said. 'Reminiscent of Goering's with the frozen men and the naked gypsy girls.'

'You are a filthy Nazi. She'll be using electrophoresis and deep suggestion, if I know anything.'

'How will you be able to know anything, *Liebchen*, if she switches on the couch curtains, as I perceive she is preparing to do?'

'Filthy Nazi I said and meant.'

'Precisely.' He clicked his heels and bowed a millimetre. 'Erich Friederich von Hohenwald, *Oberleutnant* in the army of the Third Reich. Fell at Narvik, where he was Recruited by the Spiders. Lifeline lengthened by a Big Change after his first death and at the latest report Commandant of Toronto, where he maintains extensive baby farms to provide him with breakfast meat, if you believe the handbills of the *voyageurs* underground. At your service.'

'Oh, Erich, it's all so lousy,' I said, touching his hand, reminded that he was one of the unfortunates Resurrected from a point in their lifeline well before their deaths – in his case, because the date of his death had been shifted forward by a Big Change after his Resurrection. And as every Demon finds out, if he can't imagine it beforehand, it is pure hell to remember your future, and the shorter the time between your Resurrection and your death back in the cosmos, the better. Mine, bless Bab-ed-Din, was only an action-packed ten minutes on North Clark Street.

Erich put his other hand lightly over mine. 'Fortunes of the Change War, *Liebchen*. At least I'm a Soldier and sometimes assigned to future operations – though why we should have this monomania about our future personalities back there, I don't know. Mine is a stupid *Oberst*, thin as paper – and frightfully indignant at the *voyageurs*! But it helps me a little if I see him in perspective and at least I get back to the cosmos pretty regularly, *Gott sei Dank*, so I'm better off than you Entertainers.'

I didn't say aloud that a Changing cosmos is worse than none, but I found myself sending a prayer to the Bonny Dew for my father's repose, that the Change Winds would blow lightly across the lifeline of Anton A. Forzane, professor of physiology, born in Norway and buried in Chicago. Woodlawn Cemetery is a nice grey spot.

'That's all right, Erich,' I said. 'We Entertainers Got Mittens too.'

He scowled around at me suspiciously, as if he were wondering whether I had all my buttons on.

'Mittens?' he said. 'What do you mean? I'm not wearing any. Are you trying to say something about Bruce's gloves – which incidentally seem to annoy him for some reason. No, seriously, Greta, why do you Entertainers need mittens?'

'Because we get cold feet sometimes. At least I do. Got Mittens, as I say.'

A sickly light dawned in his Prussian puss. He muttered, 'Got mittens . . . *Gott mit uns* . . . God with us,' and roared softly, 'Greta, I don't know how I put up with you the way you murder a great language for cheap laughs.'

'You've got to take me as I am,' I told him, 'mittens and all, thank the Bonny Dew—' and hastily explained, 'That's French – *le bon Dieu* – the good God – don't hit me. I'm not going to tell you any more of my secrets.'

He laughed feebly, like he was dying.

'Cheer up,' I said. 'I won't be here forever, and there are worse places than the Place.'

He nodded grudgingly, looking around. 'You know what, Greta, if you'll promise not to make some dreadful joke out of it: on operations, I pretend I'll soon be going backstage to court the world-famous ballerina Greta Forzane.'

He was right about the backstage part. The place is a regular theatre-in-the-round with the Void for an audience, the Void's grey hardly disturbed by the screens masking Surgery (Ugh!), Refresher and Stores. Between the last two are the bar and kitchen and Beau's piano. Between Surgery and the sector where the Door usually appears are the shelves and and taborets of the Art Gallery. The control divan is stage centre. Spaced around at a fair distance are six big low couches – one with its curtains now shooting up into the grey – and a few small tablets. It is like a ballet set and the crazy costumes and characters that turn up don't ruin the illusion. By no means. Diaghilev would have hired most of them for the Ballet Russe on first sight, without even asking them whether they could keep time to music.

Two

Last week in Babylon,
Last night in Rome,
– Hodgson

A Right-hand Clove

Beau had gone behind the bar and was talking quietly at Doc, but with his eyes elsewhere, looking very sallow and professional in his white, and I thought – Damballa! – I'm in the French Quarter. I couldn't see the New Girl. Sid was at last getting to the New Boy after the fuss about Mark. He threw me a sign and I started over with Erich in tow.

'Welcome, sweet lad. Sidney Lessingham's your host, and a fellow Englishman. Born in King's Lynn, 1564, schooled at Cambridge, but London was the life and death of me, though I outlasted Bessie, Jimmie, Charlie and Ollie almost. And what a life! By turns a clerk, a spy, a bawd – the two trades are hand in glove – a poet of no account, a beggar, and a peddlar of resurrection tracts. Beau Lassiter, our throats are tinder!'

At the word 'poet', the New Boy looked up, but resentfully, as if he had been tricked into it.

'And to spare your throat for drinking, sweet gallant, I'll be so bold as to guess and answer one of your questions,' Sid rattled on. 'Yes, I knew Will Shakespeare – we were of an age – and he was such a modest, mind-your-business rogue that we all wondered whether he really did write those plays. Your pardon, faith, but that scratch might be looked to.'

Then I saw that the New Girl hadn't lost her head, but gone to Surgery (Ugh!) for a first-aid tray. She reached a swab towards the New Boy's sticky cheek, saying rather shrilly, 'If I might . . .'

Her timing was bad. Sid's last words and Erich's approach had darkened the look in the young Soldier's face and he angrily swept her arm aside without even glancing at her. Erich squeezed my arm. The tray clattered to the floor – and one of the drinks that Beau was bringing almost followed it. Ever since the New Girl's arrival, Beau had been figuring that she was his responsibility, though I don't think the two of them had reached an agreement yet. Beau was especially set on it because I was thick with Sid at the time and Maud with Doc, she loving tough cases.

'Easy now, lad, and you love me!' Sid thundered, again shooting Beau the 'Hold it' look. 'She's just a poor pagan trying to comfort you. Swallow your bile, you black villain and perchance it will turn to poetry. Ah, did I touch you there? Confess, you are a poet.'

There isn't much gets by Sid, though for a second I forgot my psychology and wondered if he knew what he was doing with his insights.

'Yes, I'm a poet, all right,' the New Boy roared. 'I'm Bruce Marchant, you bloody Zombies. I'm a poet in a world where even the lines of the King James and your precious Will whom you use for laughs aren't safe from Snakes' slime and the Spiders' dirty legs. Changing our history, stealing our certainties, claiming to be so blasted all-knowing and best intentioned and efficient, and what does it lead to? This bloody SI glove!'

He held up his black-gloved left hand which still held the mate and he shook it.

'What's wrong with the Spider Issue gauntlet, heart of gold?' Sid demanded. 'And you love us, tell us.' While Erich laughed, 'Consider yourself lucky, *Kamerad*. Mark and I didn't draw any gloves at all.'

'What's wrong with it?' Bruce yelled. 'The bloody things are both lefts!' He slammed it down on the floor.

We all howled, we couldn't help it. He turned his back on us and stamped off, though I guessed he would keep out of the

Void. Erich squeezed my arm and said between gasps, '*Mein Gott, Liebchen*, what have I always told you about Soldiers? The bigger the gripe, the smaller the cause! It is infallible!'

One of us didn't laugh. Ever since the New Girl heard the name Bruce Marchant, she'd had a look in her eyes like she'd been given the sacrament. I was glad she'd got interested in something, because she'd been pretty much of a snoot and a wet blanket up until now, although she'd come to the Place with the recommendation of having been a real whoopee girl in London and New York in the Twenties. She looked disapprovingly at us as she gathered up the tray and stuff, not forgetting the glove, which she placed on the centre of the tray like a holy relic.

Beau cut over and tried to talk to her, but she ghosted past him and once again he couldn't do anything because of the tray in his hands. He came over and got rid of the drinks quick. I took a big gulp right away because I saw the New Girl stepping through the screen into Surgery and I hate to be reminded we have it and I'm glad Doc is too drunk to use it, some of the Arachnoid surgical techniques being very sickening as I know only too well from a personal experience that is number one on my list of things to be forgotten.

By that time, Bruce had come back to us, saying in a carefully hard voice, 'Look here, it's not the dashed glove itself, as you very well know, you howling Demons.'

'What is it then, noble heart?' Sid asked, his grizzled gold beard heightening the effect of innocent receptivity.

'It's the principle of the thing,' Bruce said, looking around sharply, but none of us cracked a smile. 'It's this mucking inefficiency and death of the cosmos – and don't tell me that isn't in the cards! – masquerading as benign omniscient authority. The Spiders – and we don't know who they are ultimately; it's just a name; we see only agents like ourselves – the Spiders pluck us from the quiet graves of our lifelines—'

'Is that bad, lad?' Sid murmured, innocently straightfaced.

'—and Resurrect us if they can and then tell us we must fight another time-travelling power called the Snakes – just a name, too – which is bent on perverting and enslaving the whole cosmos, past, present and future.'

'And isn't it, lad?'

'Before we're properly awake, we're Recruited into the Big Time and hustled into tunnels and burrows outside our space-time, these miserable closets, grey sacks, puss pockets – no offence to this Place – that the Spiders have created, maybe by gigantic implosions, but no one knows for certain, and then we're sent off on all sorts of missions into the past and future to change history in ways that are supposed to thwart the Snakes.'

'True, lad.'

'And from then on, the pace is so flaming hot and heavy, the shocks come so fast, our emotions are wrenched in so many directions, our public and private metaphysics distorted so insanely, the deepest thread of reality we cling to tied in such bloody knots, that we never can get things straight.'

'We've all felt that way, lad,' Sid said soberly; Beau nodded his sleek death's head; 'You should have seen me, *Kamerad*, my first fifty sleeps,' Erich put in; while I added, 'Us girls, too, Bruce.'

'Oh, I know I'll get hardened to it, and don't think I can't. It's not that,' Bruce said harshly. 'And I wouldn't mind the personal confusion, the mess it's made of my spirit, I wouldn't even mind remaking history and destroying priceless, once-called imperishable beauties of the past, if I felt it were for the best. The Spiders assure us that, to thwart the Snakes, it is all-important that the West ultimately defeat the East. But what have they done to achieve this? I'll give you some beautiful examples. To stabilize power in the early

Mediterranean world, they have built up Crete at the expense of Greece, making Athens a ghost city, Plato a trivial fabulist, and putting all Greek culture in a minor key.'

'You got time for culture?' I heard myself say and I clapped my hand over my mouth in gentle reproof.

'But *you* remember the dialogues, lad,' Sid observed. 'And rail not at Crete – I have a sweet Keftian friend.'

'For how long will I remember Plato's dialogues? And who after me?' Bruce challenged. 'Here's another. The Spiders want Rome powerful and, to date, they've helped Rome so much that she collapses in a blaze of German and Parthian invasions a few years after the death of Julius Caesar.'

This time it was Beau who butted in. Most everybody in the Place loves these bull sessions. 'You omit to mention, sir, that Rome's newest downfall is directly due to the Unholy Triple Alliance the Snakes have fomented between the Eastern Classical World, Mohammedanized Christianity, and Marxist Communism, trying to pass the torch of power futurewards by way of Byzantium and the Eastern Church, without ever letting it pass into the hands of the Spider West. That, sir, is the Snakes' Three-Thousand-Year Plan which we are fighting against, striving to revive Rome's glories.'

'Striving is the word for it,' Bruce snapped. 'Here's yet another example. To beat Russia, the Spiders kept England and America out of World War Two, thereby ensuring a German invasion of the New World and creating a Nazi empire stretching from the salt mines of Siberia to the plantations of Iowa, from Nizhni Novgorod to Kansas City!'

He stopped and my short hairs prickled. Behind me, someone was chanting in a weird spiritless voice, like footsteps in hard snow.

'*Salz, Salz, bringe Salz. Kein' Peitsch', gnädige Herren. Salz, Salz, Salz.*'

I turned and there was Doc waltzing towards us with little

tiny steps, bent over so low that the ends of his shawl touched the floor, his head crooked up sideways and looking through us.

'I knew then, but Erich translated softly. ' "Salt, salt, I bring salt. No whip, merciful sirs." He is speaking to my countrymen in their language.' Doc had spent his last months in a Nazi-operated salt mine.

He saw us and got up, straightening his top hat very carefully. He frowned hard while my heart thumped half a dozen times. Then his face slackened, he shrugged his shoulders and muttered, 'Nichevo'.

'And it does not matter, sir,' Beau translated, but directing his remark at Bruce. 'True, great civilizations have been dwarfed or broken by the Change War. But others, once crushed in the bud, have bloomed. In the 1870s, I travelled a Mississippi that had never known Grant's gunboats. I studied piano, languages, and the laws of chance under the greatest European masters at the University of Vicksburg.'

'And you think your pipsqueak steamboat culture is compensation for—' Bruce began but, 'Prithee none of that lad,' Sid interrupted smartly. 'Nations are as equal as so many madmen or drunkards, and I'll drink dead drunk the man who disputes me. Hear reason: nations are not so puny as to shrivel and vanish at the first tampering with their past, no, nor with the tenth. Nations are monsters, boy, with guts of iron and nerves of brass. Waste not your pity on them.'

'True indeed, sir,' Beau pressed, cooler and keener for the attack on his Greater South. 'Most of us enter the Change World with the false metaphysic that the slighest change in the past – a grain of dust misplaced – will transform the whole future. It is a long while before we accept with our minds as well as our intellects the law of the Conservation of Reality: that when the past is changed, the future changes barely enough to adjust, barely enough to admit the new data. The

Change Winds meet maximum resistance always. Otherwise the first operation in Babylonia would have wiped out New Orleans, Sheffield, Stuttgart, and Maud Davies' birthplace on Ganymede!

'Note how the gap left by Rome's collapse was filled by the imperialistic and Christianized Germans. Only an expert Demon historian can tell the difference in most ages between the former Latin and the present Gothic Catholic Church. As you yourself, sir, said of Greece, it is as if an old melody were shifted into a slightly different key. In the wake of a Big Change, cultures and individuals are transposed, it's true, yet in the main they continue much as they were, except for the usual scattering of unfortunate but statistically meaningless accidents.'

'All right, you bloody savants – maybe I pushed my point too far,' Bruce growled. 'But if you want variety, give a thought to the rotten methods we use in our wonderful Change War. Poisoning Churchill and Cleopatra. Kidnapping Einstein when he's a baby.'

'The Snakes did it first,' I reminded him.

'Yes, and we copied them. How resourceful does that make us?' he retorted, arguing like a woman. 'If we need Einstein, why don't we Resurrect him, deal with him as a man?'

Beau said, serving his culture in slightly thicker slices, '*Pardonnez-moi*, but when you have enjoyed your status as Doubleganger a *soupçon* longer, you will understand that greater men can rarely be Resurrected. Their beings are too crystallized, sir, their lifelines too tough.'

'Pardon me, but I think that's rot. I believe that most great men refuse to make the bargain with the Snakes, or with us Spiders either. They scorn Resurrection at the price demanded.'

'Brother, they ain't that great,' I whispered, while Beau glided on with, 'However that may be, you have accepted

Resurrection, sir, and so incurred an obligation which you as a gentleman must honour.'

'I accepted Resurrection all right,' Bruce said, a glare coming into his eyes. 'When they pulled me out of my line at Passchendaele in '17 ten minutes before I died, I grabbed at the offer of life like a drunkard grabs at a drink the morning after. But even then I thought I was also seizing a chance to undo historic wrongs, work for peace.' His voice was getting wilder all the time. Just beyond our circle, I noticed the New Girl watching him worshipfully. 'But what did I find the Spiders wanted me for? Only to fight more wars, over and over again, make them crueller and stinkinger, cut the swath of death a little wider with each Big Change, work our way a little closer to the death of the cosmos.'

Sid touched my wrist and, as Bruce raved on, he whispered to me. 'What kind of ball, think you, will please and so quench this fire-brand rogue? And you love me, discover it.'

I whispered back without taking my eyes of Bruce either, 'I know somebody who'll be happy to put on any kind of ball he wants, if he'll just notice her.'

'The New Girl, sweetling? 'Tis well. This rogue speaks like an angry angel. It touches my heart and I like it not.'

Bruce was saying hoarsely but loudly, 'And so we're sent on operations in the past and from each of those operations the Change Winds blow futurewards, swiftly or slowly according to the opposition they breast, sometimes rippling into each other, and any one of those Winds may shift the date of our own death ahead of the date of our Resurrection, so that in an instant – even here, outside the cosmos – we may moulder and rot or crumble to dust and vanish away. The wind with our name in it may leak through the Door.'

Faces hardened at that, because it's bad form to mention Change Death, and Erich flared out with, *'Halt's Maul, Kamerad!* There's always another Resurrection.'

But Bruce didn't keep his mouth shut. He said, 'Is there? I know the Spiders promise it, but even if they do go back and cut another Doubleganger from my lifeline, is he me?' He slapped his chest with his bare hand. 'I don't think so. And even if he is me, with unbroken consciousness, why's he been Resurrected again? Just to refight more wars and face more Change Death for the sake of an almighty power—' his voice was rising to a climax '—an almighty power so bloody ineffectual, it can't furnish one poor Soldier pulled out of the mud of Passchendaele, one miserable Change Commando, one Godforsaken Recuperee a proper issue of equipment!'

And he held out his bare right hand towards us, fingers spread a little, as if it were the most amazing object and most deserving of outraged sympathy in the whole world.

The New Girl's timing was perfect. She whisked through us, and before he could so much as wiggle the fingers, she whipped a black gauntleted glove on it and anyone could see that it fitted his hand perfectly.

This time our laughing beat the other. We collapsed and slopped our drinks and pounded each other on the back and then started all over.

'*Ach, der Handschuh, Liebchen!* Where'd she get it?' Erich gasped in my ear.

'Probably just turned the other one inside out – that turns a left into a right – I've done it myself,' I wheezed, collapsing again at the idea.

'That would put the lining outside,' he objected.

'Then I don't know,' I said. 'We got all sorts of junk in Stores.'

'It doesn't matter, *Liebchen,*' he assured me. '*Ach, der Handschuh!*'

All through it, Bruce just stood there admiring the glove, moving the fingers a little now and then, and the New Girl stood watching him as if he were eating a cake she'd baked.

When the hysteria quieted down, he looked up at her with a big smile. 'What did you say your name was?'

'Lili,' she said, and believe you me, she was Lili to me even in my thoughts from then on, for the way she'd handled that lunatic.

'Lilian Foster,' she explained. 'I'm English also. Mr Marchant, I've read *A Young Man's Fancy* I don't know how many times.'

'You have? It's wretched stuff. From the Dark Ages – I mean my Cambridge days. In the trenches, I was working up some poems that were rather better.'

'I won't hear you say that. But I'd be terribly thrilled to hear the new ones. Oh Mr Marchant, it was so strange to hear you call it Passiondale.'

'Why, if I may ask?'

'Because that's the way I pronounce it to myself. But I looked it up and it's more like Pas-ken-DA-luh.'

'Bless you! All the Tommies called it Passiondale, just as they called Ypres Wipers.'

'How interesting. You know, Mr Marchant, I'll wager we were Recruited in the same operation, summer of 1917. I'd got to France as a Red Cross nurse, but they found out my age and were going to send me back.'

'How old were you – are you? Same thing, I mean to say.'

'Seventeen.'

'Seventeen in '17,' Bruce murmured, his blue eyes glassy.

It was real corny dialogue and I couldn't resent the humorous leer Erich gave me as we listened to them, as if to say, 'Ain't it nice, *Liebchen*, Bruce has a silly little English schoolgirl to occupy him between operations?'

Just the same, as I watched Lili in her dark bangs and pearl necklace and tight little grey dress that reached barely to her knees, and Bruce hulking over her tenderly in his snazzy hussar's rig, I knew that I was seeing the start of something that hadn't been part of me since David died fighting Franco years before I got on the Big Time, the sort of thing that almost made me wish there could be children in the Change World. I wondered why I'd never thought of trying to work things so that Dave got Resurrected and I told myself: no, it's all changed, I've changed, better the Change Winds don't disturb Dave or I know about it.

'No, I didn't die in 1917 – I was merely Recruited then,' Lili was telling Bruce. 'I lived all through the Twenties, as you can see from the way I dress. But let's not talk about that, shall we? Oh, Mr Marchant, do you think you can possibly remember any of those poems you started in the trenches? I can't fancy them bettering your sonnet that concludes with, "The bough swings in the wind, the night is deep; Look at the stars, poor little ape, and sleep".'

That one almost made me whoop – what monkeys we are, I thought – though I'd be the first to admit that the best line to use on a poet is one of his own – in fact as many as possible. I decided I could safely forget our little Britons and devote myself to Erich or whatever needed me.

Three

Hell is the place for me. For to Hell go the fine churchmen, and the fine knights, killed in the tourney or in some grand war, the brave soldiers and the gallant gentlemen. With them will I go. There go also the fair gracious ladies who have lovers two or three beside their lord. There go the gold and the silver, the sables and ermine. There go the harpers and the minstrels and the kings of the earth.

—Aucassin

Nine for a Party

I exchanged my drink for a new one from another tray Beau was bringing around. The grey of the Void was beginning to look real pleasant, like warm thick mist with millions of tiny diamonds floating in it. Doc was sitting grandly at the bar with a steaming tumbler of tea – a chaser, I guess, since he was just putting down a shot glass. Sid was talking to Erich and laughing at the same time and I said to myself it begins to feel like a party, but something's lacking.

It wasn't anything to do with the Major Maintainer; its telltale was glowing a steady red like a nice little home fire amid the tight cluster of dials that included all the controls except the lonely and frightening Introversion switch that was never touched. Then Maud's couch curtains winked out and there were she and the Roman sitting quietly side by side.

He looked down at his shiny boots and the rest of his black duds like he was just waking up and couldn't believe it all, and he said, '*Omnia mutantur, nos et mutamur in illis,*' and I raised my eyebrows at Beau, who was taking the tray back, and he did proud by old Vicksburg by translating 'All things change and we change them.'

Then Mark slowly looked around at us, and I can testify that a Roman smile is just as warm as any other nationality, and he finally said, 'We are nine, the proper number for a party. The couches, too. It is good.'

Maud chuckled proudly and Erich shouted, 'Welcome back from the Void, *Kamerad*,' and then, because he's German and thinks all parties have to be noisy and satirically pompous, he jumped on a couch and announced, '*Herren und Damen*, permit me to introduce the noblest Roman of them all, Marcus Vipsaius Niger, legate to Nero Claudius (called Germanicus in a former time stream) and who in 763 A.U.C. (Correct, Mark? It means A.D. 10, you meatheads!) died bravely fighting the Parthians and the Snakes in the Battle of Alexandria. *Hoch, hoch, hoch!*'

We all swung our glasses and cheered with him and Sid yelled at Erich, 'Keep your feet off the furniture, you unschooled rogue,' and grinned and boomed at all three hussars, 'Take your ease, Recuperees,' and Maud and Mark got their drinks, the Roman paining Beau by refusing Falernian wine in favour of scotch and soda, and right away everyone was talking a mile a minute.

We had a lot to catch up on. There was the usual yak about the war – 'The Snakes are laying minefields in the Void,' 'I don't believe it, how can you mine nothing?' – and the shortages – bourbon, bobby pins, and the stabilitin that would have brought Mark out of it faster – and what had become of people – 'Marcia? Oh, she's not around any more,' (She'd been caught in a Change Gale and green and stinking in five seconds, but I wasn't going to say that) – and Mark had to be told about Bruce's glove, which convulsed us all over again, and the Roman remembered a legionary who had carried a gripe all the way to Octavius because he'd accidentally been issued the unbelievable luxury item sugar instead of the usual salt, and Erich asked Sid if he had any new Ghost-girls in stock and Sid sucked his beard like the old goat he is. 'Dost thou ask me, lusty Allemand? Nay, there are several great beauties, amongst them an Austria countess from Strauss's Vienna, and if it were not for sweetling here . . . Mnnnn.'

I poked a finger in Erich's chest between two of the bright buttons with their tiny death's heads. 'You, my little von Hohenwald, are a menace to us real girls. You have too much of a thing about the unawakened, ghost kind.'

He called me his little Demon and hugged me a bit too hard to prove it wasn't so, and then he suggested we show Bruce the Art Gallery. I thought this was a real brilliant idea, but when I tried to argue him out of it, he got stubborn. Bruce and Lili were willing to do anything anyone wanted them to, though not so willing to pay any attention while doing it. The sabre cut was just a thin red line on his cheek; she'd washed away all the dried blood.

The Gallery gets you, though. It's a bunch of paintings and sculptures and especially odd knick-knacks, all made by Soldiers recuperating here, and a lot of them telling about the Change War from the stuff they're made of – brass cartridges, flaked flint, bits of ancient pottery glued into futuristic shapes, mashed-up Incan gold rebeaten by a Martian, whorls of beady Lunan wire, a picture in tempera on a crinkle-cracked thick round of quartz that had filled a starship porthole, a Sumerian inscription chiselled into a brick from an atomic oven.

There are lots of things in the Gallery and I can always find some I haven't ever seen before. It gets you, as I say, thinking about the guys that made them and their thoughts, and the far times and places they came from, and sometimes, when I'm feeling low, I'll come and look at them so I'll feel still lower and get inspired to kick myself back into a good temper. It's the only history of the Place there is and it doesn't change a great deal, because the things in it and the feelings that went into them resist the Change Winds better than anything else.

Right now, Erich's witty lecture was bouncing off the big ears I hide under my pageboy bob and I was thinking how awful it is that for us that there's not only change but Change. You don't know from one minute to the next whether a mood or idea you've got is really new or just welling up into you because the past has been altered by the Spiders or Snakes.

Change Winds can blow not only death but anything short of it, down to the featheriest fancy. They blow thousands of times faster than time moves, but no one can say how much faster or how far one of them will travel or what damage it'll do or how soon it'll damp out. The Big Time isn't the little time.

And then, for the Demons, there's the fear that our personality will just fade and someone else climb into the driver's seat and us not even know. Of course, we Demons are supposed to be able to remember through Change and in spite of it; that's why we are Demons and not Ghosts like the other Doublegangers, or merely Zombies or Unborn and nothing more, and as Beau truly said, there aren't any great men among us – and blamed few of the masses, either – we're a rare sort of people and that's why the Spiders have to Recruit us where they find us without caring about our previous knowledge and background, a Foreign Legion of time, a strange kind of folk, bright but always in the background, with built-in nostalgia and cynicism, as adaptable as Centaurian shape-changers but with memories as long as a Lunan's six arms, a kind of Change People, you might say, the cream of the damned.

But sometimes I wonder if our memories are as good as we think they are and if the whole past wasn't once entirely different from anything we remember, and we've forgotten that we forgot.

As I say, the Gallery gets you feeling real low, and so now I said to myself, 'Back to your lousy little commandant, kid,' and gave myself a stiff boot.

Erich was holding up a green bowl with gold dolphins or spaceships on it and saying, 'And, to my mind, this proves that Etruscan art is derived from Egyptian. Don't you agree, Bruce?'

Bruce looked up, all smiles from Lili, and said, 'What was that, dear chap?'

Erich's forehead got dark as the Door and I was glad the hussars had parked their sabres along with their shakos, but before he could even get out a Jerry cuss-word, Doc breezed up in that plateau-state of drunkenness so like hypnotized sobriety, moving as if he were on a dolly, ghosted the bowl out of Erich's hand, said, 'A beautiful specimen of Middle Systemic Venusian. When Eightaitch finished it, he told me you couldn't look at it and not feel the waves of the Northern Venusian Shallows ripping around your hoofs. But it might look better inverted. I wonder. Who are you, young officer? *Nichevo,*' and he carefully put the bowl back on its shelf and rolled on.

It's a fact that Doc knows the Art Gallery better than any of us, really by heart, he being the oldest inhabitant, though he maybe picked a bad time to show off his knowledge. Erich was going to take out after him, but I said, 'Nix, *Kamerad,* remember gloves and sugar,' and he contended himself with complaining, 'That *nichevo* – it's so gloomy and hopeless, *ungeheuerlich.* I tell you, *Liebchen,* they shouldn't have Russians working for the Spiders, not even as Entertainers.'

I grinned at him and squeezed his hand. 'Not much entertainment in Doc these days, is there?' I agreed.

He grinned back at me a shade sheepishly and his face smoothed and his blue eyes looked sweet again for a second and he said, 'I shouldn't want to claw out at people that way, Greta, but at times I am just a jealous old man,' which is not entirely true, as he isn't a day over thirty-three, although his hair is nearly white.

Our lovers had drifted on a few steps until they were almost fading into the Surgery screen. It was the last spot I would have picked for the formal preliminaries to a little British smootching, but Lili probably didn't share my prejudices, though I remembered she'd told me she'd served a brief hitch in an Arachnoid Field Hospital before being transferred to the Place.

But she couldn't have had anything like the experience I'd had during my short and sour career as a Spider nurse, when I'd acquired my best-hated nightmare and flopped completely (jobwise, but on the floor, too) at seeing a doctor flick a switch and a being, badly injured but human, turn into a long cluster of glistening strange fruit – ugh, it always makes me want to toss my cookies and my buttons. And to think that dear old Daddy Anton wanted his Greta chile to be a doctor.

Well, I could see this wasn't getting me anywhere I wanted to go, and after all there was a party going on.

Doc was babbling something at a great rate to Sid – I just hoped Doc wouldn't get inspired to go into his animal imitations, which sound pretty fierce and once seriously offended some recuperating ETs.

Maud was demonstrating to Mark a 23rd Century twostep and Beau sat down at the piano and improvised softly on her rhythm.

As the deep-thrumming relaxing notes hit us, Erich's face brightened and he dragged me over. Pleasantly soon I had my feet off the diamond-rough floor, which we don't carpet because most of the ETs, the dear boys, like it hard, and I was shouldering back deep into the couch nearest the piano, with cushions all around me and a fresh drink in my hand, while my Nazi boy friend was getting ready to discharge his *Weltschmerz* as song, which didn't alarm me too much, as his baritone is passable.

Things felt real good, like the Maintainer was just idling to keep the Place in existence and moored to the cosmos, not exerting itself at all or at most taking an occasional lazy paddle stroke. At times the Place's loneliness can be happy and comfortable.

Then Beau raised an eyebrow at Erich, who nodded, and next thing they were launched into a song we all know, though I've never found out where it originally came from. This time it made me think of Lili, and I wondered why – and why it's a tradition at Recuperation Stations to call the new Lili, though in this case it happened to be her real name.

> *Standing in the Doorway just*
> *   outside of space,*
> *Winds of Change blow 'round*
> *   you but don't touch your face;*
> *You smile as you whisper*
> *   tenderly,*
> *'Please cross to me, Recuperee;*
> *'The operation's over, come*
> *   in and close the Door.'*

Four

De Bailhache, Fresca, Mrs Cammel, whirled
Beyond the circuit of the shuddering Bear
In fractured atoms.

—Eliot

SOS From Nowhere

I realized the piano had deserted Erich and I cranked my head
up and saw Beau, Maud and Sid streaking for the control
divan. The Major Maintainer was blinking emergency-green
and fast, but the mode was plain enough for even me to
recognize the Spider distress call and for a second I felt just
sick. Then Erich blew out his reserve breath in the middle of
'Door' and I gave myself another of those helpful mental
boots at the base of the spine and we hurried after them
towards the centre of the Place along with Mark.

The blinks faded as we got there and Sid told us not to
move because we were making shadows. He glued an eye to
the telltale and we held still as statues as he caressed the dials
like he was making love.

One sensitive hand flicked out past the Introversion switch
over to the Minor Maintainer and right away the Place was as
dark as your soul and there was nothing for me but Erich's
arm and the knowledge that Sid was nursing a green light I
couldn't even see, although my eyes had plenty of time to
accommodate.

Then the green light finally came back very slowly and I
could see the dear reliable old face – the green-gold making
him look like a merman – and then the telltale flared bright
and Sid flicked on the Place lights and I leaned back.

'That nails them, lads, whoever and whenever they may be.
Get ready for a pick-up.'

Beau, who was closest of course, looked at him sharply. Sid

shrugged uneasily. 'Meseemed at first it was from our own globe a thousand years before our Lord, but that indication flickered and faded like witchfire. As it is, the call comes from something smaller than the Place and certes adrift from the cosmos. Meseemed too at one point I knew the first of the caller – an antipodean atomicist named Benson-Carter – but that likewise changed.'

Beau said, 'We're not in the right phase of the cosmos-Places rhythm for a pick-up, are we, sir?'

Sid answered, 'Ordinarily not, boy.'

Beau continued, 'I didn't think we had any pick-ups scheduled. Or stand-by orders.'

Sid said, 'We haven't.'

Mark's eyes glowed. He tapped Erich on the shoulder. 'An octavian denarius against ten Reichsmarks it is a Snake trap.'

Erich's grin showed his teeth. 'Make it first through the Door next operation and I'm on.'

It didn't take that to tell me things were serious, or the thought that there's always a first time for bumping into something from really outside the cosmos. The Snakes have broken our code more than once. Maud was quietly serving our weapons and Doc was helping her. Only Bruce and Lili stood off. But they were watching.

The telltale brightened. Sid reached towards the Maintainer, saying, 'All right, my hearties. Remember, through this Doorway pass the fishiest finaglers in and out of the cosmos.'

The Door appeared to the left and above where it should be and darkened much too fast. There was a gust of stale salt seawind, if that makes sense, but no stepped-up Change Winds I could tell – and I had been bracing myself against them. The Door got inky and there was a flicker of grey fur whips and a flash of copper flesh and gilt and something dark and a clump of hoofs and Erich was sighting a stun gun across his left forearm, and then the Door had vanished like that and a tentacled silvery Lunan and a Venusian satyr were coming straight towards us.

The Lunan was hugging a pile of clothes and weapons. The satyr was helping a wasp-waisted woman carry a heavy-looking bronze chest. The woman was wearing a short skirt and high-collared bolero jacket of leather so dark brown it was almost black. She had a two-horned *petsofa* hairdress and she was boldly gilded here and there and wore sandals and copper anklets and wristlets – one of them a copper-plated Caller – and from her wide copper belt hung a short-handled, double-headed axe. She was dark complexioned and her forehead and chin receded, but the effect was anything but weak; she had a face like a beautiful arrowhead – and a familiar one, by golly!

But before I could say, 'Kabysia Labrys,' Maud shrilly beat me to it with, 'It's Kaby with two friends. Break out a couple of Ghostgirls.'

And then I saw it really was old-home week because I recognized my Lunan boy-friend Ilhilihis, and in the midst of all the confusion I got a nice kick out of knowing I was getting so I could tell the personality of one silver-furred muzzle from another.

They reached the control divan and Illy dumped his load and the others let down the chest, and Kaby staggered but shook off the two ETs when they started to support her, and she looked daggers at Sid when he tried to do the same, although she's his 'sweet Keftian friend' he'd mentioned to Bruce.

She leaned straight-armed on the divan and took two gasping breaths so deep that the ridges of her spine showed through her brown-skinned waist, and then she threw up her head and commanded, 'Wine!'

While Beau was rushing it, Sid tried to take her hand again, saying, 'Sweetling, I'd never heard you call before and knew not this pretty little fist,' but she ripped out, 'Save your comfort for the Lunan,' and I looked and saw – Hey, Zeus! – that one of Ilhilihis' six tentacles was lopped off half-way.

That was for me, and, going to him, I fast briefed myself: 'Remember, he only weighs fifty pounds for all he's seven feet high; he doesn't like low sounds or to be grabbed; the two legs aren't tentacles and don't act the same; uses them for long walks, tentacles for leaps; uses tentacles for close vision too and for manipulation, of course; extended, they mean he's at ease; retracted, on guard or nervous; sharply retracted, disgusted; greeting—'

Just then, one of them swept across my face like a sweet smelling feather duster and I said, 'Illy, man, it's been a lot of sleeps,' and brushed my fingers across his muzzle. It still took a little self-control not to hug him, and I did reach a little cluckingly for his lopped tentacle, but he wafted it away from me and the little voicebox belted to his side squeaked, 'Naughty, naughty. Papa will fix his little old self. Greta girl, ever bandaged even a Terra octopus?'

I had, an intelligent one from around a quarter billion A.D., but I didn't tell him so. I stood and let him talk to the palm of my hand with one of his tentacles – I don't savvy feather-talk but it feels good, though I've often wondered who taught him English – and watched him use a couple others to whisk a sort of Lunan band-aid out of his pouch and cap his wound with it.

Meanwhile, the satyr knelt over the bronze chest, which was decorated with little death's heads and crosses with hoops at the top and swastikas, but looking much older than Nazi, and the satyr said to Sid, 'Quick thinkin, Gov, when ya saw the Door comin in high n soffened up gravty unner it, but cud I have sum hep now?'

Sid touched the Minor Maintainer and we all got very light

and my stomach did a flip-flop while the satyr piled on the chest the clothes and weapons that Illy had been carrying and pranced off with it all and carefully put it down at the end of the bar. I decided the satyr's English instructor must have been quite a character, too. Wish I'd met him – her – it.

Sid thought to ask Illy if he wanted Moon-normal gravity in one sector, but my boy likes to mix, and being such a lightweight, Earth-normal gravity doesn't bother him. As he said to me once, 'Would Jovian gravity bother a beetle, Greta girl?'

I asked Illy about the satyr and he squeaked that his name was Sevensee and that he'd never met him before this operation. I knew the satyrs were from a billion years in the future, just as the Loonies were from a billion years in the past, and I thought – Kreesed us! – but it must have been a special big or emergency-like operation to have the Spiders using those two for it, with two billion years between them – a time-difference that gives you a feeling of awe for a second, you know.

I started to ask Illy about it, but just the Beau came scampering back from the bar with a big red-and-black earthenware goblet of wine – we try to keep a variety of drinking tools in stock so folks will feel more at home. Kaby grabbed it from him and drained most of it in one swallow and then smashed it on the floor. She does things like that, though Sid's tried to teach her better. Then she stared at what she was thinking about until the whites showed all around her eyes and her lips pulled way back from her teeth and she looked a lot less human than the two ETs, just like a fury. Only a time traveller knows how like the wild murals and engravings of them some of the ancients can look.

My hair stood up at the screech she let out. She smashed a fist into the divan and cried, 'Goddess! Must I see Crete destroyed, revived, and now destroyed again? It is too much for your servant.'

Personally, I thought she could stand anything.

There was a rush of questions at what she said about Crete – I asked one of them, for the news certainly frightened me – but she shot up her arm straight for silence and took a deep breath and began.

'In the balance hung the battle. Rowing like black centipedes, the Dorian hulls bore down on our outnumbered ships. On the bright beach, masked by rocks, Sevensee and I stood by the needle gun, ready to give the black hulls silent wounds. Beside us was Ilhilihis, suited as a sea monster. But then . . . then . . .'

Then I saw she wasn't altogether the iron babe, for her voice broke and she started to shake and to sob rackingly, although her face was still a mask of rage, and she threw up the wine. Sid stepped in and made her stop, which I think he'd been wanting to do all along.

Five

When I take up a newspaper and read it, I fancy I see
ghosts creeping between the lines. There must be ghosts all
over the world. They must be as countless as the grains of
the sands, it seems to me.

—Ibsen

Sid Insists on Ghostgirls

My Elizabethan boy-friend puts his fists on his hips and laid
down the law to us as if we were a lot of nervous children
who'd been playing too hard.

'Look you, masters, this is a Recuperation Station and I am
running it as such. A plague of all operations! I care not if the
frame of things disjoints and the whole Change World goes to
ruin, but you, warrior maid, are going to rest and drink more
wine slowly before you tell your tale and your colleagues are
going to be properly companioned. No questions, anyone.
Beau, and you love us, give us a lively tune.'

Kaby relaxed a little and let him put his hand carefully
against her back in token of support and she said grudgingly,
'All right, Fat Belly.'

Then, so help me, to the tune of the Muskrat Ramble,
which I'd taught Beau, we got girls for those two ETs and
everybody properly paired up.

Right here I want to point out that a lot of the things they
say in the Change World about Recuperation Stations simply
aren't so – and anyway they always leave out nine-tenths of it.
The Soldiers that come through the Door are looking for a
good time, sure, but they're hurt real bad too, every one of
them, deep down in their minds and hearts, if not always in
their bodies or so you can see it right away.

Believe me, a temporal operation is no joke, and to start
with, there isn't one person in a hundred who can endure to

be cut from his lifeline and become a really wide-awake Doubleganger – a Demon, that is – let alone a Soldier. What does a badly hurt and mixed-up creature need who's been fighting hard? One *individual* to look out for him and feel for him and patch him up, and it helps if the one is of the opposite sex – that's something that goes beyond species.

There's your basis for the Place and the wild way it goes about its work, and also for most other Recuperation Stations or Entertainment Spots. The name Entertainer can be misleading, but I like it. She's got to be a lot more than a good party girl – or boy – though she's got to be that too. She's got to be a nurse and a psychologist and an actress and a mother and a practical ethnologist and a lot of things with longer names – and a reliable friend.

None of us are all those things perfectly or even near it. We just try. But when the call comes, Entertainers have to forget grudges and gripes and envies and jealousies – and remember, they're lively people with sharp emotions – because there isn't any time then for anything but *help and don't ask who!*

And, deep inside her, a good Entertainer doesn't care who. Take the way it shaped up this time. It was pretty clear to me I ought to shift to Illy, although I wasn't quite easy in my mind about leaving Erich, because the Lunan was a long time from home and, after all, Erich was among anthropoids. Ilhilihis needed someone who was *simpatico*.

I like Illy and not just because he is a sort of tall cross between a spider monkey and a persian cat – though that is a handsome combo when you come to think of it. I like him for himself. So when he came in all lopped and shaky after a mean operation, I was the right person to look out for him. Now I've made my little speech and know-nothings in the Change World can go on making their bum jokes. But I ask you, how could an arrangement between Illy and me be anything but Platonic?

We might have had some octopoid girls and nymphs in stock – Sid couldn't be sure until he checked – but Ilhilihis and Sevensee voted for real people and I knew Sid saw it their way. Maud squeezed Mark's hand and tripped over the Sevensee ('Those are sharp hoofs you got, man' – she's picked up some of my language, like she has everything else), though Beau did frown over his shoulder at Lili from the piano, maybe to argue that she ought to take on the ET, as Mark had been a real casualty and could use live nursing. But it was plain as day to anybody but Beau that Bruce and Lili were a big thing and the last to be disturbed.

Erich acted stiffly hurt at losing me, but I knew he wasn't. He thinks he has a great technique with Ghostgirls and he likes to show it off, and he really is pretty slick at it, if you go for that sort of thing and – yang my yin! – who doesn't at times?

And when Sid formally wafted the Countess out of Stores – a real blonde stunner in a white satin hobble skirt with a white egret swaying up from her tiny hat, way ahead of Maud and Lili and me when it came to looks, though transparent as cigarette smoke – and when Erich clicked his heels and bowed over her hand and proudly conducted her to a couch, black Svengali to her Trilby, and started to Germantalk some life into her with much head cocking and toothy smiling and a flow of witty flattery, and when she began to flirt back and the dream look in her eyes sharpened hungrily and focused on him – well, then I knew that Erich was happy and felt he was doing proud by the *Reichswehr*. No, my little commandant wasn't worrying me on that score.

Mark had drawn a Greek hetaera name of Phryne; I suppose not the one who maybe still does the famous courtroom striptease back in Athens, and he was waking her up with little sips of his scotch and soda, though, from some looks he'd flashed, I got the idea Kaby was the kid he really went for. Sid was coaxing the fighting gal to take some high-energy bread and olives along with the wine, and, for a wonder, Doc seemed to be carrying on an animated and rational conversation with Svensee and Maud, maybe comparing notes on the Northern Venusian Shallows, and Beau had got on to Panther Rag, and Bruce and Lili were leaning on the piano, smiling very appreciatively, but talking to each other a mile a minute.

Illy turned back from inspecting them all and squeaked, 'Animals with clothes are so refreshing, dahling! Like you're all carrying banners!'

Maybe he had something there, though my banners were kind of Ash Wednesday, a charcoal grey sweater and skirt. He looked at my mouth with a tentacle to see how I was smiling and he squeaked softly, 'Do I seem dull and commonplace to you, Greta girl, because I haven't got banners? Just another Zombie from a billion years in your past, as grey and lifeless as Luna is today, not as when she was a real dreamy sister planet simply bursting with air and water and feather forests. Or am I as strangely interesting to you as you are to me, girl from a billion years in my future?'

'Illy, you're sweet,' I told him, giving him a little pat. I noticed his fur was still vibrating nervously and I decided to heck with Sid's orders, I'm going to pump him about what he was doing with Kaby and the satyr. Couldn't have him a billion years from home and bottled up, too. Besides, I was curious.

Six

Maiden, Nymph, and Mother are the eternal royal Trinity of the island, and the Goddess, who is worshipped there on each of these aspects, as New Moon, Full Moon, and Old Moon, is the sovereign Deity.

—Graves

Crete Circa 1300 B.C.

Kaby pushed back at Sid some seconds of bread and olives, and, when he raised his bushy eyebrows, gave him a curt nod that meant she knew what she was doing. She stood up and sort of took a position. All the talk quieted down fast, even Bruce's and Lili's. Kaby's face and voice weren't strained now, but they weren't relaxed either.

'Woe to Spider! Woe to Cretan! Heavy is the news I bring you. Bear it bravely, like a strong women. When we got the gun unlimbered, I heard seaweed fry and crackle. We three leaped behind the rock wall, saw our gun grow white as sunlight in a heat-ray of the Serpents! Natch, we feared we were outnumbered and I called upon my Caller.'

I don't know how she does it, but she does – in English too. That is, when she figures she's got something important to report, and maybe she needs a little time to get ready.

Beau claims that all the ancients fit their thoughts into measured lines as naturally as we pick a work that will do, but I'm not sure how good the Vicksburg language department is. Though why I should wonder about things like that when I've got Kaby spouting the stuff right in front of me, I don't know.

'But I didn't die there, kiddos. I still hoped to hurt the Greek ships, maybe with the Snake's own heat gun. So I quick tried to outflank them. My two comrades crawled beside me – they are males, but they have courage. Soon we spied the ambush-setters. They were Snakes and they were many, filthily disguised as Cretans.'

There was an indignant murmur at this, for our cut-throat Change War has its code, the Soldiers tell me. Being an Entertainer, I don't have to say what I think.

'They had seen us when we saw them,' Kaby swept on, 'and they loosed a killing volley. Heat- and knife-rays struck about us in a storm of wind and fire, and the Lunan lost a feeler, fighting for Crete's Triple Goddess. So we dodged behind a sand hill, steered our flight back towards the water. It was awful, what we saw there; Crete's brave ships all sunk or sinking, blue sky sullied by their death-smoke. Once again the Greeks had licked us! – aided by the filthy Serpents.

'Round our wrecks, their black ships scurried, like black beetles, filth their diet, yet this day they dine on heroes. On the quiet sunlit beach there, I could feel a Change Gale blowing, working changes deep inside me, aches and pains that were a stranger's. Half my memories were doubled, half my lifeline crooked and twisted, three new moles upon my swordhand. Goddess, Goddess, Triple Goddess—'

Her voice wavered and Sid reached out a hand, but she straightened her back.

'Triple Goddess, give me courage to tell everything that happened. We ran down into the water, hoping to escape by diving. We had hardly got under when the heat-rays hit above us, turning all the cool green surface to a roaring white inferno. But as I believe I told you, I was calling on my Caller, and a Door now opened to us, deep below the deadly steam-clouds. We dived in like frightened minnows and a lot of water with us.'

Off Chicago's Gold Coast, Dave once gave me a lesson in skin-diving and, remembering it, I got a flash of Kaby's Door in the dark depths.

'For a moment all was chaos. Then the Door slammed shut

behind us. We'd been picked up in time's nick by – an Express Room of our Spiders! – sloshing two feet deep in water, much more cramped for space than this Place. It was manned by a magician, an old coot named Benson-Carter. He dispelled the water quickly and reported on his Caller. We'd got dry, were feeling human, Illy here had shed his swimsuit, when we looked at the Maintainer. It was glowing, changing, melting! And when Benson-Carter touched it, he fell backward – death was in him. Then the Void began to darken, narrow, shrink and close around us, so I called upon my caller – without wasting time, let me tell you!

'We can't say for sure what was it slowly squeezed that sweet Express Room, but we fear the dirty Snakes have found a way to find our Places and attack outside the cosmos! – found the Spiderweb that links us in the Void's grey less-than-nothing.'

No murmur this time. This reaction was genuine; we'd been hit where we lived and I could see everybody was scared as sick as I was. Except maybe Bruce and Lili, who were still holding hands and beaming gently. I decided they were the kind that love makes brave, which it doesn't do to me. It just gives me two people to worry about.

'I can see you dig our feelings,' Kaby continued. 'This thing scared the pants off us. If we could have, we'd have even Introverted the Maintainer, broken all the ties that bind us, chanced it incommunicado. But the little old Maintainer was a seething red-hot-puddle filled with bubbles big as handballs. We sat tight and watched the Void close. I kept calling on my Caller.'

I squeezed my eyes shut, but that made it easier to see the three of them with the Void shutting down on them. (Was ours still behaving? Yes, Bibi Miriam.) Poetry or no poetry, it got me.

'Benson-Carter, lying dying, also thought the Snakes had done it. And he knew that death was in him, so he whispered me his mission, giving me precise instructions: how to press the seven death's hands, starting lockside counterclockwise, one, three, five, six, two, four, seven, then you have a half an hour; after you have pressed the seven, do not monkey with the buttons – get out fast and don't stop moving.'

I wasn't getting this part and I couldn't see that anyone else was, though Bruce was whispering to Lili. I remembered seeing skulls engraved on the bronze chest. I looked at Illy and he nodded a tentacle and spread two to say, I guessed, that yes, Benson-Carter had said something like that, but no, Illy didn't know much about it.

'All these things and more he whispered,' Kaby went on, 'with the last gasps of his life-force, telling all his secret orders – for he'd not been sent to get us, he was on a separate mission, when he heard my SOSs. Sid, it's you he was to contact, as the first leg of his mission, pick up from you three black hussars, death's-head Demons, daring Soldiers, then to wait until the Places next match rhythm with the cosmos – the matter of two mealtimes, barely – and to tune in northern Egypt in the age of the last Caesar, in the year of Rome's swift downfall, there to start on operation in a battle near a city named for Thrace's Alexander, there to change the course of battle, blow sky-high the stinking Serpents, all their agents, all their Zombies!

'Goddess, pardon, now I savvy how you've guided my least foot-step, when I thought you'd gone and left me –for I flubbed your three-mole signal We've found Sid's Place, that's the first leg, and I see the three black hussars, and we've brought with us the weapon and the Parthian disguises, salvaged from the doomed Express Room when your Door appeared in time's nick, and the Room around us closing spewed us through before it vanished with the corpse of

Benson-Carter. Triple Goddess, draw the milk now from the womanhood I flaunt here and inject the blackest hatred! Vengeance now upon the Serpents, vengeance sweet in northern Egypt, for your island, Crete, Goddess! – and a victory for the Spiders! Goddess, Goddess, we can swing it!'

The roar that made me try to stop my ears with my shoulders didn't come from Kaby – she'd spoken her piece – but from Sid. The dear boy was purple enough to make me want to remind him you can die of high blood pressure just as easy in the Change World.

'Dump me with ops! 'Sblood, I'll not endure it! Is this a battle post? They'll be mounting operations from field hospitals next. Kabysia Labrys, though art mad to suggest it. And what's this prattle of locks, clocks, and death's heads, buttons and monkeys? This brabble, this farrago, this hocus-pocus! And where's the weapon you prate of? In that whoreson bronze casket, I suppose.'

She nodded, looking blank and almost a little shy as poetic possession faded from her. Her answer came like its faltering last echo.

'It is nothing but a tiny tactical atomic bomb.'

Seven

After about 10.1 milliseconds (one ten-thousandth part of a second) has elapsed, the radius of the ball of fire is some 45 feet, and the temperature is then in the vicinity of 300,000 degrees Centigrade. At this instant, the luminosity, as observed at a distance of 100,000 yards (5.7 miles), is approximately 100 times that of the sun as seen at the earth's surface . . . the ball of fire expands very rapidly to its maximum radius of 450 feet within less than a second from the explosion.

—Los Alamos

Time to Think

Brother, that was all we needed to make everybody but Kaby and the two ETs start yelping at once, me included. It may seem strange that Change People, able to whiz through time and space and roust around outside the cosmos and knowing at least by hearsay of weapons a billion years in the future, like the Mindbomb, should panic at being shut in with a little primitive mid-20th Century gadget. Well, they feel the same as atomic scientists would feel if a Bengal tiger were brought into their laboratory, neither more nor less scared.

I'm a moron at physics, but I do now the Fireball is bigger than the Place. Remember that, besides the bomb, we'd recently been presented with a lot of other fears we hadn't had time to cope with, especially the business of the Snakes having learned how to get at our Place and melt the Maintainers and collapse them. Not to mention the general impression – first St Petersburg, the Crete – that the whole Change War was going against the Spiders.

Yet, in a free corner of my mind, I was shocked at how badly we were all panicking. It made me admit what I didn't like to: that we were all in pretty much the same state as Doc, except that the bottle didn't happen to be our out.

And had the rest of us been controlling our drinking so well lately?

Maud yelled 'Jettison it!' and pulled away from the satyr and ran from the bronze chest. Beau, harking back to what they'd thought of doing in the Express Room when it was too late, hissed, 'Sirs, we must Introvert,' and vaulted over the piano bench and legged it for the control divan. Erich seconded him with a white-faced '*Gott in Himmel, ja!*' from beside the surly, forgotten Countess, holding by its slim stem, an empty, rose-stained wine glass.

I felt my mind flinch, because Introverting a Place is several degrees worse than foxholing. It's supposed not only to keep the Door tight shut, but also to lock it so even the Change Winds can't get through – cut the Place loose from the cosmos altogether.

I'd never talked with anyone from a Place that had been Introverted.

Mark dumped Phryne off his lap and ran after Maud. The Greek Ghostgirl, quite solid now, looked around with sleepy fear and fumbled her apple-green chiton together at the throat. She wrenched my attention away from everyone else for a moment, and I couldn't help wondering whether the person or Zombie back in the cosmos, from whose lifeline the Ghost has been taken, doesn't at least have strange dreams or thoughts when something like this happens.

Sid stopped Beau, though he almost got bowled over doing it, and he held the gambler away from the Maintainer in a bear hug and bellowed over his shoulders, 'Masters, are you mad? Have you lost your wits? Maud! Mark! Marcus! Magdalene! On your lives, unhand that casket!'

Maud had swept the clothes and bows and quivers and stuff off it and was dragging it out from the bar towards the Door sector, so as to dump it through fast when we got one, I guess, while Mark acted as if he were trying to help her and wrestle it away from her at the same time.

They kept on as if they hadn't hear a word Sid said, with Mark yelling, 'Let go, *meretrix!* This holds Rome's answer to Parthia on the Nile.'

Kaby watched them as if she wanted to help Mark but scorned to scuffle with a mere – well, Mark had said it in Latin, I guess – call girl.

Then, on the top of the bronze chest, I saw those seven lousy skulls starting at the lock as plain as if they'd been under a magnifying glass, though ordinarily they'd have been a vague circle to my eyes at the distance, and I lost my mind and started to run in the opposite direction, but Illy whipped three tentacles around me, gentle-like, and squeaked, 'Easy now, Greta girl, don't you be doing it, too. Hold still or Papa spank. My, my, but you two-leggers can whirl about when you have a mind to.'

My stampede had carried his featherweight body a couple of yards, but it stopped me and I got my mind back, partly.

'Unhand it, I say!' Sid repeated without accomplishing anything, and he released Beau, though he kept a hand near the gambler's shoulder.

Then my fat friend from Lynn Regis looked real distraught at the Void and blustered at no one in particular, ''Sdeath, think you I'd mutiny against my masters, desert the Spiders, go to ground like a spent fox and pull my hole in after me? A plague of such cowardice! Who suggests it? Introversion's no mere last-ditch device. Unless ordered, supervised and sanctioned, it means the end. And why if I'd Introverted 'ere we got Kaby's call for succour, hey?'

His warrior maid nodded with harsh approval and he noticed it and shook his free hand at her and scolded her, 'Not that I say yea to your mad plan for the Devil's casket, you half-clad clackwit. And yet to jettison . . . Oh, ye gods, ye gods—' he wiped his hand across his face '—grant me a minute in which I may think!'

Thinking time wasn't an item even on the strictly limited list at the moment, although Sevensee, squatting dourly on his hairy haunches where Maud had left him threw in a deadpan 'Thas tellin em, Gov.'

Then Doc at the bar stood up tall as Abe Lincoln in his top hat and shawl and 19th Century duds and raised an unwavering arm for silence and said something that sounded like: 'Introversh, inversh, glovsh,' and then his enunciation switched to better than perfect as he continued, 'I know to an absolute certainty what we must do .'

It showed me how rabbity we were that the Place got quiet as a church while we all stopped whatever we were doing and waited breathless for a poor drunk to tell us how to save ourselves.

He said something like, 'Inversh . . . bosh . . .' and held our eyes for a moment longer. Then the light went out of his and he slobbered out a *'Nichevo'* and slid an arm far along the bar for a bottle and started to pour it down his throat without stopping sliding.

Before he completed his collapse to the floor, in the split second while our attention was still focused on the bar, Bruce vaulted up on top of it, so fast it was almost like he'd popped up from nowhere, though I'd seen him start from behind the piano.

'I've a question. Has anyone here triggered that bomb?' he said in a voice that was very clear and just loud enough. 'So it can't go off,' he went on after just the right pause, his easy grin and brisk manner putting more heart into me all the time. 'What's more, if it were to be triggered, we'd still have half an hour. I believe you said it had that long a fuse?'

He stabbed a finger at Kaby. She nodded.

'Right,' he said. 'It'd have to be that long for whoever plants it in the Parthian camp to get away. There's another safety margin.

'Second question. Is there a locksmith in the house?'

For all Bruce's easiness, he was watching us like a golden eagle and he caught Beau's and Maud's affirmatives before they had a chance to explain or hedge them and said, 'That's very good. Under certain circumstances, you two'd be the ones to go to work on the chest. But before we consider that, there's Question Three: Is anyone here an atomics technician?'

That one took a little conversation to straighten out, Illy having to explain that, yes, the Early Lunans had atomic power – hadn't they blasted the life off their planet with it and made all those ghastly craters? – but no, he wasn't a technician exactly, he was a 'thinger' (I thought at first his squeakbox was lisping); what was a thinger? – well, a thinger was someone who manipulated things in a way that was truly impossible to describe, but no, you couldn't possibly thing atomics; the idea was quite ridiculous, so he couldn't be an atomics thinger; the term was worse than a contradiction, well, really! – while Sevensee, from his two-thousand-millennia advantage of the Lunan, grunted to the effect that his culture didn't rightly use any kind of power, but just sort of moved satyrs and stuff by wrastling spacetime around, 'or think em roun ef we hafta. Can't think em in the Void, tho, wus luck. Hafta have – I dunno wut. Dun havvit anyhow.'

'So we don't have an A-tech,' Bruce summed up, 'which makes it worse than useless, downright dangerous, to tamper with the chest. We wouldn't know what to do if we did get inside safely. One more question.' He directed it towards Sid. 'How long before we can jettison anything?'

Sid, looking a shade jealous, yet mostly grateful for the way Bruce had calmed his chickens, started to explain, but Bruce didn't seem to be taking any chance of losing his audience and as soon as Sid got to the word 'rhythm', he pulled the answer away from him.

'In brief, not until we can effectively tune in on the cosmos again. Thank you, Master Lessingham. That's at least five hours – two mealtimes, as the Cretan officer put it,' and he threw Kaby a quick soldierly smile. 'So, whether the bomb goes to Egypt or elsewhere, there's not a thing we can do about it for five hours. All right then!'

His smile blinked out like a light and he took a couple of steps up and down the bar, as if measuring the space he had. Two or three cocktail glasses sailed off and popped, but he didn't seem to notice them and we hardly did either. It was creepy the way he kept staring from one to another of us. We had to look up. Behind his face, with the straight golden hair flirting around it, was only the Void.

'All right then,' he repeated suddenly. 'We're twelve Spiders and two Ghosts, and we've time for a bit of a talk, and we're all in the same bloody boat, fighting the same bloody war, so we'll all know what we're talking about. I raised the subject a while back, but I was steamed up about a glove, and it was a big jest. All right! But now the gloves are off!'

Bruce ripped them out of his belt where they'd been tucked and slammed them down on the bar, to be kicked off the next time he paced back and forth, and it wasn't funny.

'Because,' he went right on, 'I've been getting a completely new picture of what this Spiders' war has been doing to each one of us. Oh, it's jolly good sport to slam around in space and time and then have a rugged little party outside both of them when the operation's over. It's sweet to know there's no cranny of reality so narrow, no privacy so intimate or sacred, no wall of was or will be strong enough, that we can't shoulder in. Knowledge is a glamorous thing, sweeter than lust or gluttony or the passion of fighting and including all three, the ultimate insatiable hunger, and it's great to be Faust, even in a pack of other Fausts.

'It's sweet to jigger reality, to twist the whole course of a man's life or a culture's, to ink out his or its past and scribble in a new one, and be the only one to know and gloat over the changes – hah! killing men or carrying off women isn't in it for glutting the sense of power. It's sweet to feel the Change Winds blowing through you and know the pasts that were and the past that is and the pasts that may be. It's sweet to wield the Atropos and cut a Zombie or Unborn out of his lifeline and look the Doubleganger in the face and see the Resurrection-glow on it and Recruit a brother, welcome a newborn fellow Demon into our ranks and decide whether he'll best fit as Soldier, Entertainer, or what.

'Or he can't stand Resurrection, it fries or freezes him, and you've got to decide whether to return him to his lifeline and his Zombie dreams, only they'll be a little greyer and horrider than they were before, or whether, if she's got that tantalizing something, to bring her shell along for a Ghostgirl – that's sweet, too. It's even sweet to have Change Death poised over your neck, to know that the past isn't the precious indestructible thing you've been taught it was, to know that there's no certainty about the future either, whether there'll even be one, to know that no part of reality is holy, that the cosmos itself may wink out like a flicked switch and God be not and nothing left but nothing.'

He threw out his arms against the Void. 'And knowing all that, it's doubly sweet to come through the Door into the Place and be out of the worst of the Change Winds and enjoy a well-earned Recuperation and share the memories of all these sweetnesses I've been talking about, and work out all the fascinating feeling you've been accumulating back in the cosmos, layer by black layer, in the company of and with the help of the best bloody little bank of fellow Fausts and Faustines going!

'Oh, it's a sweet life, all right, but I'm asking you—' and here his eyes stabbed us again, one by one, fast '—I'm asking you what it's done to us. I've been getting a completely new picture, as I said, of what my life was and what it could have been if there'd been changes of the sort that even we Demons can't make, and what my life is. I've been watching how we've all been responding to things just now, to the news of St Petersburg and to what the Cretan officer told beautifully – only it wasn't beautiful what she had to tell – and mostly to that bloody box of bomb. And I'm simply asking each one of you, what's happened to you?'

He stopped his pacing and stuck his thumbs in his belt and seemed to be listening to the wheels turning in at least eleven other heads – only I stopped mine pretty quick, with Dave and Father and the Rape of Chicago coming up out of the dark on the turn and Mother and the Indiana Dunes and Jazz Limited just behind them followed by the unthinkable thing the Spider doctor had flicked into existence when I flopped as a nurse, because I can't stand that to be done to my mind by anybody but myself.

I stopped them by using the old infallible Entertainers' gimmick, a fast survey of the most interesting topic there is – other people's troubles.

Offhand, Beau looked as if he had most troubles, shamed by his boss and his girl given her heart to a Soldier; he was hugging them to himself very quiet.

I didn't stop for the two ETs – they're too hard to figure – or for Doc; nobody can tell whether a fallen-down drunk's at the black or bright end of his cycle; you just know it's cycling.

Maud ought to be suffering as much as Beau, called names and caught out in a panic, which always hurt her because she's plus three hundred years more future than the rest of us and figures she ought to be that much wiser, which she isn't always – not to mention she's over fifty years old, though her home-century cosmetic science keeps her looking and acting teen-age most of the time. She'd backed away from the bronze chest so as not to stand out, and now Lili came from behind the piano and stood beside her.

Lili had the opposite of troubles, a great big glow for Bruce, proud as a promised princess watching her betrothed. Erich frowned when he saw her, for he seemed proud too, proud of the way his *Kamerad* had taken command of us panicky whacks *Führer*-fashion. Sid still looked mostly grateful and inclined to let Bruce keep on talking.

Even Kaby and Mark, those two dragons hot for battle, standing a little in front and to one side of us by the bronze chest, like its guardians, seemed willing to listen. They made me realize one reason Sid had for letting Bruce run on, although the path his talk was leading us down was flashing with danger signals: When it was over, there'd still be the problem of what to do with the bomb, and a real opposition shaping up between Soldiers and Entertainers, and Sid was hoping a solution would turn up in the meantime or at least was willing to put off the evil day.

But beyond all that, and like the rest of us, I could tell from the way Sid was squinting his browy eyes and chewing his beardy lip that he was shaken and moved by what Bruce had said. This New Boy had dipped into our hearts and counted our kicks so beautifully, better than most of us could have done, and then somehow turned them around so that we had to think of what messes and heels and black sheep and lost lambs we were – well, we wantd to keep on listening.

Eight

Give me a place to stand, and I will move the world.
                                    —Archimedes

A Place to Stand

Bruce's voice had a faraway touch and he was looking up left at the Void as he said, 'Have you ever really wondered why the two sides of this war are called the Snakes and the Spiders? Snakes may be clear enough – you always call the enemy something dirty. But Spiders – our name for ourselves? Bear with me, Ilhilihis; I know that no being is created dirty or malignant by Nature, but this is a matter of anthropoid feelings and folkways. Yes, Mark, I know that some of your legions have nicknames like the Drunken Lions and the Snails, and that's about as insulting as calling the British Expeditionary Force the Old Contemptibles.

'No, you'd have to go to bands of vicious youths in cities slated for ruin to find a habit of naming like ours, and even they would try to brighten up the black a bit. But simply – Spiders. And Snakes, for that's their name for themselves too, you know. Spiders and Snakes. What are our masters, that we give them names like that?'

It gave me the shivers and set my mind working in a dozen directions and I couldn't stop it, although it made the shivers worse.

Illy beside me now – I'd never given it a thought before, but he did have eight legs of a sort, and I remembered thinking of him as a spider monkey, and hadn't the Lunans had wisdom and atomic power and a billion years in which to get the Change War rolling?

Or suppose, in the far future, Terra's own spiders evolved intelligence and a cruel cannibal culture. They'd be able to keep their existence secret. I had no idea of who or what would be on Earth in Sevensee's day, and wouldn't it be perfect black hairy poisoned spider-mentality to spin webs secretly through the world of thought and all of space and time?

And Beau – wasn't there something real Snaky about him, the way he moved and all?

Spiders and Snakes. *Spinne und Schlange,* as Erich called them. S & S. But SS stood for Nazi *Schutzstaffel,* the Black Shirts, and what if some of those cruel, crazy Jerries had discovered time travel and – I brought myself up with a jerk and asked myself, 'Greta, how nuts can you get?'

From where he was on the floor, the front of the bar his sounding board, Doc shrieked up at Bruce like one of the damned from the pit, 'Don't speak against the Spiders! Don't blaspheme! They can hear the Unborn whisper. Others whip only the skin, but they whip the naked brain and heart,' and Erich called out, 'That's enough, Bruce!'

But Bruce didn't spare him a look and said, 'But whatever the Spiders are and no matter how much they use, it's plain as the telltale on the Maintainer that the Change War is not only going against them, but getting away from them. Dwell for a bit on the current flurry of stupid slugging and panicky anachronism, when we all know that anachronism is what gets the Change Winds out of control. This punch-drunk pounding on the Cretan-Dorian fracas as if it were the only battle going and the only way to work things. Whisking Constantine from Britain to the Bosphorus by rocket, sending a pocket submarine back to sail with the Armada against Drake's woodensides – I'll wager you hadn't heard those! And now, to save Rome, an atomic bomb.

'Ye gods they could have used Greek fire or even dynamite, but a fission weapon . . . I leave you to imagine what gaps and scars that will make in what's left of history – the smothering of Greece and the vanishment of Provence and the troubadours and the Papacy's Irish Captivity won't be in it!'

The cut on his cheek had opened again and was oozing a little, but he didn't pay any attention to it, and neither did we, as his lips thinned in irony and he said, 'But I'm forgetting that this is a cosmic war and that the Spiders are conducting operations on billions, trillions of planets and inhabited gas clouds through millions of ages and that we're just one little world – one little solar system, Sevensee – and we can hardly expect our inscrutable masters, with all their pressing preoccupations and far-flung responsibilities, to be especially understanding or tender in their treatment of our pet books and centuries, our favourite prophets and periods, or unduly concerned about preserving any of the trifles that we just happen to hold dear.

'Perhaps there are some sentimentalists who would rather die forever than go on living in a world without the *Summa*, the Field Equations, *Process and Reality*, *Hamlet*, Matthew, Keats, and the *Odyssey*, but our masters are practical creatures, ministering to the needs of those rugged souls who want to go on living no matter what.'

Erich's 'Bruce, I'm telling you that's enough,' was lost in the quickening flow of the New Boy's words. 'I won't spend much time on the minor signs of our major crack-up – the cancelling of leaves, the sharper shortages, the loss of the Express Room the use of Recuperation Stations for ops and all the other frantic patchwork – last operation but one, we were saddled with three Soldiers from outside the Galaxy and, no fault of theirs, they were no earthly use. Such little things might happen at a bad spot in any war and are perhaps only local. But there's a big thing.'

He paused again, to let us wonder, I guess. Maud must have worked her way over to me, for I felt her dry little hand on my arm and she whispered out of the side of her mouth, 'What do we do now?'

'We listen,' I told her the same way. I felt a little impatient with her need to be doing something about things.

She cocked a gold-dusted eyebrow at me and murmured, 'You, too?'

I didn't get to ask her me, too, what? Crush on Bruce? Nuts! – because just then Bruce's voice took up again in the faraway range.

'Have you ever asked yourself how many operations the fabric of history can stand before it's all stitches, whether too much Change won't one day wear out the past? And the present and the future, too, the whole bleeding business. Is the law of the Conservation of Reality any more than a thin hope given a long name, a prayer of theoreticians? Change Death is as certain as Heat Death, and far faster. Every operation leaves reality a bit cruder, a bit uglier, a bit more makeshift, and a whole lot less rich in those details and feeling that are our heritage, like the crude pencilled sketch on canvas when you've stripped off the paint.

'If that goes on, won't the cosmos collapse into a outline of itself, then nothing? How much thinning can reality stand, having more and more Doublegangers cut out of it? And there's another thing about every operation – it wakes up the Zombies a little more, and as its Change Winds die, it leaves them a little more disturbed and nightmare-ridden and frazzled. Those of you who have been on operations in heavily worked-over temporal areas will know what I mean – that look they give you out of the sides of their eyes as if to say, 'You again? For Christ's sake, go away. We're the dead. We're the ones who don't want to wake up, who don't want to be Demons and hate to be Ghosts. Stop torturing us'.''

I looked around at the Ghostgirls; I couldn't help it. They'd somehow got together on the control divan, facing us, their backs to the Maintainers. The Countess had dragged along the bottle of wine Erich had fetched her earlier and they were passing it back and forth. The Countess had a big rose splotch across the ruffled white lace of her blouse.

Bruce said, 'There'll come a day when all the Zombies and all the Unborn wake up and go crazy together and figuratively come marching at us in their numberless hordes, saying, "We've had enough".'

But I didn't turn back to Bruce right away. Phryne's chiton had slipped off one shoulder and she and the Countess were sitting sagged forward, elbows on kness, legs spread – at least, as far as the Countess's hobble skirt would let her – and swayed towards each other a little They were still surprisingly solid, although they hadn't had any personal attention for a half-hour, and they were looking up over my head with half-shut eyes and they seemed, so help me, to be listening to what Bruce was saying and maybe hearing some of it.

'We make a careful distinction between Zombies and Unborn, between those troubled by our operations whose lifelines lie in the past and those whose lifelines lie in the future. But is there any distinction any longer? Can we tell the difference between the past and the future? Can we any longer locate the now, the real now of the cosmos? The Places have their own nows, the now of the Big Time we're on, but that's different and it's not made for real living.

'The Spiders tell us that the real now is somewhere in the last half of the 20th Century, which means that several of us here are also alive in the cosmos, have lifelines along which the now is travelling. But do you swallow that story quite so easily, Ilhilihis, Sevensee? How does it strike the servants of the Triple Goddess? The spiders of Octavian Rome? The Demons of Good Queen Bess? The gentlemen Zombies of the Greater South? Do the Unborn man the starships, Maud?

'The Spiders also tell us that, although the fog of battle makes the now hard to pin down precisely, it will return with the unconditional surrender of the Snakes and the establishment of cosmic peace, and roll on as majestically towards the future as before, quickening the continuum with its passage. Do you really believe that? Or do you believe, as I do, that we've used up all the future as well as the past, wasted it in premature experience, and that we've had the real now smudged out of existence, stolen from us forever, the precious now of true growth, the child-moment in which all life lies, the moment like a newborn baby that is the only home for hope there is?'

He let that start to sink in, then took a couple of quick steps and went on, his voice rising over Erich's 'Bruce, for the last time—' and seeming to pick up a note of hope from the very word he had used, 'But although things look terrifyingly black, there remains a chance – the slimmest chance, but still a chance – of saving the cosmos from Change Death and restoring reality's richness and giving the Ghosts good sleep and perhaps even regaining the real now. We have the means right at hand. What if the power of time travelling were used not for war and destruction, but for healing, for the mutual enrichment of the ages, for quiet communication and growth, in brief, to bring a peace message—'

But my little commandant is quite an actor himself and knows a wee bit about the principles of scene-stealing and he was not going to let Bruce drown him out as if he were just another extra playing a Voice from the Mob. He darted across our front, between us and the bar, took a running leap, and landed bang on the bloody box of bomb.

A bit later, Maud was silently showing me the white ring above her elbow where I'd grabbed her and Illy was teasing a clutch of his tentacle out of my other hand and squeaking reproachfully, 'Greta girl, don't ever do that.'

Erich was standing on the chest and I notice that his boots carefully straddled the circle of skulls, and I should have known anyway you could hardly push them in the right order by jumping on them, and he was pointing at Bruce and saying, '—and that means mutiny, my young sir. *Um Gottes willen,* Bruce, listen to me and step down before you say anything worse. I'm older than you, Bruce. Mark's older.

Trust in your *Kameraden*. Guide yourself by their knowledge.'

He had got my attention, but I had much rather have him black my eye.

'You older than me?' Bruce was grinning. 'When your twelve-years' advantage was spent in soaking up the wisdom of a race of sadistic dreamers gone paranoid, in a world whose thought-stream had already been muddied by one total war? Mark older than me? When all his ideas and loyalties are those of a wolf pack of unimaginative sluggers two thousand years younger than I am? Either of you older because you have more of the killing cynicism that is all the wisdom the Change World ever gives you? Don't make me laugh!

'I'm an Englishman, and I come from an epoch when total war was still a desecration and the flowers and buds of thoughts not yet whacked off or blighted. I'm a poet and poets are wiser than anyone because they're the only people who have the guts to think and feel at the same time. Right, Sid? When I talk to all of you about a peace message, I want you to think about it correctly in terms of using the Places to bring help across the mountains of time when help is really needed, not to bring help that's undeserved or knowledge that's premature or contaminating, sometimes not to bring any-thing at all, but just to check with infinite tenderness and concern that everything's safe and the glories of the universe unfolding as they were intended to—'

'Yes, you are a poet, Bruce,' Erich broke in. 'You can tootle soulfully on the flute and make us drip tears. You can let out the stops on the big organ pipes and make us tremble as if at Jehovah's footsteps. For the last twenty minutes, you have been giving us some very *charmante* poetry But what are you? An Entertainer? Or are you a Soldier?'

Right then – I don't know what it was, maybe Sid clearing his throat – I could sense our feelings beginning to turn against Bruce. I got the strangest feeling of reality clamping down and bright colours going dull and dreams vanishing. Yet it was only then I also realized how much Bruce had moved us, maybe some of us to the verge of mutiny, even. I was mad at Erich for what he was doing, but I couldn't help admiring his cockiness.

I was still under the spell of Bruce's words and the more-than-words behind them, but then Erich would shift around a bit and one of his heels would kick near the death's head pushbuttons and I wanted to stamp with spike heels on every death's-head button on his uniform. I didn't know exactly what I felt yet.

'Yes, I'm a Soldier,' Bruce told him, 'and I hope you won't ever have to worry about my courage, because it's going to take more courage than any operation we've ever planned, ever dreamed of, to carry the peace message to the other Places and to the wound-spots of the cosmos. Perhaps it will be a fast wicket and we'll be bowled down before we score a single run, but who cares? We may at least see our real masters when they come to smash us, and for me that will be a deep satisfaction. And we may do some smashing of our own.'

'So you're a Soldier,' Erich said, his smile showing his teeth. 'Bruce, I'll admit that the half-dozen operations you've been on were rougher than anything I drew in my first hundred sleeps. For that, I am all honest sympathy. But that you should let them get you into such a state that love and a girl can turn you upside down and start you babbling about peace messages—'

'Yes, by God, love and a girl have changed me!' Bruce shouted at him, and I looked around at Lili and I remembered Dave saying, 'I'm going to Spain,' and I wondered if anything would ever again make my face flame like that. 'Or, rather, they've made me stand up for what I've believed in all along. They've made me—'

'*Wunderbar,*' Erich called and began to do a little sissy dance on the bomb that set my teeth on edge. He bent his wrists and elbows at arty angles and stuck out a hip and ducked his head simperingly and blinked his eyes very fast. 'Will you invite me to the wedding, Bruce? You'll have to get another best man, but I will be the flower girl and throw pretty little posies to all the distinguished guests. Here, Mark. Catch, Kaby. One for you, Greta. *Danke schön. Ache, zwei Herzen in dreivierteltakt . . . ta-ta . . . ta-ta . . . ta-ta-ta-ta-ta . . .'*

'What the hell do you think a woman is?' Bruce raged. 'Something to mess around with in your spare time?'

Erich kept on humming 'Two hearts in Waltz Time' – and jigging around to it, damn him – but he slipped in a nod to Bruce and a 'Precisely.' So I knew where I stood, but it was no news to me.

'Very well,' Bruce said, 'let's leave this Brown Shirt *maricón* to amuse himself and get down to business. I made all of you a proposal and I don't have to tell you how serious it is or how serious Lili and I are about it. We not only must infiltrate and subvert other Places, which luckily for us are made for infiltration, we also must make contact with the Snakes and establish working relationships with their Demons at our level as one of our first steps.'

That stopped Erich's jig and got enough of a gasp from some of us to make it seem to come from practically everybody. Erich used it to work a change of pace.

'Bruce! We've let you carry this foolery further than we should. You seem to have the idea that because anything goes in the Place – duelling, drunkenness, *und so weiter* – you can say what you have and it will all be forgotten with the hangover. Not so. It is true that among such a set of monsters and free spirits as ourselves, and working as secret agents to boot, there cannot be the obvious military discipline that would obtain in a Terran army.

'But let me tell you, Bruce, let me grind it home into you – Sid and Kaby and Mark will bear me out in this, as officers of equivalent rank – that the Spider line of command stretches into and through this Place just as surely as the word of *der Führer* rules Chicago. And as I shouldn't have to emphasize to you, Bruce, the Spiders have punishments that would make my countrymen in Belsen and Buchenwald – well, pale a little. So while there is still a shadow of justification for our interpreting your remarks as utterly tasteless clowning—'

'Babble on,' Bruce said, giving him a loose downward wave of his hand without looking. 'I made you people a proposal.' He paused. 'How do you stand, Sidney Lessingham?'

Then I felt my legs getting weak, because Sid didn't answer right away. The old boy swallowed and started to look around at the rest of us. Then the feeling of reality clamping down got something awful, because he didn't look around, but straightened his back a little. Just then, Mark cut in fast.

'It grieves me, Bruce, but I think you are possessed. Erich, he must be confined.'

Kaby nodded, almost absently. 'Confine or kill the coward, whichever is easier, whip the woman, and let's get on to the Egyptian battle.'

'Indeed, yes,' Mark said. 'I died in it. But now perhaps no longer.'

Kaby said to him 'I like you, Roman.'

Bruce was smiling, barely, and his eyes were moving and fixing. 'You, Ilhilihis?'

Illy's squeak box had never sounded mechanical to me before, but it did as he answered, 'I'm a lot deeper into borrowed time that the rest of you, tra-la-la, but Papa still loves living. Include me very much out, Bruce.'

'Miss Davies?'

Beside me, Maud said flatly, 'Do you think I'm a fool?' Beyond her, I saw Lili and I thought, 'My God, I might look as proud if I were in her shoes, but I sure as hell wouldn't look as confident.'

Bruce's eyes hadn't quite come to Beau when the gambler

spoke up. 'I have no cause to like you, sir, rather the opposite. But this Place has come to bore me more than Boston and I have always found it difficult to resist a long shot. A very long one, I fear. I am with you, sir.'

There was a pain in my chest and a roaring in my ears and through it I heard Sevensee grunting, 'Sicka these lousy Spiders. Deal me in.'

And then Doc reared up in front of the bar and he'd lost his hat and his hair was wild and he grabbed an empty fifth by the neck and broke the bottom of it all jagged against the bar and he waved it and screeched, *'Ubivaytye Pauki-i Nyemetzi!'*

And right behind his words, Beau sang out fast the English of it, 'Kill the Spiders – and the Germans!'

And Doc didn't collapse then, though I could see he was hanging on to the bar tight with his other hand, and the Place got stiller, inside and out, than I've ever known it, and Bruce's eyes were finally moving back towards Sid.

But the eyes stopped short of Sid and I heard Bruce say, 'Miss Forzane?' and I thought, 'That's funny,' and I started to look around at the Countess, and felt all the eyes and I realized, 'Hey, that's me! But this can't happen to me. To the others, yes, but not to me. I just work here. Not to Greta, no, no, no!'

But it had, and the eyes didn't let go, and the silence and the feeling of reality were Godawful, and I said to myself, 'Greta, you've got to say something, if only a suitable four-letter word,' and then suddenly I knew what the silence was like. It was like that of a big city if there were some way of shutting off all the noise in one second. It was like Erich's singing when the piano had deserted him. It was as if the Change Winds should ever die completely . . . and I knew beforehand what had happened when I turned my back on them all.

The Ghostgirls were gone. The Major Maintainer hadn't merely been switched to Introvert. It was gone, too.

Nine

'We examined the moss between the bricks, and found it
undisturbed.'

'You looked among D—'s papers of course, and into the
books of the library?'

'Certainly; we opened every package and parcel; we not
only opened every book, but we turned over every half leaf
in each volume . . .'

—Poe

A Locked Room

Three hours later, Sid and I plumped down on the couch
nearest the kitchen, though too tired to want to eat for a while
yet. A tighter search than I could ever have cooked up had
shown that the Maintainer was not in the Place.

Of course it had to be in the Place, as we kept telling each
other for the first two hours. It had to be, if circumstances and
the theories we lived by in the Change World meant anything.
A Maintainer is what maintains a Place. The Minor
Maintainer takes care of oxygen, temperature, humidity,
gravity, and other little life-cycle and matter-cycle things
generally, but it's the Major Maintainer that keeps the walls
from buckling and the ceiling from falling in. It is little, but
oh my, it does so much.

It doesn't work by wires or radio or anything complicated
like that. It just hooks into local space-time.

I have been told that its inside working part is made up of
vastly tough, vastly hard giant molecules, each one of which is
practically a vest-pocket cosmos in itself. Outside, it looks like
a portable radio with a few more dials and some telltales and
switches and plug-ins for earphones and a lot of other sensory
thingumajigs.

But this Maintainer was gone and the Void hadn't closed

in, yet. By this time, I was so fagged, I didn't care much whether it did or not.

One thing for sure, the Maintainer had been switched to Introvert before it was spirited away or else its disappearance automatically produced Introversion, take your choice, because we sure were Introverted – real nasty martinet-school-master grip of reality on my thoughts that I knew, without trying, liquor wouldn't soften, not a breath of Change Wind, absolutely stifling, and the grey of the Void seeming so much inside my head that I think I got a glimmering of what the science boys mean when they explain to me that the Place is a kind of interweaving of the material and the mental – a Giant Monad, one of them called it.

Anyway, I said to myself, 'Greta, if this is Introversion, I want no part of it. It is not nice to be cut adrift from the cosmos and know it. A lifeboat in the middle of the Pacific and a starship between galaxies are not in it for loneliness.'

I asked myself why the Spiders had ever equipped Maintainers with Introversion switches anyway, when we couldn't drill with them and weren't supposed to use them except in an emergency so tight that it was either Introvert or surrender to the Snakes, and for the first time the obvious explanation came to me:

Introversion must be the same as scuttling, its main purpose to withhold secrets and material from the enemy. It put a place into a situation from which even the Spider high command couldn't rescue it, and there was nothing left but to sink down, down (out? up?), down into the Void.

If that was the case, our chances of getting back were about those of my being a kid again playing in the Dunes on the Small Time.

I edged a little closer to Sid and sort of squunched under his shoulder and rubbed my cheek against the smudged, gold-worked grey velvet. He looked down and I said, 'A long way to Lynn Regis, eh, Siddy?'

'Sweetling, thou spokest a mouthful,' he said. He knows very well what he is doing when he mixes his language that way, the wicked old darling.

'Siddy,' I said, 'why this goldwork? It'd be a lot smoother without it.'

'Marry, men must prick themselves out and, 'faith I know not, but it helps if there's metal in it.'

'And girls get scratched.' I took a little sniff. 'But don't put this doublet through the cleaner yet. Until we get out of the woods, I want as much around as possible.'

'Marry, why should I?' he asked blankly, and I think he wasn't fooling me. The last think time travellers find out is how they do or don't smell. Then his face clouded and he looked as though he wanted to squunch under my shoulder. 'But 'faith, sweetling, your forest has a few more trees than Sherwood.'

'Thou saidst it,' I agreed, and wondered about the look. He oughtn't to be interested in my girlishness now. I knew I was a mess, but he had stuck pretty close to me during the hunt and you never can tell. Then I remembered that he was the other one who hadn't declared himself when Bruce was putting it to us, and it probably troubled his male vanity. Not me, though – I was still grateful to the Maintainer for getting me out of the spot, whatever other it had got us all into. It seemed ages ago.

We'd all jumped to the conclusion that the two Ghostgirls had run away with the Maintainer, I don't know where or why, but it looked so much that way. Maud had started yiping about how she'd never trusted Ghosts and always know that some day they'd start doing things on their own, and Kaby had got it firmly fixed in her head, right between the horns, that Phryne, being a Greek, was the ringleader and was going to wreak havoc on us all.

But when we were checking Stores the first time, I had

noticed that the Ghostgirl envelopes looked flat. Ectoplasm doesn't take up much space when it's folded, but I had opened one anyway, then another, and then called for help.

Every last envelope was empty. We had lost over a thousand Ghostgirls, Sid's whole stock.

Well, at least it proved what none of us had ever seen or heard of being demonstrated: that there is a spooky link – a sort of Change Wind contact – between a Ghost and its lifeline; and when that umbilicus, I've heard it called, is cut, the part away from the lifeline dies.

Interesting, but what had bothered me was whether we Demons were going to evaporate too, because we are as much Doublegangers as the Ghosts and our apron strings had been cut as surely. We're more solid, of course, but that would only mean we'd take a little longer. Very logical.

I remember I had looked up at Lili and Maud – us girls had been checking the envelopes; it's one of the proprieties we frequently maintain and anyway, if men check them they're apt to trot out that old wheeze about 'instant women' which I'm sick to death of hearing, thank you.

Anyway, I had looked up and said, 'It's been nice knowing you,' and Lili had said, 'Twenty-three, skiddoo,' and Maud had said, 'Here goes nothing,' and we had shook hands all around.

We figured that Phryne and the Countess had faded at the same time as the other Ghostgirls, but an idea had been nibbling at me and I said, 'Siddy, do you suppose it's just barely possible that, while we were all looking at Bruce, those two Ghostgirls would have been able to work the Maintainer and get a Door and lam out of here with the thing?'

'Thou speakst my thoughts, sweetling. All weighs against it: Imprimis, 'tis well known that Ghosts cannot lay plots or act on them. Secundo, the time forbade getting a Door. Tercio – and here's the real meat of it – the Place folds without the Maintainer. Quadro, 'twere folly to depend on not one of

– how many of us? ten, elf – not looking around in all the time it would have taken them—'

'I looked around once, Siddy. There were drinking and they had got to the control divan under their own power. Now when was that? Oh, yes, when Bruce was talking about Zombies.'

'Yes, sweetling. And as I was about to cap my argument with quinquo when you 'gan prattle. I could have sworne none could touch the Maintainer, much less work it and purloin it, without my certain knowledge. Yet . . .'

'Eftsoons yet,' I seconded him.

Somebody must have got a door and walked out with the thing. It certainly wasn't in the Place. The hunt had been a lulu. Something the size of a portable typewriter is not easy to hide and we had been inside everything from Beau's piano to the renewer link of the Refresher.

We had even flúoroscoped everybody, though it had made Illy writhe like a box of worms, as he'd warned us; he said it tickled terribly and I insisted on smoothing his fur for five minutes afterwards, although he was a little standoffish towards me.

Some areas, like the bar, kitchen and Stores, took a long while, but we were thorough. Kaby helped Doc check Surgery: since she last made the Place, she has been stationed in a Field Hospital (it turns out the Spiders actually are mounting operations from them) and learned a few nice new wrinkles.

However, Doc put in some honest work on his own, though, of course, every check was observed by at least three people, not including Bruce or Lili. When the Maintainer vanished, Doc had pulled out of his glassy-eyed drunk in a way that would have surprised me if I hadn't seen it happen to him before, but when we finished Surgery and got on to the Arts Gallery, he had started to putter and I noticed him hold out his coat and duck his head and whip out a flask and take a swig and by now he was well on his way towards another peak.

The Art Gallery had taken time too, because there's such a jumble of strange stuff, and it broke my heart but Kaby took her axe and split a beautiful blue woodcarving of a Venusian medusa because, although there wasn't a mark in the paw-polished surface, she claimed it was just big enough. Doc cried a little and we left him fitting the pieces together and mooning over the other stuff.

After we'd finished everything else, Mark had insisted on tackling the floor. Beau and Sid both tried to explain how this is a one-sided Place, that there is nothing, but nothing, under the floor, it just gets a lot harder than the diamonds crusting it and soon as you get a quarter inch down – that being the solid equivalent of the Void. But Mark was knuckleheaded (like all Romans, Sid assured me on the q.t.) and broke four diamond-plus drills before he was satisfied.

Except for some trick hiding places, that left the Void, and things don't vanish if you throw them at the Void – they half melt and freeze forever unless you can fish them out. Back of the Refresher, at about eye level, are three Venusian coconuts that a Hittite strongman threw there during a major brawl. I try not to look at them because they are so much like witch heads they give me the woolies. The parts of the Place right up against the Void have strange spatial properties which one of the gadgets in Surgery makes use of in a way that gives me the worse woolies, but that's beside the point.

During the hunt, Kaby and Erich had used their Callers as direction finders to point out the Maintainer, just as they're used in the cosmos to locate the Door – and sometimes in the Big Places, people tell me. But the Callers only went wild – like a compass needle whirling around without stopping – and nobody knew what that meant.

The trick hiding places were the Minor Maintainer, a cute idea, but it is no bigger than the Major and has its own mysterious insides and had obviously kept on doing its own work, so that was out for several reasons, and the bomb chest, though it seemed impossible for anyone to have opened it, granting they know the secret of its lock, even before Erich jumped on it and put it in the limelight double. But when you've ruled out everything else, the word impossible changes meaning.

Since time travel is our business, a person might think of all sorts of tricks for sending the Maintainer into the past or future, permanently or temporarily. But the Place is strictly on the Big Time and everybody that should know tells me that time travelling *through* the Big Time is out. It's this way: the Big Time is a train, and the Little Time is the countryside and we're on the train, unless we go out a Door, and as Gertie Stein might put it, you can't time travel through the time you time travel in when you time travel.

I'd also played around with the idea of some fantastically obvious hiding place, maybe something that several people could pass back and forth between them, which could mean a conspiracy, and, of course, if you assume a big enough conspiracy, you can explain anything, including the cosmos itself. Still, I'd got a sort of shell-game idea about the Soldiers' three big black shakos and I hadn't been satisfied until I'd got the three together and looked in them all at the same time.

'Wake up, Greta, and take something. I can't stand here forever.' Maud had brought us a tray of hearty snacks from then and yon, and I must say they were tempting; she whips up a mean hors d'oeuvre.

I looked them over and said, 'Siddy, I want a hot dog.'

'And I want a venison pasty! Out upon you, you finical jill, you o'erscrupulous jade, you whimsic and tyrannous poppet!'

I grabbed a handful and snuggled back against him.

'Go on, call me some more, Siddy,' I told him. 'Real juicy ones.'

Ten

My thought, whose murder yet is but fantastical,
Shake so my single state of man that function
Is smother'd in surmise, and nothing is
But what is not.

—Macbeth

Motives and Opportunities

My big bad waif from King's Lynn had set the tray on his
knees and started to wolf the food down. The others were
finishing up. Erich, Mark and Kaby were having a quietly
furious argument I couldn't overhear at the end of the bar
nearest the bronze chest, and Illy was draped over the piano
like a real octopus, listening in.

Beau and Sevensee were pacing up and down near the
control divan and throwing each other a word now and then.
Beyond them Bruce and Lili were sitting on the opposite
couch from us, talking earnestly about something. Maud had
sat down at the other end of the bar and was knitting – it's one
of the habits like chess and quiet drinking, or learning to talk
by squeak box, that we pick up to pass the time in the Place in
the long stretches between parties. Doc was fiddling around
the Gallery, picking things up and setting them down, still
managing to stay on his feet at any rate.

Lili and Bruce stood up, still gabbing intensely at each
other, and Illy began to pick out with one tentacle a little tune
in the high keys that didn't sound like anything on God's
earth. 'Where do they get all the energy?' I wondered.

As soon as I asked myself that, I knew the answer and I
began to feel the same way myself. It wasn't energy; it was
nerves, pure and simple.

Change is like a drug, I realized – you get used to the facts
never staying the same, and one picture of the past and future
dissolving into another maybe not very different but still

different, and your mind being constantly goosed by strange moods and notions, like nightclub lights of shifting colour with weird shadows between shining right on your brain.

The endless swaying and jogging is restful, like riding on a train.

You soon get to like the movement and to need it without knowing, and when it suddenly stops and you're just you and the facts you think from and feel from are exactly the same when you go back to them – boy, that's rough, as I found out now.

The instant we got Introverted, everything that ordinarily leaks into the Place, wake or sleep, had stopped coming, and we were nothing but ourselves and what we meant to each other and what we could make of that, an awfully lonely, scratchy situation.

I decided I felt like I'd dropped into a swimming pool full of cement and held under until it hardened.

I could understand the others bouncing around a bit. It was a wonder they didn't hit the Void. Maud seemed to be standing it the best, maybe she'd got a little preparation from the long watches between stars; and then she is older than all of us, even Sid, though with a small 'o' in 'older'.

The restless work of the search for the Maintainer had masked the feeling, but now it was beginning to come full force. Before the search, Bruce's speech and Erich's interruptions had done a passable masking job too. I tried to remember when I'd first got the feeling and decided it was after Erich had jumped on the bomb, about the time he mentioned poetry. Though I couldn't be sure. Maybe the Maintainer had been Introverted even earlier, when I'd turned to look at the Ghostgirls. I wouldn't have known. Nuts!

Believe me, I could feel that hardened cement on every inch of me. I remembered Bruce's beautiful picture of a universe without Big Change and decided it was the worst idea going. I went on eating, though I wasn't so sure now it was a good idea to keep myself strong.

'Does the Maintainer have an Introversion telltale, Siddy?'

''Sdeath, chit, and you love me, speak lower. Of a sudden, I feel not well, as if I'd drunk a butt of Rhenish and slept inside it. Marry yes, blue. In short flashes, saith the manual. Why ask'st thou?'

'No reason. God, Siddy, what I'd give for a breath of Change Wind.'

'Thou can'st say that eftsoons,' he groaned. I must have looked pretty miserable myself, for he put his arm around my shoulder and whispered gruffly, 'Comfort thyself sweetling, that while we suffer thus sorely, we yet cannot die the the Change Death.'

'What's that?' I asked him.

I didn't want to bounce around like the others. I had a suspicion I'd carry it too far. So, to keep myself from going batty, I started to rework the business of who had done what to the Maintainer.

During the hunt there had been some pretty wild suggestions tossed around as to its disappearance or at least its Introversion: a feat of Snake science amounting to sorcery; the Spider high command bunkering the Places from above, perhaps in reaction to the loss of the Express Room, in such a hurry that they hadn't even time to transmit warnings; the hand of the Late Cosmicians, those mysterious hypothetical beings who are supposed to have successfully resisted the extension of the Change War into the future much beyond Sevensee's epoch – unless the Late Cosmicians are the ones fighting the Change War.

One thing these suggestions had steered very clear of was naming any one of us as a suspect, whether acting as Snake spy, Spider political police, agent of – who knows, after

Bruce? – a secret Change World Committee of Public Safety or Spider revolutionary underground, or strictly on our own. Just as no one had piped a word, since the Maintainer had been palmed, about the split between Erich's and Bruce's factions.

Good group thinking probably, to sink differences in the emergency, but that didn't apply to what I did with my own thoughts.

Who wanted to escape so bad they'd Introvert the Place, cutting off all possible contact and communication either way with the cosmos and running the very big risk of not getting back to the cosmos at all?

Leaving out what had happened since Bruce had arrived and stirred things up, Doc seemed to me to have the strongest motive. He knew that Sid couldn't keep covering up for him forever and that Spider punishments for derelictions of duty are not just the clink of a firing squad, as Erich had reminded us. But Doc had been flat on the floor in front of the bar from the time Bruce had jumped on top of it, though I certainly hadn't had my eye on him every second.

Beau? Beau had said he was bored with the Place at a time when what he said counted, so he'd hardly lock himself in it maybe forever, not to mention locking Bruce in with himself and the babe he had a yen for.

Sid loves reality, Changing or not, and at least everything in it, people especially, more than any man or woman I've every known – he's like a big-eyed baby who wants to grab every object and put it in his mouth – and it was hard to imagine him ever cutting himself off from the cosmos.

Maud, Kaby, Mark and the two ETs? None of them had any motive I knew of, though Sevensee's being from the very far future did tie in with that idea about Late Cosmicians, and there did seem to be something developing between the Cretan and the Roman that could make them want to be Introverted together.

'Stick to the facts, Greta,' I reminded myself with a private groan.

That left Erich, Bruce, Lili and myself.

Erich, I thought – now we're getting somewhere. The little commandant has the nervous system of a coyote and the courage of a crazy tomcat, and if he thought it would help him settle his battle with Bruce better to be locked in with him, he'd do it in a second.

But even before Erich had danced on the bomb, he'd been heckling Bruce from the crowd. Still, there would have been time between heckles for him to step quietly back from us, Introvert the Maintainer and . . . well, that was nine-tenths of the problem.

If I was the guilty party, I was nuts and that was best explanation of all. Gr-r-r!

Bruce's motives seemed so obvious, especially the mortal (or was it immortal?) danger he'd put himself in by inciting mutiny, that it seemed a shame he'd been in full view on the bar so long. Surely, if the Maintainer had been Introverted before he jumped on the bar, we'd all have noticed the flashing blue telltale. For that matter, I'd have noticed it when I looked back at the Ghostgirls – if it worked as Sid claimed, and he said he had never seen it in operation, just read in the manual – oh, 'sdeath!

But Bruce didn't need opportunity, as I'm sure all the males in the Place would have told me right off, because he had Lili to pull the job for him and she had as much opportunity as any of the rest of us. Myself, I have large reservations to this woman-is-putty-in-the-hands-of-the-man-she-loves-madly theory, but I had to admit there was something to be said for it in this case, and it had seemed quite natural to me when the rest of us had decided, by unspoken agreement, that neither Lili's nor Bruce's checks counted when we were hunting for the Maintainer.

That took care of all of us and left only the mysterious stranger, intruding somehow through a Door (how'd he get it without using our Maintainer?) or from an unimaginable hiding place or straight out of the Void itself. I know that last is impossible – nothing can step out of nothing – but if anything ever looked like it was specially built for something not at all nice to come looming out of, it's the Void – misty, foggily churning, slimy grey . . .

'Wait a second,' I told myself, 'and hang on to this, Greta. It should have smacked you in the face at the start.'

Whatever came out of the Void, or, more to the point, whoever slipped back from our crowd to the Maintainer, Bruce would have seen them. He was looking at the Maintainer past our heads the whole time, and whatever happened to it, he saw it.

Erich wouldn't have, even after he was on the bomb, because he'd been stagewise enough to face Bruce most of the time to build up his role as tribune of the people.

But Bruce would have – unless he got so caught up in what he was saying . . .

No, kid, a Demon is always an actor, no matter how much he believed in what he's saying, and there never was an actor yet who wouldn't instantly notice a member of the audience starting to walk out on his big scene.

So Bruce knew, which made him a better actor than I'd have been willing to grant, since it didn't look as if anyone else had thought of what had just occurred to me, or they'd have gone over and put it to him.

Not me, though – I don't work that way. Besides, I didn't feel up to it – Nervy Anna enfold me, I felt like pure hell.

'Maybe,' I told myself encouragingly, 'the Place is Hell,' but added, 'Be your age, Greta – be a real rootless, ruleless, ruthless twenty-nine.'

Eleven

The barrage roars and lifts. Then, clumsily bowed
With bombs and guns and shovels and battle gear,
Men jostle and climb to meet the bristling fire.
Lines of grey, muttering faces, masked with fear,
They leave their trenches, going over the top,
While time ticks blank and busy on their wrists.

—Sassoon

The Western Front, 1917

'Please don't Lili.'

'I shall, my love.'

'Sweetling, wake up! Hast the shakes?'

I opened my eyes a little and lied to Siddy with a smile, locked my hands together tight and watched Bruce and Lili quarrel nobly near the control divan and wished I had a great love to blur my misery and provide me with a passable substitute for Change Winds.

Lili won the argument, judging from the way she threw her head back and stepped away from Bruce's arms while giving him a proud, tender smile. He walked off a few steps; praise be, he didn't shrug his shoulders at us like an old husband, though his nerves were showing and he didn't seem to be standing Introversion well at all, as who of us were?

Lili rested a hand on the head of the control divan and pressed her lips together and looked around at us, mostly with her eyes. She'd wound a grey silk bandeau around her bangs. Her short grey silk dress without a waistline made her look, not so much like a flapper, though she looked like that all right, as like a little girl, except the neckline was scooped low enough to show she wasn't.

Her gaze hesitated and then stopped at me and I got a sunk feeling of what was coming, because women are always picking on me for an audience. Besides, Sid and I were the centrist party of two in our fresh-out-of-the-shell Place politics.

She took a deep breath and stuck out her chin and said in a voice that was even a little higher and Britisher than she usually uses, 'We girls have often cried, "Shut the Door!" But now the Door is jolly well shut for keeps!'

I knew I'd guessed right and I felt crawly with embarrassment, because I know about this love business of thinking you're the other person and trying to live their life – and grab their glory, though you don't know that – and carry their message for them, and how it can foul things up. Still, I couldn't help admitting what she said wasn't too bad a start – unpleasantly apt to be true, at any rate.

'My fiancé believes we may yet be able to open the Door. I do not. He thinks it is a bit premature to discuss the peculiar pickle in which we all find ourselves. I do not.'

There was a rasp of laughter from the bar. The militarists were reacting. Erich stepped out, looking very happy. 'So now we have to listen to women making speeches,' he called. 'What is this Place, anyhow? Sidney Lessingham's Saturday Evening Sewing Circle?'

Beau and Sevensee, who'd stopped their pacing halfway between the bar and the control divan, turned towards Erich, and Sevensee looked a little burlier, a little more like half a horse, than satyrs in mythology book illustrations. He stamped – medium hard, I'd say – and said, 'Ahh, go flya kite.' I'd found out he'd learned English from a Demon who'd been a longshoreman with syndicalist-anarchist sympathies. Erich shut up for a moment and stood there grinning, his hands on his hips.

Lili nodded to the satyr and cleared her throat, looking scared. But she didn't speak; I could see she was thinking and feeling something, and her face got ugly and haggard, as if she were in a Change Wind that hadn't reached me yet, and her mouth went into a snarl to fight tears, but some spurted out, and when she did speak her voice was an octave lower and it wasn't just London talking but New York too.

'I don't know how Resurrection felt to you people, because I'm new and I loathe asking questions, but to me it was pure torture and I wished only I'd had the courage to tell Suzaku, "I wish to remain a Zombie, if you don't mind. I'd rather the nightmares." But I accepted Resurrection because I've been taught to be polite and because there is a Demon in me I don't understand that always wishes to live, and I found that I still felt like a Zombie, although I could flit about, and that I still had the nightmares, except they'd grown a deal vivider.

'I was a young girl again, seventeen, and I suppose every woman wishes to be seventeen, but I wasn't seventeen inside my head – I was a woman who had died of Bright's disease in New York in 1929 and also, because a Big Change blew my lifeline into a new drift, a woman who had died of the same disease in Nazi-occupied London in 1955, but rather more slowly because, as you can fancy, the liquor was in far shorter supply. I had to live with both those sets of memories and the Change World didn't blot them out any more that I'm told it does those of any Demon, and it didn't even push them into the background as I'd hoped it would.

'When some Change Fellow would say to me, "Hello, beautiful, how about a smile?" or "That's a posh frock, kiddo," I'd be back at Bellevue looking down at my swollen figure and the light getting like spokes of ice, or in that dreadful gin-steeped Stepney bedroom with Phyllis coughing herself to death beside me, or at best, for a moment, a little girl in Glamorgan looking at the Roman road and wondering about the wonderful life that lay ahead.'

I looked at Erich, remembering he had a long nasty future back in the cosmos himself, and at any rate he wasn't smiling, and I thought maybe he's getting a little humility, knowing someone else has two of those futures, but I doubted it.

'Because, you see,' Lili kept forcing it out, 'all my three lives I'd been a girl who fell in love with a great young poet she'd never met, the voice of the new youth and all youth, and she'd told her first big lie to get in the Red Cross and across to France to be nearer him, and it was all danger and dark magics and a knight in armour, and she pictured how she'd find him wounded but not seriously, with a little bandage around his head, and she'd light a fag for him and smile lightly, never letting him guess what she felt, but only being her best self and watching to see if that made something happen to him . . .

'And then the Boche machine-guns cut him down at Passchendaele and there couldn't ever have been bandages big enough and the girl stayed seventeen inside and messed about and tried to be wicked, though she wasn't very good at that, and to drink, and she had a bit more talent there, though drinking yourself to death is not nearly as easy as it sounds, even with a kidney weakness to help. But she turned the trick.

'Then a cock crows. She wakes up with a tearing start from the grey dreams of death that fill her lifeline. It's cold daybreak. There's the smell of a French farm. She feels her ankles and they're not at all like huge rubber boots filled with water. They're not swollen the least bit. They're young legs.

'There's a little window and the tops of rows of trees that may be poplars when there's more light, and what there is shows cots like her own and heads under blankets, and hanging uniforms make large shadows and a girl is snoring. There's a very distant rumble and it moves the window a bit. Then she remembers they're Red Cross girls many, many kilometers from Passchendaele and that Bruce Marchant is going to die at dawn today.

'In a few more minutes, he's going over the top where there's a crop-headed machine-gunner in the sights and swinging the gun a bit. But she isn't going to die today. She's going to die in 1929 and 1955.

'And just as she's going mad, there's a creaking and out of the shadows tiptoes a Jap with a woman's hairdo and the whitest face and the blackest eyebrows. He's wearing a rose robe and a black sash which belts to his sides two samurai swords, but in his right hand he has a strange silver pistol. And he smiles at her as if they were brother and sister and lovers at the same time and he says, "*Voulez-vous vivre, mademoiselle?*" and she stares and he bobs his head and says, "Missy wish live, yes, no?" '

Sid's paw closed quietly around my shaking hands. It always gets me to hear about anyone's Resurrection, and although mine was crazier, it also had the Krauts in it. I hoped she wouldn't go through the rest of the formula and she didn't.

'Five minutes later, he's gone down a stairs more like a ladder to wait below and she's dressing in a rush. Her clothes resist a little, as if they were lightly gummed to the hook and the stained wall, and she hates to touch them. It's getting lighter and her cot looks as if someone were still sleeping there, although it's empty and she couldn't bring herself to put her hand on the place if her new life depended on it.

'She climbs down and her long skirt doesn't bother her because she knows how to swing it. Suzaku conducts her past a sentry who doesn't see them and a puffy-faced farmer in a smock coughing and spitting the night out of his throat. They cross the farmyard and it's filled with rose light and she sees the sun is up and she knows that Bruce Marchant has just bled to death.

'There's an empty open touring car chugging loudly, waiting for someone; it has huge muddy wheels with wooden spokes and a brass radiator that says "Simplex". But Suzaku leads her past it to a dunghill and bows apologetically and she steps through a Door.'

I heard Erich say to the others at the bar, 'How touching! Now shall I tell everyone about my operation?' But he didn't get much of a laugh.

'That's how Lilian Foster came into the Change World with its steel-engraved nightmares and its deadly pace and deadlier lassitudes. I was more alive than I ever had been before, but it was the kind of life a corpse might get from unending electrical shocks and I couldn't summon any purpose or hope and Bruce Marchant seemed farther away than ever.

'Then not six hours ago, a Soldier in a black uniform came through the Door and I thought, "It can't be, but it does look like his photographs," and then I thought I heard someone say the name Bruce, and then he shouted as if to all the world that he was Bruce Marchant, and I knew there was a Resurrection beyond Resurrection, a true resurrection. Oh, Bruce—'

She looked at him and he was crying and smiling and all the young beauty flooded back into her face, and I thought, 'It has to be Change Winds, but it can't be. Face it without slobbering, Greta – there's something that works bigger miracles than Change.'

And she went on, 'And then the Change Winds died when the Snakes vaporized the Maintainer or the Ghostgirls Introverted it and all three of them vanished so swiftly and silently that even Bruce didn't notice – those are the best explanations I can summon and I fancy one of them is true. At all events, the Change Winds died and my past and even my futures became something I could bear lightly, because I have someone to bear them with me, and because at last I have a true future stretching out ahead of me, an unknown future which I shall create by living. Oh, don't you see that all of us have it now, this big opportunity?'

'*Hussa* for Sidney's suffragettes and the W.C.T.U.!' Erich cheered. 'Beau, will you play us a medley of "Hearts and Flowers" and "Onward Christian Soldiers"? I'm deeply moved, Lili. Where do the rest of us queue up for the Great Love Affair of the Century?'

Twelve

Now is a bearable burden. What buckles the back is the added weight of the past's mistakes and the future's fears.

I had to learn to close the front door of tomorrow and the back door to yesterday and settle down to here and now.

—Anonymous

The Big Opportunity

Nobody laughed at Erich's screwball sarcasms and still I thought, 'Yes, perish his hysterical little grey head, but he's half right – Lili's got the big thing now and she wants to serve it up to the rest of us on a platter, only love doesn't cook and cut that way.'

Those weren't bad ideas she had about the Maintainer, though, especially the one about the Ghostgirls doing the Introverting – it would explain why there couldn't be Introversion drill, the manual stuff about blue flashes being window-dressing, and something disappearing without movement or transition is the sort of thing that might not catch the attention – and I guess they gave the others something to think about too, for there wasn't any follow-up to Erich's frantic sniping.

But I honestly didn't see where there was the big opportunity being stuck away in a grey sack in the Void and I began to wonder and I got the strangest feeling and I said to myself, 'Hang on to your hat, Greta. It's hope.'

'The dreadful thing about being a Demon is that you have all time to range through,' Lili was saying with a smile. 'You can never shut the back door to yesterday or the front door to tomorrow and simply live in the present. But now that's been done for us: the Door is shut, we need never again rehash the past or the future. The Spiders and Snakes can never find us, for who ever heard of a Place that was truly lost being rescued? And as those in the know have told me, Introversion is the end as far as those outside are concerned. So we're safe from the Spiders and Snakes, we need never be slaves or enemies again, and we have a Place in which to live our new lives, the Place prepared for us from the beginning.'

She paused. 'Surely you understand what I mean? Sidney and Beauregard and Dr Pyeshkov are the ones who explained it to me. The Place is a balanced aquarium, just like the cosmos. No one knows how many ages of Big Time it has been in use, without a bit of new material being brought in – only luxuries and people – and not a bit of waste cut off. No one knows how many more ages it may not sustain life. I never heard of Minor Maintainers wearing out. We have all the future, all the security, anyone can hope for. We have a place to live together.'

You know, she was dead right and I realized that all the time I'd had the conviction in the back of my mind that we were going to suffocate or something if we didn't get a Door open pretty quick. I should have known differently, if anybody should, because I'd once been in a Place without a Door for as long as a hundred sleeps during the foxhole stretch of the Change War and we'd had to start cycling our food and it had been okay.

And then, because it is also the way my mind works, I started to picture in a flash the consequences of our living together all by ourselves like Lili said.

I began to pair people off; I couldn't help it. Let's see, four women, six men, two ETs.

'Greta,' I said, 'you're going to be Miss Polly Andry for sure. We'll have a daily newspaper and folk-dancing classes, we'll shut the bar except evenings, Bruce'll keep a rhymed history of the Place.'

I even thought, though I knew this part was strictly silly,

about schools and children. I wondered what Siddy's would look like, or my little commandant's. 'Don't go near the Void, dears.' Of course that would be specially hard on the two ETs, but Sevensee at least wasn't so different and the genetics boys had made some wonderful advances and Maud ought to know about them and there were some amazing gadgets in Surgery when Doc sobered up. The patter of little hoofs . . .

'My fiancé spoke to you about carrying a peace message to the rest of the cosmos,' Lili added, 'and bringing an end to the Big Change, and healing all wounds that have been made in the Little Time.'

I looked at Bruce. His face was set and strained, as will happen to the best of men when a girl starts talking about her man's business, and I don't know why, but I said to myself, 'She's crucifying him, she's nailing him to his purpose as a woman will, even when there's not much point to it, as now.'

And Lili went on, 'It was a wonderful thought, but now we cannot carry or send any message and I believe it is too late in any event for a peace message to do any good. The cosmos is too ravelled by change, too far gone. It will dissolve, fade "leave not a rack behind". We're the survivors. The torch of existence has been put in our hands.

'We may already be all that's left in the cosmos, for have you thought that the Change Winds may have died at their source? We may never reach another cosmos, we may drift forever in the Void, but who of us has been Introverted before and who knows what we can or cannot do? We're a seed for a new future to grow from. Perhaps all doomed universes cast off seeds like this Place. It's a seed, it's an embryo, let it grow.'

She looked swiftly at Bruce and then at Sid and she quoted, '"Come, my friends, 'tis not too late to seek a newer world."'

I squeezed Sid's hand and I started to say something to him, but he didn't know I was there; he was listening to Lili quote Tennyson with his eyes entranced and his mouth open, as if he were imagining new things to put into it – oh, Siddy!

And then I saw the others were looking at her the same way. Ilhilihis was seeing finer feather forests than long-dead Luna's grow. The greenhouse child Maud ap-Ares Davies was stowing away on a starship bound for another galaxy, or thinking how different her life might have been, the children she might have had, if she'd stayed on the planets and out of the Change World. Even Erich looked as though he might be blitzing new universes, and Mark subduing them, for an eight-legged *Führer-imperator*. Beau was throbbing up a wider Mississippi in a bigger-than-life side-wheeler.

Even I – well, I wasn't dreaming of a Greater Chicago. 'Let's not go hog-wild on this sort of thing,' I told myself, but I did look up at the Void and I got a shiver because I imagined it drawing away and the whole Place starting to grow.

'I truly meant what I said about a seed,' Lili went on slowly. 'I know, as you all do, that there are no children in the Change World, that there cannot be, that we all become instantly sterile, that what they call a curse is lifted from us girls and we are no longer in bondage to the moon.'

She was right, all right – if there's one thing that's been proved a million times in the Change World, it's that.

'But we are no longer in the Change World,' Lili said softly, 'and its limitations should no longer apply to us, including that one. I feel deeply certain of it, but—' she looked around slowly – 'we are four women here and I thought one of us might have a surer indication.'

My eyes followed her around like anybody's would. In fact, everybody was looking around except for Maud, and she had the silliest look of surprise on her face and it stayed there, and then, very carefully, she got down from the bar stool with her knitting. She looked down at the half-finished pink bra with the long white needles stuck in it, and her eyes bugged bigger yet, as if she were expecting it to turn into a baby sweater right then and there. Then she walked across the Place to Lili and stood beside her. While she was walking, the look of surprise changed to a quiet smile. The only other thing she did was throw her shoulders back a little.

I was jealous of her for a second, but it was a double miracle for her, considering her age, and I couldn't grudge her that. And to tell the truth, I was a little frightened, too. Even with Dave, I'd been bothered about this business of having babies.

Yet I stood up with Siddy – I couldn't stop myself and I guess he couldn't either – and hand in hand we walked to the control divan. Beau and Sevensee were there with Bruce, of course, and then, so help me, those Soldiers to the death, Kaby and Mark, started over from the bar and I couldn't see anything in their eyes about the greater glory of Crete and Rome, but something, I think, about each other, and after a moment Illy slowly detached himself from the piano and followed, lightly trailing his tentacles on the floor.

I couldn't exactly see him hoping for little Illies in this company, unless it was true what the jokes said about Lunans but maybe he was being really disinterested and maybe he wasn't; maybe he was simply figuring that Illy ought to be on the side with the biggest battalions.

I heard dragging footsteps behind us and here came Doc from the Gallery, carrying in his folded arms an abstract sculpture as big as a newborn baby. It was an agglomeration of perfect shiny grey spheres the size of golfballs, shaping up to something like a large brain, but with holes showing through here and there. He held it out to us like an infant to be admired and worked his lips and tongue as if he were trying hard to say something, though not a word came out that you could understand, and I thought, 'Maxey Aleksevich may be speechless drunk and have all sorts of holes in his head, but he's got the right instincts, bless his soulful little Russian heart.'

We were all crowded around the control divan like a football team huddling. The Peace Packers, it came to me. Sevensee would be fullback or centre and Illy left end – what a receiver! The right number, too. Erich was alone at the bar, but now even he – 'Oh no, this can't be,' I thought – even he came towards us. Then I saw that his face was working the worst ever. He stopped halfway and managed to force a smile, but it was the worst, too. 'That's my little commandant,' I thought, 'no team spirit.'

'So now Lili and Bruce – yes, and *Grossmutterchen* Maud – have their little nest,' he said, and he wouldn't have had to push his voice very hard to get a screech. 'But what are the rest of us supposed to be – cowbirds?'

He crooked his neck and flapped his hands and croaked, 'Cuc-koo! Cuc-koo!' And I said to myself, 'I often thought you were crazy, boy, but now I know.'

'*Teufelsdreck!* – yes, Devil's dirt – but you all seem to be infected with this dream of children. Can't you see that the Change World is the natural and proper end of evolution? – a period of enjoyment and measuring, an ultimate working out of things, which women call destruction – "Help, I'm being raped!" "Oh, what are they doing to my children?" – but which men know as fulfilment.

'You're given good parts in *Götterdämmerung* and you go up to the author and tap him on the shoulder and say, "Excuse me, Herr Wagner, but this Twilight of the Gods is just a bit morbid. Why don't you write an opera for me about the little ones, the dear little blue-eyed curly-tops? A plot? Oh, boy meets girl and they settle down to breed, something like that."

'Devil's dirt doubled and damned! Have you thought what life will be without a Door to go out of to find freedom and adventure, to measure your courage and keenness? Do you want to grow long grey beards hobbling around this asteroid turned inside out? Putter around indoors to the end of your days, mooning about little baby cosmoses? – incidentally, with a live bomb for company. The cave, the womb, the little grey home in the nest – is that what you want? It'll grow? Oh, yes, like the city engulfing the wild wood, a proliferation of *Kinder, Kirche, Küche* – I should live so long!

'Women – how I hate their bright eyes as they look at me from the fireside, bent-shouldered, rocking, deeply happy to be old, and say, "He's getting weak, he's giving out, soon I'll have to put him to bed and do the simplest things for him." Your filthy Triple Goddess, Kaby, the birther, bride, and burier of man! Woman, the enfeebler, the fetterer, the crippler! Woman! – and the curly-headed little cancers she wants!'

He lurched towards us, pointing at Lili. 'I never knew one who didn't want to cripple a man if you gave her the chance. Cripple him, swaddle him, clip his wings, grind him to sausage to mould another man, hers, a doll man. You hid the Maintainer, you little smother-hen, so you could have your nest and your Brucie!'

He stopped, gasping and I expected someone to bop him one on the schnozzle, and I think he did, too. I turned to Bruce and he was looking, I don't know how, sorry, guilty, anxious, angry, shaken, inspired, all at once, and I wished people sometimes had simple suburban reactions like magazine stories.

Then Erich made the mistake, if it was one, of turning towards Bruce and slowly staggering towards him, pawing the air with his hands as if he were going to collapse into his arms, and saying 'Don't let them get you, Bruce. Don't let them tie you down. Don't let them clip you – your words or your deeds. You're a Soldier. Even when you talked about a peace message, you talked about doing some smashing of your own. No matter what you think and feel, Bruce, no matter how much lying you do and how much you hide, you're really not on their side.'

That did it.

It didn't come soon enough or, I think, in the right spirit to please me, but I will say it for Bruce that he didn't muck it up by tipping or softening his punch. He took one step forward and his shoulders spun and his fist connected sweet and clean.

As he did it, he said only one word, 'Loki!' and darn if that didn't switch me back to a campfire in the Indiana Dunes and my mother telling me out of the Elder Saga about the malicious sneering, all-spoiling Norse god and how, when the other gods came to trap him in his hideaway by the river, he was on the point of finishing knotting a mysterious net big enough, I had imagined, to snare the whole universe, and that if they'd come a minute later, he would have.

Erich was stretched out on the floor, his head hitched up, rubbing his jaw and glaring at Bruce. Mark, who was standing beside me, moved a little and I thought he was going to do something, maybe even clobber Bruce in the old spirit of you can't do that to my buddy, but he just shook his head and said, '*Omnia vincit amor.*' I nudged him and said, 'Meaning?' and he said, 'Love licks everything.'

I'd never have expected it from a Roman, but he was half right at any rate. Lili had her victory: marriage by laying out the woman-hating boy-friend who would be trying to get him to go out nights. At that moment, I think Bruce wanted Lili and a life with her more than he wanted to reform the Change World. Sure, us women have our little victories – until the legions come or the Little Corporal draws up his artillery or the Panzers roar down the road.

Erich scrambled to his feet and stood there in a half-slump, half-crouch, still rubbing his jaw and glaring at Bruce over his hand, but making no move to continue the fight, and I studied his face and said to myself, 'If he can get a gun, he's going to shoot himself, I know.'

Bruce started to say something and hesitated, like I would have in his shoes, and just then Doc got one of his unpredictable inspirations and went weaving out towards Erich, holding out the sculpture and making deaf-and-dumb noises like he had to us. Erich looked at him as if he were going to kill him, and then grabbed the sculpture and swung it up over his head and smashed it down on the floor, and for a wonder, it didn't shatter. It just skidded along in one piece and stopped inches from my feet.

That thing not breaking must have been the last straw for Erich. I swear I could see the red surge up through his eyes towards his brain. He swung around into the Stores sector and ran the few steps between him and the bronze bomb chest.

Everything got slow motion for me, though I didn't do any moving. Almost every man started out after Erich. Bruce didn't, though, and Siddy turned back after the first surge forward, while Illy squunched down for a leap, and it was between Sevensee's hairy shanks and Beau's scissoring white pants that I saw that under-the-microscope circle of death's heads and watched Erich's finger go down on them in the order Kaby had given: one, three, five, six, two, four, seven. I was able to pray seven distinct times that he'd make a mistake.

He straightened up. Illy landed by the box like a huge silver spider and his tentacles whipped futilely across its top. The others surged to a frightened halt around them.

Erich's chest was heaving, but his voice was cool and collected as he said, 'You mentioned something about our having a future, Miss Foster. Now you can make that more specific. Unless we get back to the cosmos and dump this box, or find a Spider A-tech, or manage to call headquarters for guidance on disarming the bomb, we have a future exactly thirty minutes long.'

Thirteen

But whence he was, or of what whombe ybore,
Of beasts, or of the earth, I have not read;
But certes was with milke of wolves and tygres fed.
                                        —Spencer

The Tiger is Loose

I guess when they really push the button or throw the switch
or spring the trap or focus the beam or what have you, you
don't faint or go crazy or anything else convenient. I didn't.
Everything, everybody, every move that was made, every
word that was spoken, was painfully real to me, like a hand
twisting and squeezing things deep inside me, and I saw every
last detail spotlighted and magnified like I had the seven
skulls.

Erich was standing beyond the bomb chest; little smiles
were ruffling his lips. I'd never seen him look so sharp. Illy
was beside him, but not on his side, you understand. Mark,
Sevensee and Beau were around the chest to the nearer side.
Beau had dropped to a knee and was scanning the chest
minutely, terror-under-control making him bend his head a
little closer than he needed to for clear vision, but with his
hands locked together behind his back, I guess to restrain the
impulse to push any and everything that looked like a
disarming button.

Doc was sprawled face down on the nearest couch, out like
a light, I suppose.

Us four girls were still by the control divan. With Kaby,
that surprised me, because she didn't look scared or frozen,
but almost as intensely alive as Erich.

Sid had turned his back, as I'd said, and had one hand
stretched out towards but not touching the Minor Maintainer, and a look on his beardy face as if he were calling down

death and destruction on every boozy rogue who had ever
gone up from King's Lynn to Cambridge and London, and I
realized why: if he'd thought of the Minor Maintainer a
second sooner, he could have pinned Erich down with heavy
gravity before he could touch the buttons.

Bruce was resting one hand on the head of the control divan
and was looking towards the group around the chest, towards
Erich, I think, as if Erich had done something wonderful for
him, though I can't imagine myself being tickled at being
included in anybody's suicide surprise party. Bruce looked
altogether too dreamy, Brahma blast him, for someone who
must have the same steel-spiked thought in his head that I
know darn well the rest of us had: that in twenty-nine minutes
or so, the Place would be a sun in a bag.

Erich was the first to get down to business, as I'd have laid any
odds he would be. He had the jump on us and he wasn't going
to lose it.

'Well, when are you going to start getting Lili to tell us
where she hid the Maintainer? It has to be her – she was too
certain it was gone forever when she talked. And Bruce must
have seen from the bar who took the Maintainer, and who
would he cover up for but his girl?'

There he was plagiarizing my ideas, but I guess I was
willing to sign them over to him in full if he got the right pail
of water for that time-bomb.

He glanced at his wrist. 'According to my Caller, you have
twenty-nine and a half minutes, including the time it will take
to get a Door or contact headquarters. When are you going to
get busy on the girl?'

Bruce laughed a little – deprecatingly, so help me – and
started towards him. 'Look here, old man,' he said, 'there's no
need to trouble Lili, or to fuss with headquarters, even if you
could. Really not at all. Not to mention that your surmises are

quite unfounded, old chap, and I'm a bit surprised at your advancing them. But that's quite all right because, as it happens, I'm an atomics technician and I even worked on that very bomb. To disarm it, you just have to fiddle a bit with some of the ankhs, those hoopy little crosses. Here, let me—'

Allah il allah, but it must have struck everybody as it did me as being just too incredible an assertion, too bloody British a barefaced bluff, for Erich didn't have to say a word; Mark and Sevensee grabbed Bruce by the arms, one on each side, as he stooped towards the bronze chest, and they weren't gentle about it. Then Erich spoke.

'Oh, no, Bruce. Very sporting of you to try to cover up for your girl-friend, but we aren't going to let ourselves be blown to stripped atoms twenty-eight minutes too soon while you monkey with the buttons, the very thing Benson-Carter warned against, and pray for a guesswork miracle. It's too thin, Bruce, when you come from 1917 and haven't been on the Big Time for a hundred sleeps and were calling for an A-Tech yourself a few hours ago. Much too thin. Bruce, something is going to happen that I'm afraid you won't like, but you're going to have to put up with it. That is, unless Miss Foster decided to be co-operative.'

'I say, you fellows, let me go,' Bruce demanded, struggling experimentally. 'I know it's a bit thick to swallow and I did give you the wrong impression calling for an A-Tech, but I just wanted to capture your attention then; I didn't want to have to work on the bomb. Really, Erich, would they have ordered Benson-Carter to pick us up unless one of us were an A-Tech? They'd be sure to include one in the bally operation.'

'When they're using patchwork tactics?' Erich grinningly quoted back at him.

Kaby spoke up beside me and said, 'Benson-Carter was a magician of matter and he was going on the operation disguised as an old woman. We have the cloak and hood with the other garments,' and I wondered how this cold fish of a she-officer could be the same girl who was giving Mark slurpy looks not ten minutes ago.

'Well?' Erich asked, glancing at his Caller and then swinging his eyes around at us as if there must be some of the old *Wehrmacht* iron somewhere. We all found ourselves looking at Lili and she was looking so sharp herself, so ready to jump and so at bay, that it was all *I* needed, at any rate, to make Erich's theory about the Maintainer a rock-bottom certainty.

Bruce must have realized the way our minds were working, for he started to struggle in earnest and at the same time called, 'For God's sake, don't do anything to Lili! Let me loose, you idiots! Everything's true I told you – I can save you from that bomb. Sevensee, you took my side against the Spiders: you've nothing to lose. Sid, you're an Englishman. Beau, you're a gentleman and you love her, too – for God's sake, stop them!'

Beau glanced up over his shoulder at Bruce and the others surging around close to his ankles and he had on his poker face. Sid I could tell was once more going through the purgatory of decision. Beau reached his own decision first and I'll say it for him that he acted on it fast and intelligently. Right from his kneeling position and before he'd even turned his head quite back, he jumped Erich.

But other things in this cosmos besides Man can pick sides and act fast. Illy landed on Beau midway and whipped his tentacles around him tight and they went wobbling around like a drunken white and silver barber pole. Beau got his hands each around a tentacle, and at the same time his face began to get purple, and I winced at what they were both going through.

Maybe Sevensee had a hoof in Sid's purgatory, because

Bruce shook loose from the satyr and tried to knock out Mark, but the Roman twisted his arm and kept him from getting in a good punch.

Erich didn't make a move to mix into either fight, which is my little commandant all over. Using his fists on anybody but me is beneath him.

Then Sid made his choice but there was no way for me to tell what it was, for, as he reached for the Minor Maintainer, Kaby contemptuously snatched it away from his hands and gave him a knee in the belly that doubled me up in sympathy and sent him sprawling on his knees towards the fighters. On the return, Kaby gave Lili, who'd started to grab too, an effortless backhand smash that set her down on the divan.

Erich's face lit up like an electric sign and he kept his eyes fixed on Kaby.

She crouched a little, carrying her weight on the balls of her feet and firmly cradling the Minor Maintainer in her left arm, like a basketball captain planning an offensive. Then she waved her free hand decisively to the right. I didn't get it, but Erich did and Mark too, for Erich jumped for the Refresher sector and Mark let go of Bruce and followed him, ducking around Sevensee's arms, who was coming back into the fight on which side I don't know. Illy unwhipped for Beau and copied Erich and Mark with one big spring.

Then Kaby twisted a dial as far as it would go and Bruce, Beau, Sevensee and poor Siddy were slammed down and pinned to the floor by about eight gravities.

It should have been lighter near us – I hoped it was, but you couldn't tell from watching Siddy; he went flat on his face, spread-eagled, one hand stretched towards me so close, I could have touched it (but not let go!), and his mouth was open against the floor and he was gasping through a corner of it and I could see his spine trying to sink through his belly.

Bruce just managed to get his head and one shoulder up a bit, and they all made me think of a Doré illustration of the *Inferno* where the cream of the damned are frozen up to their necks in ice in the innermost circle of Hell.

The gravity didn't catch me, although I could feel it in my left arm. I was mostly in the Refresher sector, but I dropped down flat, too, partly out of a crazy compassion I have, but mostly because I didn't want to take a chance of having Kaby knock me down.

Erich, Mark and Illy had got clear and they headed towards us. Maud picked the moment to make her play; she hadn't much choice of times, if she wanted to make one. The Old Girl was looking it for once, but I guess the thought of her miracle must have survived alongside the fear of the sacked sun and must have meant a lot to her, for she launched out fast, all set to straight-arm Kaby into the heavy gravity and grab the Minor Maintainer with the other hand.

Fourteen

Like diamonds, we are cut with our own dust.
—Webster

'Now Will You Talk?'

Cretans have eyes under their back hair, or let's face it, Entertainers aren't Soldiers. Kaby waved to one side and flicked a helpful hand and poor old Maud went where she'd been going to send Kaby. It sickened me to see the gravity take hold and yank her down.

I could have jumped up and made it four in a row for Kaby, but I'm not a bit brave when things like my life are at stake.

Lili was starting to get up, acting a little dazed. Kaby gently pushed her down again and quietly said, 'Where is it?' and then hauled off and slapped her across the face. What got me was the matter-of-fact way Kaby did it. I can understand somebody getting mad and socking someone, or even deliberately working up a rage so as to be able to do something nasty, but this cold-blooded way turns my stomach.

Lili looked as if half her face were about to start bleeding, but she didn't look dazed any more and her jaw set. Kaby grabbed Lili's pearl necklace and twisted it around her neck and it broke and the pearls went bouncing around like ping-pong balls, so Kaby yanked down Lili's grey silk bandeau until it was around the neck and tightened that. Lili started to choke through her tight-pressed lips. Erich, Mark and Illy had come up and crowded around, but they seemed content with the job Kaby was doing.

'Listen, slut,' she said, 'we have no time. You have a healing room in this place. I can work the things.'

'Here it comes,' I thought, wishing I could faint. On top of everything, on top of death even, they had to drag in the nightmare personally stylized for me, the horror with my name on it. I wasn't going to be allowed to blow up peacefully. They weren't satisfied with an A-bomb. They had to write my private hell into the script.

'There is a thing called an Invertor,' Kaby said exactly as I'd known she would, but as I didn't really hear it just then – a mental split I'll explain in a moment. 'It opens you up so they can cure your insides without cutting your skin or making you bleed anywhere. It turns the big parts of you inside out, but not the blood tubes. All your skin – your eyes, ears, nose, toes, all of it – becoming the lining of a little hole that's half-filled with your hair.

'Meantime, your insides are exposed for whatever the healer wants to do to them. You live for a while on the air inside the hole. First the healer gives you an air that makes you sleep, or you go mad in about fifty heartbeats. We'll see what ten heartbeats do to you without the sleepy air. Now will you talk?'

I hadn't been listening to her, though, not the real me, or I'd have gone made without getting the treatment. I once heard Doc say your liver is more mysterious and farther away from you that the stars, because although you live with your liver all your life, you never see it or learn to point to it instinctively, and the thought of someone messing around with that intimate yet unknown part of you is just too awful.

I knew I had to do something quick. Hell, at the first hint of Inversion, before Kaby had even named it, Illy winced so that his tentacles were all drawn up like fat feather-sausages. Erich had looked at him questioningly, but that lousy Looney had unendeared himself to me by squeaking, 'Don't mind me, I'm just sensitive. Get on with the girl. Make her tell.'

Yes, I knew I had to do something, and here on the floor that meant thinking hard and in high gear about something else. The screwball sculpture Erich had tried to smash was a foot from my nose and I saw a faint trail of white stuff where it had skidded. I reached out and touched the trail; it was finely gritty, like powdered glass. I tipped up the sculpture and the part on which it had skidded wasn't marred at all, not even dulled; the grey spheres were as glisteningly bright as ever. So I knew the trail was diamond dust rubbed off the diamonds in the floor by something even harder.

That told me the sculpture was something special and maybe Doc had had a real idea in his pickled brain when he'd been pushing the thing at all of us and trying to tell us something. He hadn't managed to say anything then, but he had earlier when he'd been going to tell us what to do about the bomb, and maybe there was a connection.

I twisted my memory hard and let it spring back and I got 'Inversh . . . bosh . . .' Bosh, indeed! Bosh and inverse bosh to all boozers, Russki or otherwise.

So I quick tried the memory trick again and this time I got 'glovsh' and then I grasped and almost sneezed on the diamond dust as I watched the pieces fit themselves together in my mind like a speeded-up movie reel.

It all hung on that black right-hand hussar's glove Lili had produced for Bruce. Only she couldn't have found it in Stores, because we'd searched every fractional pigeon-hole later on and there hadn't been any gloves there, not even the left-hand mate there would have been. Also, Bruce had had two left-hand gloves to start with, and we had been through the whole Place with a fine-tooth comb, and there had been only two black gloves on the floor where Bruce had kicked them off the bar – those two and those two only, the left-hand glove he'd brought from outside and the right-hand glove Lili had produced for him.

So a left-hand glove had disappeared – the last I'd seen of it, Lili had been putting it on her tray – and a right-hand glove had appeared. Which could only add up to one thing: Lili had turned the left-hand glove into an identical right. She couldn't have done it by turning it inside out the ordinary way, because the lining was different.

But as I knew only too sickeningly well, there was an extraordinary way to turn things inside out, things like human beings. You merely had to put them on the Invertor in Surgery and flick the switch for full Inversion.

Or you could flick it for partial Inversion and turn something into a perfect three-dimensional mirror image of itself, just what a right-hand glove is of a left. Rotation through the fourth dimension, the science boys call it; I've heard of it being used in surgery on the highly asymmetric Martians, and even to give a socially impeccable right hand to a man who'd lost one, by turning an amputated right arm into an amputated left.

Ordinarily, nothing but live things are ever Inverted in Surgery and you wouldn't think of doing it to an inanimate object, especially in a Place where the Doc's a drunk and the Surgery hasn't been used for hundreds of sleeps.

But when you've just fallen in love, you think of wonderful crazy things to do for people. Drunk with love, Lili had taken Bruce's extra left-hand glove into Surgery, partially Inverted it, and got a right-hand glove to give him.

What Doc had been trying to say with his 'Inversh . . . bosh . . .' was 'Invert the box', meaning we should put the bronze chest through full Inversion to get at the bomb inside to disarm it. Doc too had got the idea from Lili's trick with the glove. What an inside-out tactical atomic bomb would look like, I could not imagine and did not particularly care to see. I might have to, though, I realized.

But the fast-motion film was still running in my head. Later on, Lili had decided like I had that her lover was going to lose out in his plea for mutiny unless she could give him a

really captive audience – and maybe, even then, she had been
figuring on creating the nest for Bruce's chicks and . . . all
those other things we'd believed in for a while. So she'd taken
the Major Maintainer and remembered the glove, and not
many seconds later, she had set down on a shelf of the Art
Gallery an object that no one would think of questioning –
except someone who knew the Gallery by heart.

I looked at the abstract sculpture a foot from my nose, at
the clustered grey spheres the size of golfballs. I had known
that the inside of the Maintainer was made up of vastly tough,
vastly hard giant molecules, but I hadn't realized they were
quite *that* big.

I said to myself, 'Greta, this is going to give you a major
psychosis, but you're the one who has to do it, because no one
is going to listen to your deductions when they're all
practically on negative time already.'

I got up as quietly as if I were getting out of a bed I
shouldn't have been in – there are some things Entertainers
are good at – and Kaby was just saying 'you go mad in about
fifty heartbeats'. Everybody on their feet was looking at Lili.
Sid seemed to have moved, but I had no time for him except
to hope he hadn't done anything that might attract attention
to me.

I stepped out of my shoes and walked rapidly to Surgery –
there's one good thing about this hardest floor anywhere, it
doesn't creak. I walked through the Surgery screen that is like
a wall of opaque, odourless cigarette smoke and I
concentrated on remembering my snafued nurse's training,
and before I had time to panic, I had the sculpture positioned
on the gleaming table of the Invertor.

I froze for a moment when I reached for the Inversion
switch, thinking of the other and trying to remember what it
had been that bothered me so much about an inside-out brain
being bigger and not having eyes, but then I either thumbed

my nose at my nightmare or kissed my sanity good-bye, I don't know which, and twisted the switch all the way over, and there was the Major Maintainer winking blue about three times a second as nice as you could want it.

It must have been working sweet and steady as ever, all the time it was Inverted, except that, being inside out, it had hocused the direction finders.

Fifteen

black legged spiders with red
hearts of hell
                            —Marquis

Lord Spider

'Jesus!' I turned and Sid's face was sticking through the screen like a tinted bas-relief hanging on a grey wall and I got the impression he had peered unexpectedly through a slit in an arras into Queen Elizabeth's bedroom.

He didn't have any time to linger on the sensation even if he'd wanted to, for an elbow with a copper band thrust through the screen and dug his ribs and Kaby marched Lili in by the neck. Erich, Mark and Illy were right behind. They caught the blue flashes and stopped dead, staring at the long-lost. Erich spared me one look which seemed to say, so you did it, not that it matters. Then he stepped forward and picked it up and held it solidly to his left side in the double right-angle made by fingers, forearm and chest, and reached for the Introversion switch with a look on his face as if he were opening a fifth of whisky.

The blue light died and Change Winds hit me like a stiff drink that had been a long, long time in coming, like a hot trumpet note out of nowhere.

I felt the changing pasts blowing through me, and the uncertainties whistling past, and ice-stiff reality softening with all its duties and necessities, and the little memories shredding away and dancing off like autumn leaves, leaving maybe not even ghosts behind, and all the crazy moods like Mardi Gras dancers pouring down an evening street, and something inside me had the nerve to say it didn't care whether Greta Forzane's death was riding in those Winds because they felt so good.

I could tell it was hitting the others the same way. Even battered, tight-lipped Lili seemed to be saying, you're making me drink the stuff and I hate you for it, but I do love it. I guess we'd all had the worry that even finding and Extroverting the Maintainer wouldn't put us back in touch with the cosmos and give us those Winds we hate and love.

The thing that cut through to us as we stood there glowing was not the thought of the bomb, though that would have come in a few seconds more, but Sid's voice. He was still standing in the screen, except that now his face was out the other side and we could just see parts of his grey-doubleted back, but, of course, his 'Jesu!' came through the screen as if it weren't there.

At first I couldn't figure out who he could be talking to, but I swear I never heard his voice so courtly obsequious before, so strong and yet so filled with awe and an undernote of, yes, sheer terror.

'Lord, I am filled from top to toe with confusion that you should so honour my poor Place,' he said. 'Poor say I and mine, when I mean that I have ever busked it faithfully for you, not dreaming that you would ever condescend . . . yet knowing that your eye was certes ever upon me . . . though I am but as a poor pinch of dust adrift between the suns . . . I base myself. Prithee, how may I serve thee, sir? I know not e'en how most suitably to address thee, Lord . . . King . . . Emperor Spider!'

I felt like I was getting very small, but not a bit less visible, worse luck, and even with the Change Winds inside me to give me courage, I thought this was really too much, coming on top of everything else; it was simply unfair.

At the same time, I realized it was to be expected that the big bosses would have been watching us with their unblinking beady black eyes ever since we had Introverted waiting to pounce if we should ever come out of it. I tried to picture what was on the other side of the screen and I didn't like the assignment.

But in spite of being petrified, I had a hard time not giggling, like the zany at graduation exercises, at the way the other ones in Surgery were taking it.

I mean the Soldiers. They each stiffened up like they had the old ramrod inside them, and their faces got that important look, and they glanced at each other and the floor without lowering their heads, as if they were measuring the distance between their feet and mentally chalking alternate sets of footprints to step into. The way Erich and Kaby held the Major and Minor Maintainers became formal; the way they checked their Callers and nodded reassuringly was positively esoteric. Even Illy somehow managed to look as if he were on parade.

Then from beyond the screen came what was, under the circumstances, the worst noise I've ever heard, a seemingly wordless, distant-sounding howling and wailing, with a note of menace that made me shake, although it also had a nasty familiarity about it I couldn't place. Sid's voice broke into it, loud, fast and frightened.

'Your pardon, Lord, I did not think . . . certes, the gravity . . . I'll attend to it on the instant.' He whipped a hand and half a head back through the screen, but without looking back and snapped his fingers, and before I could blink, Kaby had put the Minor Maintainer in his hand.

Sid went completely out of sight then and the howling stopped, and I thought that if that was the way a Lord Spider expressed his annoyance at being subjected to incorrect gravity, I hoped the bosses wouldn't start any conversations with me.

Erich pursed his lips and threw the other Soldiers a nod and the four of them marched through the screen as if they'd

drilled a lifetime for this moment. I had the wild idea that
Erich might give me his arm, but he strode past me as if I
were . . . an Entertainer.

I hesitated a moment then, but I had to see what was
happening outside, even if I got eaten up for it. Besides, I had
a bit of the thought that if these formalities went on much
longer, even a Lord Spider was going to discover just how
immune he was to confined atomic blast.

I walked through the screen with Lili beside me.

The Soldiers had stopped a few feet in front of it. I looked
around ahead for whatever it was going to turn out to be,
prepared to drop a curtsy or whatever else, bar nothing, that
seemed expected of me.

I had a hard time spotting the beast. Some of the others
seemed to be having trouble too. I saw Doc weaving around
foolishly but the control divan, and Bruce and Beau and
Sevensee and Maud on their feet beyond it, and I wondered
whether we were dealing with an invisible monster; ought to
be easy enough for the bosses to turn a simple trick like
invisibility.

Then I looked sharply left where everyone else, even
glassy-eyed Doc, was coming to look, into the Door sector,
only there wasn't any monster there or even a Door, but just
Siddy holding a Minor Maintainer and grinning like when he
is threatening to tickle me, only fiendishly.

'Not a move, masters,' he cried his eyes dancing, 'or I'll pin
the pack of you down, marry and amen I will. It is my firm
purpose to see the Place blasted before I let this instrument
out of my hands again.'

My first thought was, ''Sblood but Siddy is a real actor! I
don't care if he didn't study under anyone later than Burbage,
that just proves how Burbage is.'

Sid had convinced us not only that the real Spiders had
arrived, but earlier that the gravity in the edge of Stores had

been a lot heavier than it actually was. He completely fooled all those Soldiers, including my swelled-headed victorious little commandant, and I kind of filed away the timing of that business of reaching out the hand and snapping the fingers without looking, it was so good.

'Beauregard!' Sid called. 'Get to the Major Maintainer and call headquarters. But don't come through Door, marry go by Refresher. I'll not trust a single Demon of you in this sector with me until much more has been shown and settled.'

'Siddy, you're wonderful,' I said, starting towards him. 'As soon as I got the Maintainer unsnarled and looked around and saw your sweet old face—'

'Back, tricksy trull! Not the breadth of one scarlet toenail nearer me, you Queen of Sleights and High Priestess of Deception!' he bellowed. 'You least of all do I trust. Why you hid the Maintainer, I know not, 'faith, but later you'll discover the truth to me or I'll have your gizzard.'

I could see there was going to have to be a little explaining.

Doc, touched off, I guess, by Sid waving his hand at me, threw back his head and let off one of those shuddery Siberian wolf-howls he does so blamed well, Sid waved towards him sharply and he shut up, beaming toothily, but at least I knew who was responsible for the Spider wail of displeasure that Sid had either called for or more likely got as a gift of the gods and used it in his act.

Beau came circling around fast and Erich shoved the Major Maintainer into his hands without making any fuss. The four Soldiers were looking pretty glum after losing their grand review.

Beau dumped some junk off one of the Art Gallery's sturdy taborets and set the Major Maintainer on it carefully but fast, and quickly knelt in front of it and whipped on some earphones and started to tune. The way he did it snatched away from me my inward glory at my big Inversion brainwave so fast, I might never have had it, and there was nothing in my mind again but the bronze bomb chest.

I wondered if I should suggest Inverting the thing, but I said to myself, 'Uh-huh, Greta, you got now diploma to show them and there probably isn't time to try two things, anyway.'

Then Erich for once did something I wanted him to, though I didn't care for its effect on my nerves, by looking at his Caller and saying quietly, 'Nine minutes to go, if Place time and cosmic time are synching.'

Beau was steady as a rock and working adjustments so that I couldn't even see his fingers move.

Then, at the other end of the Place, Bruce took a few steps towards us. Sevensee and Maud followed a bit behind him. I remembered Bruce was another of our nuts with a private programme for blowing up the place.

'Sidney,' he called, and then, when he'd got Sid's attention, 'Remember, Sidney, you and I both came down to London from Peterhouse.'

I didn't get it. Then Bruce looked towards Erich with a devil-may-care challenge and towards Lili as if he were asking her forgiveness for something. I couldn't read her expression; the bruises were blue on her throat and her cheek was puffy.

Then Bruce once more shot Erich that look of challenge and he spun and grabbed Sevensee by a wrist and stuck out a foot – even half-horses aren't too sharp about infighting, I guess, and the satyr had every right to feel at least as confused as I felt – and sent him stumbling into Maud, and the two of them tumbled to the floor in a jumble of hairy legs and pearl-grey frock. Bruce raced to the bomb chest.

Most of us yelled, 'Stop him, Sid, pin him down,' or something like that – I know I did because I was suddenly sure that he'd been asking Lili's pardon for blowing the two of them up – and all the rest of us too, the love-blinded stinker.

Sid had been watching him all the time and now he lifted

his hand to the Minor Maintainer, but then he didn't touch any of the dials, just watched and waited, and I thought, 'Shaitan shave us! Does Siddy want in on death, too? Ain't he satisfied with all he knows about life?'

Bruce had knelt and was twisting some things on the front of the chest, and it was all as bright as if he were under a bank of Klieg lights, and I was telling myself I wouldn't know anything when the fireball fired, and not believing it, and Sevensee and Maud got unscrambled and were starting for Bruce, and the rest of us were yelling at Sid, except that Erich was just looking at Bruce very happily, and Sid was still not doing anything, and it was unbearable except just then I felt the little arteries start to burst in my brain like a string of firecrackers and the old aorta pop, and for good measure, a couple of valves come unhinged in my ticker, and I was thinking, 'Well, now I know what it's like to die of heart failure and high blood pressure,' and having a last quiet smile at having cheated the bomb, when Bruce jumped up and back from the chest.

'That does it!' he announced cheerily. 'She's as safe as the Bank of England.'

Sevensee and Maud stopped themselves just short of knocking him down and I said to myself, 'Hey, let's get a move on! I thought heart attacks were fast.'

Before anyone else could speak, Beau did. He had turned around from the Major Maintainer and pulled aside one of the earphones.

'I got headquarters,' he said crisply. 'They told me how to disarm the bomb – I merely said I thought we ought to know. What did you do, sir?' he called to Bruce.

'There's a row of four ankhs just below the lock. The first to your left you give a quarter turn to the right, the second a quarter turn to the left, same for the fourth, and you don't touch the third.'

'That is it, sir,' Beau confirmed.

The long silence was too much for me; I guess I must have the shortest span for unspoken relief going. I drew some nourishment out of my restored arteries into my brain cells and yelled, 'Siddy, I know I'm a tricksy trull and the High Vixen of all Foxes, but what the Hell is Peterhouse?'

'The oldest college at Cambridge,' he told me rather coolly.

Sixteen

'Familiar with infinite universe sheafs and open-ended postulate systems? – the notion that everything is possible – and I mean everything – and everything has happened. *Everything.*'

—Heinlein

The Possibility-Binders

An hour later, I was nursing a weak highball and a black eye in the sleepy-time darkness on the couch farthest from the piano, half watching the highlighted party going on around it and the bar, while the Place waited for rendezvous with Egypt and the Battle of Alexandria.

Sid had swept all our outstanding problems into one big bundle and, since his hand held the joker of the Minor Maintainer, he had settled them all as high-handedly as if they'd been those of a bunch of schoolkids.

It amounted to this:

We'd been Introverted when most of the damning things had happened, so presumably only we knew about them, and we were all in so deep one way or another that we'd all have to keep quiet to protect our delicate complexions.

Well, Erich's triggering the bomb did balance rather neatly Bruce's incitement to mutiny, and there was Doc's drinking, while everybody who had declared for the peace message had something to hide. Mark and Kaby I felt inclined to trust anywhere, Maud for sure, and Erich in this particular matter, damn him. Illy I didn't feel at all easy about, but I told myself there always has to be a fly in the ointment – a darn big one this time, and furry.

Sid didn't mention his own dirty linen, but he knew we knew he'd flopped badly as boss of the Place and only recouped himself by that last-minute flimflam.

Remembering Sid's trick made me think for a moment about the real Spiders. Just before I snuck out of Surgery, I'd had a vivid picture of what they must look like, but now I couldn't get it again. It depressed me, not being able to remember – oh, I probably just imagined I'd had a picture, like a hophead on a secret-of-the-universe kick. Me ever find out anything about the Spiders? – except for nervous notions like I'd had during the recent fracas? – what a laugh!

The funniest thing (ha-ha!) was that I had ended up the least-trusted person. Sid wouldn't give me time to explain how I'd deduced what had happened to the Maintainer, and even when Lili spoke up and admitted hiding it, she acted so bored I don't think everybody believed her – although she did spill the realistic detail that she hadn't used partial Inversion on the glove; she'd just turned it inside out to make it a right and then done a full Inversion to get the lining back inside.

I tried to get Doc to confirm that he'd reasoned the thing out the same way I had, but he said he had been blacked out the whole time, except during the first part of the hunt, and he didn't remember having any bright ideas at all. Right now, he was having Maud explain to him twice, in detail, everything that had happened. I decided that it was going to take a little more work before my reputation as a great detective was established.

I looked over the edge of the couch and just made out in the gloom one of Bruce's black gloves. It must have been kicked there. I fished it up. It was the right-hand one. My big clue, and was I sick of it! Got mittens, God forbid! I slung it away and, like a lurking octopus, Illy shot up a tentacle from the next couch, where I hadn't known he was resting, and snatched the glove like it was a morsel of underwater garbage. These ETs can seem pretty shuddery non-human at times.

I thought of what a cold-blooded, skin-saving louse Illy had been, and about Sid and his easy suspicions, and Erich and my black eye, and how, as usual, I'd got left alone in the end. My men!

Bruce had explained about being an A-tech. Like a lot of us, he'd had several widely different jobs during his first weeks in the Change World and one of them had been as secretary to a group of the minor atomics boys from the Manhattan-Project-Earth-Satellite days. I gathered he'd also absorbed some of his bothersome ideas from them. I hadn't quite decided yet what species of heroic heel he belonged to, but he was thick with Mark and Erich again. Everybody's Men!

Sid didn't have to argue with anybody; all the wild compulsions and mighty resolves were dead now, anyway until they'd had a good long rest. I sure could use one myself, I knew.

The party at the piano was getting wilder. Lili had been dancing the black bottom on top of it and now she jumped down into Sid's and Sevensee's arms, taking a long time about it. She'd been drinking a lot and her little grey dress looked about as innocent on her as diapers would on Nell Gwyn. She continued her dance, distributing her marks of favour equally between Sid, Erich and the satyr. Beau didn't mind a bit, but serenely pounded out 'Tonight's the Night' – which she'd practically shouted to him not two minutes ago.

I was glad to be out of the party. Who can compete with a highly experienced, utterly disillusioned seventeen-year-old really throwing herself away for the first time?

Something touched my hand. Illy had stretched a tentacle into a furry wire to return me the black glove, although he ought to have known I didn't want it. I pushed it away, privately calling Illy a washed-out moronic tarantula, and right away I felt a little guilty. What right had I to be critical of Illy? Would my own character have shown to advantage if I'd been locked in with eleven octopoids a billion years away?

For that matter, where did I get off being critical of anyone?

Still, I was glad to be out of the party, though I kept on watching it. Bruce was drinking alone at the bar. Once Sid had gone over to him and they'd had one together and I'd heard Bruce reciting from Rupert Brooke those deliberately corny lines, 'For England's the one land, I know, Where men with Splendid Hearts may go; and Cambridgeshire, of all England, The Shire for Men who Understand;' and I'd remembered that Brooke too had died young in World War One and my ideas had got fuzzy. But mostly Bruce was just calmly drinking by himself. Every once in a while Lili would look at him and stop dead in her dancing and laugh.

I'd figured out this Bruce-Lili-Erich business as well as I cared to. Lili had wanted the nest with all her heart and nothing else would ever satisfy her, and now she'd go to hell her own way and probably die of Bright's disease for a third time in the Change World. Bruce hadn't wanted the nest or Lili as much as he wanted the Change World and the chances it gave for Soldierly cavorting and poetic drunks; Lili's seed wasn't his idea of healing the cosmos; maybe he'd make a real mutiny some day, but more likely he'd stick to barroom epics.

His and Lili's infatuation wouldn't die completely, no matter how rancid it looked right now. The real-love angle might go, but Change would magnify the romance angle and it might seem to them like a big thing of a sort if they met again.

Erich had his *Kamerad*, shaped to suit him, who'd had the guts and cleverness to disarm the bomb he'd had the guts to trigger. You have to hand it to Erich for having the nerve to put us all in a situation where we'd have to find the Maintainer or fry, but I don't know anything disgusting enough to hand to him.

I had tried a while back. I had gone up behind him and said, 'Hey, how's my wicked little commandant? Forgotten your *und so weiter?*' and as he turned, I clawed my nails and slammed him across the cheek. That's how I got the black eye. Maud wanted to put an electric leech on it, but I took the old handkerchief in ice water. Well, at any rate Erich has his scratches to match Bruce's, not as deep, but four of them, and I told myself maybe they'd get infected – I hadn't washed my hands since the hunt. Not that Erich doesn't love scars.

Mark was the one was helped me up after Erich knocked me down.

'You got any omnias for that?' I snapped at him.

'For what?' Mark asked.

'Oh, for everything that's been happening to us,' I told him disgustedly.

He seemed to actually think for a moment and then he said, '*Omnia mutantur, nihil interit.*'

'Meaning?' I asked him.

He said, 'All things change, but nothing is really lost.'

It would be a wonderful philosophy to stand with against the Change Winds. Also damn silly. I wondered if Mark really believed it. I wished I could. Sometimes I come close to thinking it's a lot of baloney trying to be any decent kind of Demon, even a good Entertainer. Then I tell myself, 'That's life, Greta. You've got to love through it somehow.' But there are times when some of these cookies are not too easy to love.

Something brushed the palm of my hand again. It was Illy's tentacle, with the tendrils of the tip spread out like a little bush. I started to pull my hand away, but then I realized the Loon was simply lonely. I surrendered my hand to the patterned gossamer pressures of feather-talk.

Right away I got the words, 'Feeling lonely, Greta girl?'

It almost floored me, I tell you. Here I was understanding feather-talk, which I just didn't, and I was understanding it in English, which didn't make sense at all.

For a second, I thought Illy must have spoken, but I knew

he hadn't and for a couple more seconds I thought he was working telepathy on me, using the feather-talk as cues. Then I tumbled to what was happening: he was playing English on my palm like on the keyboard of his squeakbox, and since I could play English on a squeakbox myself, my mind translated automatically.

Realizing this almost gave my mind stage fright, but I was too fagged to be hocused by self-consciousness. I just lay back and let the thoughts come through. It's good to have someone to talk to you, even an underweight octopus, and without squeaks Illy didn't sound so silly; his phrasing was soberer.

'Feeling sad, Greta girl, because you'll never understand what's happening to us all,' Illy asked me, 'because you'll never be anything but a shadow fighting shadows – and trying to love shadows in between the battles? It's time you understood we're not really fighting a war at all, although it looks that way, but going through a kind of evolution, though not exactly the kind Erich had in mind.

'Your Terran thought has a word for it and a theory for it – a theory that recurs on many worlds. It's about the four orders of life: Plants, Animals, Men and Demons. Plants are energy-binders – they can't move through space and time, but they can clutch energy and transform it. Animals are space-binders – they can move through space. Man (Terran or ET, Lunan or non-Lunan) is a time-binder – he has memory.

'Demons are the fourth order of evolution, possibility-binders – they can make all of what might be part of what is, and that is their evolutionary function. Resurrection is like the metamorphosis of a caterpillar into a butterfly: a third-order breaks out of the chrysalis of its lifeline into fourth-order life. The leap from the ripped cocoon of an unchanging reality is like the first animal's leap when he ceases to be a plant, and the Change World is the core of meaning behind the many myths of immortality.

'All evolution looks like a war at first – octopoids against monopoids, mammals against reptiles. And it has a necessary dialectic: there must be the thesis – we call it Snake – and the antithesis – Spider – before there can be the ultimate synthesis, when all possibilities are fully realized in one ultimate universe. The Change War isn't the blind destruction it seems.

'Remember that the Serpent is your symbol of wisdom and the Spider your sign for patience. The two names are rightly frightening to you, for all high existence is a mixture of horror and delight. And don't be surprised, Greta girl, at the range of my words and thoughts; in a way I've had a billion years to study Terra and learn her languages and myths.

'Who are the real Spider and Snakes, meaning who were the first possibility-binders? Who was Adam, Greta girl? Who was Cain? Who were Eve and Lilith?

'In binding all possibility, the Demons also bind the mental with the material. All fourth-order beings live inside and outside all minds, throughout the whole cosmos. Even this Place is, after its fashion, a giant brain: its floor is the brain-pan, the boundary of the void is the cortex of grey matter – yes, even the Major and Minor Maintainers are analogues of the pineal and pituitary glands, which in some form sustain all nervous systems.

'There's the real picture, Greta girl.'

The feather-talk faded out and Illy's tendril tips merged into a soft pad on which I fingered, 'Thanks, Daddy Longlegs.'

Chewing over in my mind what Illy had just told me, I looked back at the gang around the piano. The party seemed to be breaking up; at least some of them were chopping away at it. Sid had gone to the control divan and was getting set to tune in Egypt. Mark and Kaby were there with him, all bursting with eagerness and the vision of ranks on ranks of mounted Zombie bowmen going up in a mushroom cloud; I thought of what Illy had told me and I managed a smile – seems we've got to win and lose all the battles, every which way.

Mark had just put on his Parthian costume, groaning cheerfully, 'Trousers again!' and was striding around under a hat like a fur-lined ice-cream cone and with the sleeves of his metal-stuffed candys flapping over his hands. He waved a short sword with a heart-shaped guard at Bruce and Erich and told them to get a move on.

Kaby was going along on the operation wearing the old-woman diguise intended for Benson-Carter. I got a half-hearted kick out of knowing she was going to have to cover that chest and hobble.

Bruce and Erich weren't taking orders from Mark just yet. Erich went over and said something to Bruce at the bar, and Bruce got down and went over with Erich to the piano, and Erich tapped Beau on the shoulder and leaned over and said something to him, and Beau nodded and yanked 'Limehouse Blues' to a fast close and started another piece, something slow and nostalgic.

Erich and Bruce waved to Mark and smiled, as if to show him that whether he came over and stood with them or not, the legate and the lieutenant and the commandant were very much together. And while Sevensee hugged Lili with a simple enthusiasm that made me wonder why I've wasted so much imagination on genetic treatments for him, Erich and Bruce sang:

'*To the legion of the lost ones, to the cohort of the damned,*
To our brothers in the tunnels outside time,
Sing three Change-resistant Zombies, raised from death and
*   robot-crammed,*

And Commandos of the Spiders–
Here's to crime!
We're three blind mice on the wrong time-track,
  Hush – hush – hush!
We've lost our now and will never get back,
  Hush – hush – hush!
Change Commandos out on the spree,
Damned through all possibility,
Ghostgirls, think kindly on such as we,
  Hush – hush – hush!'

While they were singing, I looked down at my charcoal skirt and over at Maud and Lili and I thought, 'Three grey hustlers for three black hussars, that's our speed.' Well, I'd never thought of myself as a high-speed job, winning all the races – I wouldn't feel comfortable that way. Come to think of it, we've got to lose and win all the races in the long run, the way the course is laid out.

I fingered to Illy, 'That's the picture, all right, Spider boy.'